FINDING
ENA

FINDING ENA

A FEDERAL AGENT SAM CAVIELLO CRIME MYSTERY

BOOK 3

STAN COMFORTI

Finding Ena

Copyright © 2022 by Stan Comforti

This book is a work of fiction. Names, characters, places, events, or incidents are created by the author's imagination and used fictitiously. Any similarity to actual persons, living or dead, events or locales is coincidental and not intended by the author.

Production & Publishing Consultant: AuthorPreneur Publishing Inc.—geoffaffleck.com

Editor: Dominic Wakeford
Cover Designer: pagatana.com
Interior Designer: Amit Dey—amitdey2528@gmail.com

ISBN
979-8-9861641-8-2 (paperback)
979-8-9861641-9-9 (hard cover)
979-8-9861641-7-5 (ebook)

FIC022020   FICTION / Mystery & Detective / Police Procedural
FIC031010   FICTION / Thrillers / Crime
FIC030000   FICTION / Thrillers / Suspense

DEDICATION

To all the federal agents killed or injured in the line of duty.
They are remembered and honored for their sacrifices.
Our thoughts and prayers are with you, always.

CHAPTER

1

On the signal, the FBI tactical team rammed the booby-trapped farmhouse door, which instantly triggered a tremendous explosion. A second explosive detonation occurred from a van parked in front of the farmhouse. It caused a piercing shock wave and conflagration, which spewed fragmentation, thermal heat, and an intense windstorm that shocked the FBI's entire tactical team. Members of the tactical squad cried out with screams of torturous pain and death. Townspeople heard the fiery blasts from miles away. It became apparent to Agent Sam Caviello that the terrorist suspects were tipped off about the raid and used the vacated farmhouse as bait to draw the government agents into a trap. Instead, the terrorist leaders had structured the barn adjacent to the farmhouse as their base to surprise the authorities, gun them down, and claim victory over their enemy, the U.S. government.

A second tactical team of state police officers synchronized their ramming of the barn door with that of the FBI at the farmhouse. However, delayed by seconds from hitting the barn door, the explosive blasts at the house disrupted them as they turned to see the horror behind them. Temporarily losing their focus on the barn door, three team members standing near it got hit by waves of bullets that sliced through the door fired from inside the barn. The rest of the team backed away from the heavily splinted door as the three members fell to the ground.

ATF agent Sam Caviello, part of the state police backup team, had forewarned the FBI to delay the raid when he learned the farm owner secretly reconstructed the barn more like a garrison in preparation for a battle. Now, seeing the catastrophic event, Sam's only words were, "They were ready for us."

Sam's whole body quivered in anxiety, not in fear for his safety but for that of Detective Juli Ospino, with whom he had begun a romantic affair. Juli was adamant about replacing the tactical team members shot at the barn door in defiance of Sam, who asked her to avoid getting near a gun battle. Juli had a mind of her own and joined her colleagues in a fight for their lives. Her action wasn't what Sam had anticipated. He had promised to watch over and protect her from harm as her partner. He instinctively joined the tactical team in their encounter with the terrorist. The skirmish lasted until the state's tactical team estimated they had the advantage after killing half the shooters inside the barn. The team leader devised an entry plan involving team members crisscrossing into the barn one after another battling the remaining terrorists until all were down.

When Sam entered the barn, he was hit twice by gunfire, once in the left arm and again in the left chest, but he kept firing at the enemy. The gun battle continued until only one terrorist, the radical field leader Rashid Al Madari, remained. Unfortunately, he got off his final shots at the team before escaping. Luckily, Sam's wounds were not fatal, and he began to chase the lone killer until his fear became real when Juli cried out to him. Juli's cry immobilized Sam before turning to see her wounded on the barn's floor. Emotional anxiety elevated inside him, accompanied by a throbbing from a wounded heart. He stood immobile for seconds while his insides twisted in agony and his eyes welled in tears. Finally, Sam cried out and cursed as he staggered down the stairs, nearly tripping over his feet while making his way to Juli's side. Sweat drenched his forehead while desperately trying to undo Juli's pain with words of love while applying bandages to her wounds.

"Stay with me, don't die on me," Sam shrieked as the darkness that encircled him suddenly glowed with bright light blinding his blurred eyes. He sprung up, screaming, "What? No! Juli!" as a familiar voice called out to him.

"Dad, are you alright? You were screaming."

Drowsy and confused, Sam scanned the room until he saw his son, Drew, standing by the open bedroom door near the light switch.

"Sorry to wake you. You don't look well, dad. You're sweating buckets. You okay?"

Sam swiped the sweat from his forehead. "Yeah, Drew. It was another awful nightmare. What time is it?"

"It's a little after four."

"Okay. I'll get up and take a shower. Go back to bed. Sorry, I woke you."

Sam sat on the edge of the bed, his hands cupping his sweaty cheeks. He thought back to the horrible event the morning of the raid that ended with countless injuries and the death of agents and state officers, including Juli. Sam had these horrendous nightmares about that dreadful morning all too often. He shook his head, trying to throw off the images he had of Juli lying on the floor, bleeding after being shot by Al Madari.

Ultimately, Sam wandered into the bathroom and threw cold water on his face. He looked into the mirror and saw a shell of himself looking back at him. He closed his eyes, seeing darkness, then a radiant glow of Juli's image, with a loving smile abruptly becoming hazy and blurred, melting into a vision of horrifying death. Sam flooded his face with cold water, trying to shake the chilling reflections of Juli. He refused to look back into the mirror. Sam, stripped of his t-shirt and shorts, stepped into a cold shower and shifted his thoughts away from Juli to planning his day. He skipped shaving until after breakfast. He wandered to the kitchen in the dark. He used the light from the open refrigerator door to find the Keurig coffee K-cups in the cabinet, pulled out the container of half and half, and brewed himself a cup of coffee.

He sat at the kitchen counter in the dark, thinking back to the hunt for the murderous Al Madari until Juli's best friend, Andrea, called to let him know that Juli didn't make it. He was heartbroken and cried like a little kid. Although crushed over her death, he focused on hunting Juli's killer. While wounded, Juli insisted Sam find the shooter. Not wanting to leave her side, he promised Juli he'd hunt down the beast and get justice for her.

Moments later, Sam heard the shower in his son's bathroom, figuring his son couldn't get back to sleep either. Twenty minutes later, Drew flicked on the kitchen light.

"Are you feeling better?"

"A little. I just can't stop thinking about it. I never envisioned that when we stopped for gas, I'd see a hostage being held in a van by several men."

"We did what we had to do. If only that rookie trooper hadn't pulled over and approached the van without backup."

"I can't help but think that if I never saw the hostage in the van and didn't report it to the state police, Juli would still be alive today."

"There's no way you could predict what would happen down the road. Besides, if you hadn't called them, you'd never have met Juli and experienced the time you had together."

"I know, but I would trade it all for knowing she would be alive today."

"Try not to blame yourself, Dad. I'm heading to work early now that I'm up. I'll talk to you later. Love you."

"Love you too. Hey, I'm going to stop at the ATF office a little later. Let's get together for lunch."

*   *   *

A man limped slowly down the basement corridor with the help of a cane. The guy lost his right leg from the knee during his third tour in Afghanistan. He shuffled toward the maintenance office in the building where he worked. He was of average height and weight and in his early thirties. He had a four-inch scar across the left side of his forehead. As he limped, his brown eyes covered with thin-framed glasses squinted, searching for the maintenance office. His long curly brown hair, tied into a ponytail, brushed the back of his neck as he reached the office marked Maintenance, Staff Only.

He stepped inside the office and saw Wilbur Adkins, the supervisor, at his desk with his Covid mask lowered to his chin.

"Hey, Max, what can I do for you, man?"

"Sorry to bother you, Wil. I spilled some coffee on my sister's rug this morning. I need something to clean it before she gets home from work tonight. She'll freak out if she sees the coffee stain. Do you have anything that will work on coffee stains?"

"Man, don't you drink your coffee at the kitchen table?"

"Uh, yeah, most of the time, but I watched the news on TV this morning and tripped. It's easy to do with this dummy leg."

"Let me find something in the storage room."

Max looked to his left, surveying the locker room. He saw two rows of metal lockers for the maintenance crew that worked the two shifts. Employees assigned to a locker attached masking tape with their names printed on it with a black magic marker. The locker room had two small bathrooms at the far end, one for the men and the other for women. When Max saw Wil enter the back storage room, he quickly shuffled into the locker room and searched the names on the lockers until he found the one he wanted. Next, he quietly opened the unlocked door and searched the jacket pockets hanging inside until he found what he was looking for. Max shoved them into his pocket and was about to return to the office when he heard Wil call out, "Max, where you at, man?"

Max froze for a second, turned, and headed toward the john in the back of the room. "I'm in the bathroom, Wil. Coming right out." He flushed the toilet for the noise effect and limped back out of the locker room. "Had to piss bad, my man."

Wil handed Max a spray bottle for rug cleaning. "This should work on the coffee stain."

"Thanks, Wil. See you later."

Max left the office and limped down the hall to the side parking lot exit. He hid the bottle of rug cleaner behind the trash can and left the building. Once on the sidewalk, Max glanced both ways, looking for the hardware store. He spotted it and headed there. He was in the store for only ten minutes before exiting and stopping at a nearby luncheonette for a sandwich and coffee. After lunch, he returned to the building and used his keycard to unlock the side entrance door. He fetched the bottle of rug cleaner he hid and headed back to the maintenance office.

"That was fast. You live next door?" asked Wil.

"It's a ten-minute drive from here. The cleaner was not perfect, but it made the stain unnoticeable on the dark rug. You want me to return it to the storage room?"

"Nah, I'll do it. You won't know where it goes on the shelf." Just then, the phone rang. Wil answered the phone with his back to Max.

Max quietly entered the locker room and returned the item he had borrowed. Then, with Wil still on the phone with his back to the locker room, Max quietly left the office, closing the door in silence. After accomplishing his covert mission, he returned to his workstation on the third floor with a grin on his lips.

CHAPTER

2

In the living room, Sam finished a forty-five-minute workout lifting fifteen-pound weights in each hand, then completed one hundred sit-ups, seventy push-ups, fifty jumping jacks, and a variety of leg lunges. When finished, he dressed for his meeting with his boss at the ATF office in Boston. As Sam was leaving Drew's apartment, his cell phone rang. He answered the call from Massachusetts State Police Major Jack Burke.

"Sam, Jack Burke. I contacted Donna Ranero regarding surveillance and wiretap plans for the remaining suspects, either out on bail or not yet arrested. She arranged for us to meet at her office today at two o'clock. She'll have FBI, State Department, and Homeland Security agents present. Are you available?"

"Absolutely. We need as many agencies as possible to help with the surveillance and wiretaps. Hopefully, something will turn up and tell us where the suspects are hiding. We need to track anything and everything the suspects use. We must find these thugs and arrest them as soon as possible before they kill again."

"Agreed. I'll see you at the federal courthouse in Boston at two this afternoon."

Sam left the apartment and drove to the O'Neill Federal Building in Boston. He took the elevator to the seventh floor for the ATF's Boston Field

Division Office. ATF was the acronym for the Bureau of Alcohol, Tobacco, Firearms, and Explosives, the federal law enforcement agency responsible for enforcing federal firearms, arson, and explosives laws. The agency began way back during Prohibition as the Alcohol Tax Unit. Its most famous agent was Eliot Ness, whose job, along with his team of only thirty-four agents, was to eradicate illegal alcohol operations by violent organized criminals, the most notorious being Al Capone.

Sam arrived just before eleven and met with the Special Agent in Charge, Gary Hopkins, and his Assistant Steve Roberts. He was there to update them on the status of his continued temporary assignment working with the state police in their investigation of the remaining terrorists at large. Sam's briefing was short and included his afternoon attendance at a meeting on the investigation that afternoon with Assistant U.S. Attorney Ranero.

Hopkins informed Sam that ATF headquarters approved an extension for him to complete his work with the state police for an additional forty-five days. "You'll need to replace the agent you assigned to act as the supervisor in your stead with another agent while you continue working in Boston."

"I'll cut the paperwork while I'm here."

Sam was the supervisory special agent at the ATF Hartford office and temporarily assigned to a Massachusetts State Police task force. The assignment arose when he was on vacation helping his son move into an apartment in Boston. He and his son, Drew, took a break from the move for dinner. Low on gas, Sam stopped to fill up at the first gas station, where a van pulled up opposite him. When the van's side door slid open, Sam observed someone inside the van, bound at the hands and feet with a black hood covering their head, seated between two men. When the van left the station, Sam and his son tailed the van while calling the Mass State Police to report he was following five men in a van who held someone hostage. He advised them to consider the men armed and proceed with caution with sufficient backup.

Unfortunately, a lone state trooper pulled over the van without backup and, while slowly approaching the van on foot, got shot by one of the van's passengers. Sam, unarmed at the time, felt angry and partially responsible for not being able to back up the trooper. He wanted to help the police find the shooter but got rebuffed by the female lead detective. So on his own, Sam found the abandoned van and crucial leads on the five suspects, which convinced the female detective to work with Sam as an investigative team. Working with an informant, they located a farmhouse where the suspects hid. An attachment grew between Sam and the detective, Juli Ospino, leading to more than a partnership but an intimate romance.

Learning that Sam was to attend the afternoon meeting with Attorney Ranero, Sam's boss wanted his assistant to attend. "I'll call Ranero and have her invite Steve to sit in on the meeting," said Hopkins. "I want to stay on top of what's going on in the investigation. I need current updates on the status of your involvement in the task force. Headquarters doesn't want surprises and hear about significant events after the fact."

Sam concurred. After the meeting with his boss, Sam called his son, Drew, who worked in the same building, to meet him for lunch in the cafeteria.

"Is it okay if my OJT, Eric Mills, joins us for lunch?" said Drew.

"Yeah. Bring him along."

"So you know, my boss got a call from Ranero requesting he send a representative to the meeting at two o'clock. He's sending Eric and me."

"Great. I'll see you both in the cafeteria in ten minutes."

*   *   *

Sam, Drew, and Eric had lunch and then drove together to the federal court-house on Fan Pier on the Boston waterfront. The newest federal courthouse was built on the pier presenting great ocean views for the judges and other ranking government officials. The three federal agents entered the confer-ence room in the U. S. Attorney's office. The officials present at the meeting were State Police Major Jack Burke and Detective Kevin Bishop, FBI SAC Austin Taylor and Supervisory Agent Dell Haskins, State Department DSS SAC Pat O'Shae, and Agents Eric Mills and Drew Caviello. Also, Homeland Security Assistant Director Roger Haywood, ATF ASAC Steve Roberts, and Sam. After Ranero had each person stand and introduce themselves. She recapped the events of the farm raid and the escape and subsequent killing of Al Madari by Detective Andrea Serrano and Sam. Al Madari's demise led to threats against Sam and Andrea and the subsequent abduction of Andrea's daughter, whom Sam and the state police succeeded in rescuing. Next, regarding the suspects, she listed those arrested and indicted, those killed during the confrontation with the authorities, and finally, the names of the leaders still at large.

Since the Massachusetts State Police initiated the investigation, Ranero asked Major Jack Burke to outline the measures they have taken to date and their recommendations going forward with the help of the agencies present.

Burke took a moment to confer with Sam before beginning. "Those suspects still at large are Shahrad Abedini, the farm owner believed to have ties to an Iranian terrorist group, his sister Tsarina Abedini Ferguson, and her husband, Tucker Ferguson, a U.S. citizen and former building inspector for the town. Last but not least, the Imam at the Lynn Mosque."

Burke paused to look at his notes. "We previously arrested State Police Lieutenant Martin Randell, whose birth name is Mateen Rahmani, believed to be a mole for the terrorist group. Randell had harbored Al Madari at his home until Sam located and killed him in self-defense. Randell has a high-level attorney representing him and is unwilling to talk to us. Secretly indicted, his wife, Sara Naceri Rahmani Randell, has been under surveillance since her husband's arrest."

Burke took a sip of water and then continued. "With the help of the FBI, we analyzed Randell's home phone, his two cell phones, his wife's two cell phones, and both of their laptops. To date, we have gone through Randell's personal and burner cell phones and came up with three numbers he frequently called. We believe those numbers belonged to others involved with this group. The FBI has wiretaps on the three burner phones, but they remain silent. We suspect they discarded the phones. Our surveillance of Sara Randell, who is pregnant, was observed purchasing four additional burner phones last night. We obtained the sales slips with the phone numbers from the store where she purchased them. The FBI has had FISA warrants authorized for wiretaps on them. To date, there has been no communication on any of them. Once a phone gets used, we hope to track its location. Agent Caviello feels that the FBI should request a FISA warrant for a wiretap on Randell's attorney's office and cell phones to monitor any calls he makes or receives from any identified burner phone numbers. This request is for monitoring only the communication unrelated to the attorney's defense of Randell in the criminal case against him."

Burke looked around the table for comments or questions but got none, so he continued. "Also, Agent Caviello and I agree that we should attempt to interview Randell and his wife with a promise of leniency in sentencing for him and no time served for his wife for their cooperation in locating, arresting, and prosecuting the others. We should also go back and interview those arrested for information that may help locate those at large. Finally, we have a cooperating person who initially led us to the farmhouse where the perps were hiding. We plan to use that source to help find out where they are hiding."

There was a knock on the conference room door. An FBI agent then appeared as the door opened. "Sorry for the intrusion. I have an important message for SAC Taylor." He quietly moved to where Taylor sat and whispered in his ear. The agent then exited the room.

Taylor stood and reported the message. "Good news, our surveillance team spotted a grey pickup truck stop a short distance past Tucker Ferguson's home in New Hampshire. The agents spotted Ferguson exiting the truck and walking to the house next door to his house. They spotted him walking behind that house and some bushes before entering the back of his home. He obviously tried avoiding arrest while returning to his house without being seen. Our team continues covering the house with one unit following the pickup."

"Will you arrest and transport Ferguson and the pickup driver to Boston for interrogation?" asked Sam.

"We'll wait to see if the pickup driver returns to get Ferguson or takes us to other suspects. If neither happens, we'll arrest Ferguson and pick up the driver for questioning."

"If you end up arresting Ferguson, I'd like the opportunity to interview him or at least sit in on the interview," said Sam.

Taylor paused and whispered to Haskins. "The best I could do is allow you to watch and listen from the adjoining room."

"If he refuses to talk to your agents, can I have an opportunity to question him? I've interviewed him before and feel he may be willing to talk to me," said Sam.

"I'll get back to you on that, Sam."

Sam was angry that inter-agency cooperation wasn't at play here. Sharing information and working as a team is critical to the success of a joint investigation. Not allowing Sam access to the suspect keeps him outside the loop. The lack of inclusion has been an issue with law enforcement agencies wanting to maintain total control of an investigation. Sam felt agency teamwork was the best formula for success.

There was quiet until Donna Ranero asked if the other agency heads had anything to add. Roger Haywood, Homeland Security, raised his hand. "Our agency teams are watching airports, train stations, and bus terminals for the fugitives if they attempt to leave the area. In addition, we have alerted our border agents with photos and descriptions of the suspects in case they try to flee the country. We'll contact Agent Taylor if our agents report anything significant regarding the suspects."

Pat O'Shae, State Department, added his agents are assisting by determining if the suspects have any relatives living in the New England area.

"Anyone else want to add anything before we adjourn?" asked Ranero.

"Yes," said Sam. "Detective Serrano and I would like an opportunity to interview Randell and his wife separately. We want to offer a deal for their cooperation, as Major Burke mentioned earlier. I want the U.S. Attorney's approval to make such a deal. Detective Serrano speaks Farsi, and being a woman may prove valuable in convincing Randell's wife to cooperate."

"We've already tried speaking to Randell, and he's not talking," remarked FBI agent Haskins.

"I understand, Dell, but Detective Serrano and I have interviewed other suspects and witnesses who initially refused to talk or lied to investigators, but we were able to gain their cooperation. So sometimes, additional efforts work out. Not everyone conducts interviews the same." countered Sam.

"I could vouch that Detective Serrano and Agent Caviello have been extremely successful in their interviews. Their interviews resulted in identifying the suspects in the van and later locating them at the farm. It would be worth giving them a try, especially with Randell's wife," interjected Major Burke.

No one spoke but looked to Ranero for her response to Sam's request. "I will confer with Austin and get back to you, Major. It may be for naught if Randell's attorney prohibits us from talking to them. Let's see what happens with Ferguson and the pickup driver. The ongoing surveillance could detect one or more of the suspects still at large. So, we'll adjourn and meet again soon."

As the group began exiting the room, Ranero asked Sam to stay. She shut the door and asked him to take a seat. "Listen, Sam. I admit I am impressed with your work. You have a talent for getting things done. I'll talk to Randell's attorney and try convincing him to allow you to interview his client. I'm not going to mention the wife. Since we didn't arrest her, it's possible he doesn't represent her. Not yet, anyway. I'm not sure if he'll agree, but it's worth a try. You have to understand the FBI lost several agents during the raid, and they want all the suspects burned at the stake."

"I understand that Randell provided information regarding the raid, but he didn't pull the trigger that killed FBI agents or state police officers. Anyway, let's set that issue aside for now and key on Randell's wife, Sara. You haven't had her arrested yet, so maybe Randell's attorney doesn't represent her. Permit Detective Serrano and me to visit her. If she is willing to listen to an offer, she may be willing to cooperate. She's young, pregnant, and may trade information if it keeps her out of jail or from getting deported. There's always a chance that she may be willing to cooperate if we promise her she won't spend time in jail and may get to stay in the U.S."

"Sounds reasonable, Sam. I'll confer with my boss and get back to you."

"Fair enough, but I don't like to wait around while these assholes plan on harming Andrea or her daughter. So, I appreciate anything you can do to push this along."

Sam left the room and saw Jack Burke and Kevin Bishop waiting for him. As they left the office, Sam explained what Ranero agreed to do but made no promises. "I want to talk to those arrested and held in jail, such as Ganani and the two arrested during the rescue of Andrea's daughter. Andrea and I will also reach out to the informant, who might help us. We need to act fast and not sit around waiting for approvals to find these bastards."

"I'll set it up, Sam. Andrea will contact you after we arrange for the interviews at the jails. But, she'll still need troopers around her for protection."

"I agree, Jack. Let's not wait until they harm anyone else. One way or another, I plan on finding every one of them."

CHAPTER
3

Doctor Mayumi Oshiro finished her long shift at Boston General Hospital and was about to catch the T, Boston's subway system. While on the subway, she ensured she had the cash to pay Angie, her neighbor who watched Mayumi's eight-year-old daughter, Ena. Because of the pandemic, Mayumi worked long hours at the hospital, and Angie, who lived next door, agreed to watch Ena after school until Mayumi got home. Mayumi got off the subway at the Porter Square Station, providing riders access to Boston and Cambridge. She walked about four blocks to her duplex apartment on West Street.

Angie Lomax was an unemployed 33-year-old woman considered overweight and suffering from various medical conditions, including high blood pressure, arthritis, and gout that caused considerable pain in her feet. She formerly worked multiple jobs, mostly stocking goods on shelves or clothing racks and at the register. Unfortunately, Angie often arrived late or didn't go to work without calling the manager. For that reason, her last boss let her go after not showing up for work for the third time.

Mayumi rang the bell to Angie's apartment and waited for the door to open, usually by Ena rushing to greet her mom. Sure enough, Ena opened the door with a happy smile, glad she could now go home with her mom. Angie followed Ena to the door and greeted Mayumi.

"Ena was a little rowdy this afternoon. We played checkers for a while and watched TV, but she started gymnastic exercises on the floor and almost knocked over a lamp that sent the ashtray flying across the floor. Nothing got broken, though."

"So sorry, Angie, and I'm sorry for being late. I'll talk to Ena when we get home."

"No problem, doctor. I enjoy having Ena here and understand your hours are crazy at the hospital. You are lucky to have such a sweet, beautiful young girl."

"Thank you, Angie. I don't know what I would do without you. How have you been feeling?"

"Most of the time, I'm fine, but my gout has flared up at the moment."

"So sorry to hear that. There's medication you can get to help with that. Oh, how is your brother doing?"

"He's fine. It's nice having him here with me, especially since he helps with the rent. But, unfortunately, he's talking about moving south. An old army buddy he stays in touch with is trying to talk him into moving near where he and a bunch of their ex-military friends live. I hope he doesn't move. I won't be able to pay all the bills without his help, but he'll do what he wants. I can't stop him."

"Well, I hope he stays. I have your money for watching Ena. Thanks again for all that you do."

"She's a good kid, doctor. I'll see Ena tomorrow. Bye, Ena."

*   *   *

Liang Wu mopped the floors on the third-floor office building hallway. Dressed in a light green coverall garment and sneakers, Liang worked for the company that contracts with the office building owners for janitorial cleaning. Liang's shift varied. He usually reported for work at eight in the morning and worked until five. Sometimes, his shift began at four in the afternoon and ended at midnight. The drive to work was frequently slower during the day shift since he faced commuter traffic and the school buses on his way to work.

His pay was only twelve dollars an hour, but few companies hired ex-cons, especially those who spent time for child sex trafficking. Liang considered himself fortunate even to have a job. At twenty-eight years old, he never wanted to spend another day in prison. Instead, he hoped to find a better-paying job by attending adult education classes to improve his English. He was eager to take courses at a community college once his English improved. Liang's a slender Chinese immigrant, five feet eight inches tall, weighing a meager hundred and twenty pounds. He lived in a studio basement apartment complex occupied mainly by those over sixty years old with no children. The maintenance company owner where Liang worked was a former ex-con who served time for petty theft and assault and now helped young cons find a place to work and live after being released from jail. The owner also lived in the same apartment building as Liang.

Although the job isn't what Liang envisioned as a vocation, he wanted to do right by the guy who hired him. He often showed up at work early and did better than an adequate job cleaning. He kept to himself and was somewhat quiet and shy but personable with those in the offices he cleaned. His shift was about to end. He put away the mop and bucket and went to the maintenance office to clean up. He left the building through the side parking lot door, unlocked the driver's door of his beat-up black van, and climbed onto the driver's seat. Often, he would sit for a moment while staring out over the steering wheel, thinking about his past arrest and how he could better himself. After snapping out of his trance, he started up the van and searched for his cell phone for a good jazz station. As the music played, he left the parking lot, drove several blocks past the MLK Elementary School, and turned right onto West Street, where he stopped at a small Asian restaurant for takeout before heading to his apartment.

CHAPTER
4

Back at state police headquarters, Detective Andrea Serrano was waiting for Major Burke to arrive from his meeting at the U.S. Attorney's office in Boston. He had called ahead and asked her to sit in on a short meeting with him, Detective Bishop, and Sam. Andrea was more than happy to meet with them. It's been a week since Andrea last saw Sam. She was deeply attracted to him and missed him terribly. She knew Sam was still not over Juli's death and partially blamed himself for not keeping his promise to keep her out of harm's way. Andrea knew Sam needed time before committing to another relationship. As Juli's best friend, she also suffered the same painful grief as Sam. She and Juli were like sisters. They knew each other's deepest secrets and spent nearly every day together on and off the job. After Juli's death, she and Sam supported each other through friendship to get through their grief from losing her.

Andrea waited near Burke's office when he, Bishop, and Sam walked through the front entrance. When Sam walked by, she wanted to pull him to her lips and kiss him, but it was only a wish that may never come true. Although she craved Sam's attention, she had to avoid her display of affection for him around police headquarters.

The meeting was short. Burke informed Andrea she'd be working with Sam interviewing Joram Haddad, Matjar Albagalih, and others who were currently in lockup.

"Bishop will be available to assist when and where needed. Andrea, you will prepare all written statements for the department and keep me updated on all meaningful results. I'll arrange for you and Sam to have access to the suspects in jail. Our detectives had just detained Tucker Ferguson when he arrived at his home. Since the state has the best case against him for submitting fraudulent building inspection reports, the FBI and our detectives are bringing Ferguson here to interview him. If Ferguson doesn't cooperate, I may have you two interview him since Sam already questioned him and is familiar with what role he played in the investigation. Any questions?"

"It's late. Andrea and I could call Haddad and meet him instead of waiting here to interview Ferguson. I assume you'll hold Ferguson in lockup overnight if he doesn't cooperate. That might give him the incentive to talk to us. We could interview tomorrow," said Sam.

Burke agreed, so Sam asked Andrea to call Joram. When she did, Joram answered in three rings.

"This is Joram."

"Joram, it's Detective Serrano. You probably remember showing my partners and me how to get to the farmhouse. We want to meet with you again. We need your help finding the Imam and the farmhouse owner. We'll pay you for your time."

"Don't know where they are."

"Okay, but you know others who you could ask. You had told us the Imam's assistant sometimes would ask you for help when they needed extra bodies. Am I right?"

"I don't want to help them."

"We don't want you to help them either. Let's meet, and we'll explain better how you can help us. Can you meet us someplace in private later today?"

"I can meet you."

"Do you know where Suffolk Downs horse racetrack is?

"Yes."

If you keep driving past it toward Boston, you will come to a traffic light. There will be a coffee shop on the right. Take a left there, and you will see a hotel. We could meet you in the hotel parking lot. No one will see us together. Can you meet us there at seven o'clock tonight?"

"Yes, but I don't know how I can help you."

"We will explain when we see you. What will you be driving?"

"My sister lets me use Akram's SUV while he's in jail."

"Okay, we know his SUV. When you drive into the parking lot, we'll flash our headlights. Follow us to the back lot and get into our car. Okay, Joram?"

"Yes. Be there at seven o'clock."

Later, Sam was uneasy driving with Andrea to the hotel lot to meet an informant. He was uncomfortable because two troopers in plain clothes followed behind for Andrea's added protection from an ongoing threat to Andrea. Although Sam agreed that her added protection was necessary, he didn't know the two troopers assigned to protect her. He thought exposing the informant's identity should be on a need-to-know basis. All he knew was one mole inside the state police had already resulted in the loss of life for many officers. Another leak identifying Joram as an informant could result in the informant's death. But, Joram had previously helped the Imam's assistant bring supplies to the suspect's farmhouse. So, Sam planned to persuade Joram to contact the Imam's assistant and offer his help, hoping it might speed up finding the suspects' whereabouts. Sam felt it was taking too long to find the suspects who remained a threat to Andrea and her daughter. Although impatient, he had to risk having Joram's identity leaked to find the remaining suspects and put an end to any potential harm to Andrea and her daughter.

Andrea and Sam arrived at the hotel parking lot at six-thirty. Andrea drove a seized silver Toyota Camry with a fictitious Rhode Island registration listed to a made-up female's name residing in that state. She maneuvered toward the far end of the lot and selected an area where four adjacent spots were open. She then parked near the entrance waiting for Joram to arrive. Twenty minutes later, they spotted Joram's SUV entering the parking lot. Andrea flashed her headlights, and he followed her to the back lot. Joram parked alongside her, exited his SUV, and entered the back seat of Andrea's car.

After handshakes, Sam spoke first. "I want to show you photos of some people who know the Imam. I want you to tell me if you know any of the persons in the photos."

Joram slowly looked at each of the ten photos. "I know only Matjar and his wife at Lugassi's store and Kazmi and his son Arian at the market. I saw this man and woman at the farmhouse but do not know them." The photos Joram had pointed out were Shahrad Abedini, the farm owner, and his sister Tsarina.

"Do you think the four you know also know the Imam and might know where he is? Might any of them bring food and other supplies to him?" asked Sam.

"The Lugassi's know the Imam, but not the farm owner and the woman. I don't think the Lugassi's know where the Imam is now."

Andrea, speaking Farsi, asked Joram a follow-up question. "Who is the Imam's closest friend at the Mosque?"

"Kasra Qazwini works at the Mosque with the Imam. They are close. Reza Kadivar also is there sometimes to help the Imam. I think Reza and Kasra are cousins."

"Do you know Reza and Kasra well enough to contact them and ask if they need help to deliver food or supplies to anyone?" You could mention you need the money," asked Andrea.

"I have helped a few times there. I could ask."

"That will help us. We need to find where the Imam and the farm owner are hiding. We will pay you good money if you can find where they are," said Sam.

"I will try but cannot promise."

"That's all we can ask of you. Anything you can do to find out where the Imam and others are will be helpful," said Andrea.

They ended their talk. Andrea gave him twenty-five dollars and her cell number. "This number is for you only. Do not give it to anyone else."

"I understand."

Once Joram left the parking lot, Andrea asked Sam if they could go to her apartment.

"I don't think I should, especially since your security team watches every move you make," expressed Sam.

"I want the team around Micaela and my sister, but I wish they didn't assign one to me."

"I'm glad they did. Unfortunately, the suspects still want revenge on us for killing their field leader, Al Madari. They took Micaela once. They could do it again, and I don't want anything to happen to her or you. If they got to you, what would happen to Micaela?"

"I know you're right, but now that Juli is gone, you've become my only close friend. I need a friend I can confide in outside of my sister."

"You can count on me for support, Andrea. I want to find those bastards soon, so you no longer need a security team watching over you. You're stuck with them right now. I don't want them to get the wrong impression when I sometimes spend the night at your place. So drive me back to my son's apartment and pick me up in the morning. We'll figure something out in the next day or two, okay?"

"Okay, Sam, I trust your judgment, but I could use your support."

Sam became exasperated with Andrea, who constantly wanted him to spend the night with her. "I'll figure something out, Andrea."

"Okay. I just wanted you to know how I feel."

*　*　*

At a secluded old colonial house near Windham, New Hampshire, the Imam was seated at a table, finishing a late dinner. Also sitting at the table were Shahrad Abedini and Kasra Qazwini, the Imam's assistant at the Lynn Mosque. They had just concluded plans for luring agent Caviello to an isolated area where he could be captured and later killed.

"The state police have heavy police security on Detective Serrano, her daughter, and her sister's family. Let's get the agent, Caviello, who does not have the same protection. We need to find someplace where he cannot escape. I will contact Rahmani's wife, Sara, to provide Kasra with what we discussed. Tsarina is staying with a cousin. We don't want all of us together in case the police find where we're staying. Once we find a private place to get the agent to meet us, we will execute our plan. In the meantime, remember to disguise yourself, watch for suspicious cars following behind, and make only short phone calls using the code words we discussed when talking on the phone. The government may be listening to our conversations. We will meet again soon. Go in peace and with Allah."

CHAPTER
5

The following morning, Andrea and Sam had breakfast at a restaurant not far from where Andrea lived. During breakfast, they decided to interview Matjar Albagalih at Lugassi's Market in Lynn first and then decide who they would interview next.

As they traveled to Lynn, Sam received a phone call from Ranero.

"Hi Sam, I spoke to Lucas Stewart, and he approved granting Sara Rahmani Randell a deal for her cooperation. Regarding her husband, Lucas is more reluctant to offer him any deal other than what you recommended. A misdemeanor charge and no prison time for his wife, and a reduced felony charge for him with a recommendation of up to five years to serve. His or his wife's cooperation must lead to the location and arrest of the Imam, Shahrad Abedini, and his sister Tsarina."

"That's good news. Will Detective Serrano and I get the chance to interview them first?"

"Lucas isn't comfortable having an ATF agent taking the lead in place of the FBI."

"Donna, this investigation was initiated by the state police and me as partners. Together, we identified and found the suspects hiding at the farmhouse, not to mention finding and killing Al Madari, their field commander. As you remember, I insisted the FBI hold off on executing the search warrant at the farm after I found out the farm owner constructed the barn as a fortress."

"I understand where you are coming from, Sam, but Lucas is adamant about not creating any resentment between our office and the FBI."

"There shouldn't be any resentment if the state police took the lead in the interview. What if you propose Detective Serrano and I interview the wife and Detective Serrano and an FBI agent interview Randell?"

"I don't know. Let me work on that with Lucas, and I'll get back to you. A caveat in all of this is whether Randell and his attorney will agree to the interview."

"Do we know if the attorney also represents Randell's wife?"

"I'll find out from the prosecutors handling Randell's case. If she's not, I'll try getting Lucas' approval for you and Andrea to approach her."

"Understood. Call me back. Andrea and I are heading to interview the grocery store owner in Lynn. The owner provided food to the five suspects sheltered at the Mosque at the Imam's request. It's a long shot, but it's possible that the Imam still uses the store to get food for himself and the others."

"You're very determined, Sam. I'll do my best to convince my boss. Call me if there's anything else I can do."

"You can help by keeping Detective Serrano and me in the loop if the wiretaps come up with something significant."

"Sure thing. I'll talk to you soon."

Andrea and Sam traveled to Lugassi's market and visited the owner, Matjar Albagalih. Matjar swore the Imam had not contacted him. He doesn't want to get involved with the Imam anymore but assured Sam he would inform them if the Imam or his associates reached out for anything. After that interview, they stopped to question Kazai Baraghani at the other market. Baraghani had previously provided help to Al Madari during his escape from the farm. Still, he insisted he has not heard from the Imam or any other person associated with him, including his associates at the Mosque in Lynn. He vowed to contact Andrea if the suspects reached out for anything. Sam informed both store owners that he would know if the

Imam or his associates called on them. "If you don't report that to us, we'll arrest you."

"Three down and a lot more interviews to do. Let's stop for coffee and discuss the sequence of who we talk to next. My list includes Randell and his wife, and Ferguson, of course. Then there's Armita Shahidi, and uh, what's the other guy's name? I forget," asked Sam.

"His name is Amir Abdullahi, who claims to be a friend of Radir and his sister Parnia at the Crescent Drive Plaza."

"Thanks, Andrea. I have his name noted somewhere, but there're too many names to remember."

During the coffee break, Sam received another call from Donna Ranero. "Sam, Lucas talked to the FBI SAC, and they agreed that if Randell's attorney consents to listen to our offer, Detective Serrano and an FBI agent can interview Randell. Regarding Sara, it doesn't seem the attorney is representing her, not yet, anyway. So you and Andrea have the okay to approach her with an offer for her cooperation. I pushed hard for this, Sam, so I hope it works for you."

"It does, and thanks for making it happen."

"Let me know if you make any progress with the wife."

Sam briefed Andrea. "After finishing our interviews at the Revere jail, let's call Burke to fill him in and ask if he wants us to interview Ferguson."

As they left the coffee cafe, Andrea called Major Burke to arrange their access to interview the suspects at the holding facilities and if Ferguson agreed to cooperate. Burke told her the detectives and FBI are still in with Ferguson, trying to get him to talk.

* * *

Doctor Mayumi Oshiro, who preferred to be called May, departed the subway at the Porter Square Station and walked to her apartment on West Street. As she approached her residence, she saw her daughter, Ena, with Angie, talking with two police officers. Concerned, Mayumi picked up her steps to get to them. When Ena saw her mom, she rushed to her, calling "mama," and tightly wrapped her arms around her.

"Angie, what happened? Is everything all right?" asked Mayumi.

Angie explained without introducing the officers. "May, when Ena got off the bus and began walking here, a man in a black van stopped and asked Ena if she wanted a ride. Ena was frightened and ran. I was sitting by the window and saw the van drive by, but I didn't know the driver had tried to get Ena into the van. I didn't notice who drove the van."

One police officer introduced himself before asking Mayumi for identification and her phone number. "Your daughter didn't get a good look at the driver, only that it was a black van and a man wearing a hat. I'll give you my number to call if you see the van nearby. I'll refer this to the detectives, and I'm sure one of them will call and want to talk to you further."

Mayumi thanked the officers and Angie, then hugged her daughter again before entering their apartment. "Ena, you did what I taught you. Never get into anybody's car if you don't know them. The only people you know are Angie, her brother Billy and baba (grandma).

CHAPTER

6

Sam and Andrea sat in the interview room at the Revere State Police Barracks to interview the suspects held there. Sam was eager, alert, and ready to get answers, while Andrea appeared edgy, drumming her fingers on her notebook.

The first suspect escorted to the room was Armita Shahidi Nazari, the wife of Ameen Nazari, a close associate of the Imam. As Armita entered the interview room, Andrea took the lead speaking in Farsi. "Good afternoon Armita. I am Detective Andrea Serrano, with my partner Sam Caviello. I hope the officers here are treating you well."

"I already talked to your other officer. I do not know where the Imam, Shahrad, and Tsarina are now. Even if I knew, I would not tell you. You people killed my husband," replied Armita in a resentful tone.

Andrea nodded her head, meaning she understood, before continuing. "We're sorry for your loss, Armita, but the police ordered your husband to surrender. Instead, he went for his weapon. The police had no choice but to stop him from shooting them. We are here to help you. The Imam and Shahrad were responsible for the death of several police officers. When found, they will spend many years in prison. They may never see freedom again. If you help us find them, we will recommend you be allowed to return to your homeland."

"They do not call me or come here to see me. Even if they did, they would not tell me where they lived. That would be stupid, no?"

"Yes, I know, but you may know where the Imam or Shahrad have other places they own or visit. Your husband was a close friend of the Imam. Maybe he visited other places where the Imam would spend time away from the Mosque. Soon, you will be brought to court and tried as part of the plan to kill police officers. You will spend many years in prison, far away from here, if found guilty. Then, after you serve all those years in prison, you will be deported. If you help us find them, you can return to your home country and not go to prison."

Armita sat there like she was contemplating how she could help. "I cannot help you. I would be called a traitor and killed by my country's government."

"No one will know you helped us."

"I cannot help you."

Andrea caught a glimpse of Sam, who motioned to leave. "My name is Andrea. If you change your mind or remember something that could help us, tell the officers you want to speak to me again." Andrea asked the officer standing outside the door to bring Armita back to her cell and bring in Amir Abdullahi next.

Once Amir arrived, Andrea proposed similar help to him if he would cooperate. Amir claimed only to be an acquaintance of Armita when both worked at a high-tech company near Boston. "I was friendly with Armita but not a close friend. Her husband, Ameen, was not friendly and was suspicious of me. Armita had invited me to their home that night when the police came and shot her husband. She only told me they were at a friend's house and needed my help with computer programming. We were to watch TV and have pizza and beer. I did not know they held a young girl upstairs. I never saw the girl until the police came."

"What kind of computer program did you work on?" asked Andrea in English since Amir understood and spoke English well.

"We never got to use the computer. The pizza arrived soon after I got to the house, and Armita wanted to watch the movie first. I do not know and never met the Imam or persons named Shahrad or Tsarina. I live in Lowell, a long distance from the home where the police arrested me. Before my arrest, I worked at a smaller tech company on Route 128. Now I do not have a job."

Sam asked Amir to listen for anything Armita or Radir mentioned about the Imam or Shahrad, specifically if they talked about where they might be living. "If you hear anything like that, ask the officers to have us come back and meet with you again. If you help us find the Imam, and we can confirm you are not part of their group, we'll get you out of jail and help get your job back."

Amir said he would cooperate if he could and thanked them. Andrea gave him a sandwich and Coke in a styrofoam cup to take with him as the officer escorted him back to his cell.

Andrea requested the guard to bring Radir in next. Once Radir entered the room, Andrea and Sam gave him the same pitch as they did to the others.

Radir said nothing while thinking about his options. "If we help you, they would harm my sister and me."

"No one will know that you and your sister helped us. We will tell no one. Do you think your sister might know where Tsarina is?" asked Sam.

Radir nodded before answering. "Parnia is close to Tsarina, and they sometimes visited with Tsarina's cousin. I only know her cousin by Ada. I have not been to where she lives in Lawrence."

"If we can arrange for you to talk to Parnia, could you find out from her where Ada lives? It might be better if you didn't tell your sister you're asking for us. If you help us find Tsarina, we'll help you go home on bail until the trial begins."

"I will ask her, but she may know it is for you. You killed Parnia's husband. I know she will not help you."

Andrea arranged for Radir to call his sister while Sam waited outside the station. After the call, Andrea thanked Radir and had him escorted back to his cell.

Andrea met Sam waiting by her car. She shook her head no while approaching Sam. "Parnia told him she didn't know, but maybe she might talk to me if I go in alone without you. It's worth a chance she might."

"Okay. Let's head to Boston and visit Parnia. I'll wait outside in the fresh air."

Andrea called ahead to the Boston Correctional Center, identified herself, and requested to meet with inmate Parnia Jahanbami. Thirty minutes later, she entered the correctional center and waited in an interview room for the officer to escort Parnia to her.

When Parnia entered the interview room, Andrea said, "Parnia, I understand you're friendly with Tsarina, and she may be staying with her cousin Ada. I want to talk to Tsarina and hoped you would tell me where she and Ada live."

"The man you were with that night killed my husband and broke my arm."

"Your husband was going to kill a young child. If your husband had dropped his gun when told to, he would be alive, and you wouldn't have had your arm broken."

Parnia stared at Andrea with fury in her expression. "I don't know where Tsarina or Ada lives. Even if I did, I would not tell you."

"I can help you and Radir if you help me. We only want to talk to Tsarina, hoping she knows where I could find her brother and the Imam."

"Tsarina won't help you."

"I would like your help, Parnia. If you help me, I will help you."

Parnia sat there glaring at Andrea. "The child was your daughter, yes?"

"Yes. Do you have children?"

"No, and now that my husband is dead, I will not have any children. What's more, Tsarina is my friend. I could never help you find her."

"Can you tell me where her cousin Ada lives in Lawrence?"

"I do not know the address. I was there maybe two times. I would not tell you, even if I knew,"

"You and Radir will be in prison for many years. But, with your help, I could help you and Radir return to your country." Knowing Parnia would not cooperate, Andrea stood from her chair and said, "If you change your mind, tell the guard you would like to speak to me."

"I won't change my mind."

Andrea left the corrections center.

"No luck, Sam. What's next?"

"Let's find out if Ferguson talked. If not, let's head back to headquarters and interview him."

Back in Andrea's car, she called Burke, listened to what he had to say, and repeated it to Sam. "Ferguson said he knew nothing and refused to answer questions, so Burke wants us to try to get him to cooperate."

It took nearly forty minutes to arrive at state police headquarters and enter the room where Ferguson sat handcuffed to the desk. Andrea brought him a sandwich and a Coke as she and Sam sat opposite him.

Sam took over the questioning. "I assume you remember me visiting at your home. So you know, the U.S. Attorney will charge you with conspiracy and aiding and abetting related to the violent death of federal agents and state police officers. Those charges include providing the means for a terrorist killer to escape capture. At your age, you will spend most of your remaining life in prison. I feel you didn't know what you were getting into when you agreed to help Shahrad Abedini and his sister, Tsarina, to set a trap for the police. But, you became a willing co-conspirator by signing off on a fraudulent building inspector's report. Tsarina and her brother used you to hide the barn's structural plan from the authorities. We want to find where Shahrad and the Imam are hiding. If you help us find them, we will talk to the prosecutor about reduced jail time for you and your wife, Tsarina."

"I don't know where they are."

Andrea then spoke. "Tucker, I don't believe you. You lied to Agent Caviello when he questioned you at your home, and you are lying to us now. I'm sure you know where your wife is staying. We are offering you a great deal, not just for you but for your wife. If convicted, you and your wife will spend years in prison, far apart from each other. You may never get out, but Tsarina is young enough that she could get released someday. However, once released, the government will likely deport her. By cooperating, you both can still have a life together in your home in New Hampshire."

Ferguson sat in silence. He appeared distressed and beaten down. Yet, Ferguson had no criminal record and had seemed happily married and content with his new wife in retirement living in comfort near the ocean. After considering his fate, he finally nervously mumbled that he didn't know where his wife or the other two were staying.

"That's hard to believe you don't know where your wife is," said Andrea.

"I don't know. I've been told not to call Tsarina or try to find her or her brother," mumbled Ferguson.

"Who told you not to call or try to find her?" asked Sam.

"The guy who drove me to my home where I got arrested. I don't know his name. I think he works for the Imam, and it wasn't a request but a warning he made to me."

"What about Tsarina's close friends or relatives she may be staying with?" asked Andrea.

"She has a cousin, Ada, but I don't know for sure where she lives or have a way to call her. I think she lives near Lawrence. Tsarina is close to Radir's sister, Parnia. Both of them have visited Ada together. If I knew, I would tell you. I'm too old to go to jail."

Andrea contacted the guard to escort Ferguson back to his cell.

"It's getting late, and I'm hungry, Sam. So let's get something to eat, okay?"

*   *   *

Liang Wu wasn't feeling well when he woke up that morning. He didn't want to go to work but didn't have sick leave. Therefore, Liang went to work early, told his boss he wasn't feeling well and asked if he could leave once he finished his work, promising to skip lunch and take no breaks.

Liang scurried around the office building, emptying wastebaskets and wiping desks clean. Max watched him from his work desk, wondering why Liang was racing to clean the office area at a rate never seen before.

"Li," Max called him, "What's going on? Why are you in such a hurry today?"

"I'm not feeling good. Got to finish work and go home early to bed. You need me to clean something for you?"

'No. If you don't feel good, go home and rest. You can clean up here another day when you're feeling better." Max sat back in his chair, thinking this could be a good day to put his plan into motion.

Liang completed all his assigned work quicker than usual. He moved to the second floor and cleaned the offices there with the help of a co-worker. Liang avoided taking any breaks or socializing with anyone. He was sweating profusely from working as fast as he could. The back of his shirt was soaked, and sweat ran down his forehead. He constantly rubbed the moisture from rolling into his eyes. Finally, Liang couldn't do anymore. He felt nauseous and wanted to get home before he vomited. He checked the time and saw it was minutes before one o'clock. Liang quickly put away the cleaning apparatus he used and headed to the maintenance office to tell his boss he had finished his work and was leaving for home.

He left the building through the side exit, climbed into his van, and drove out of the parking lot. As he drove past the MLK School, traffic moved smoothly since no school buses were on the road yet. Several blocks past the school, Liang turned right onto West Street. He was anxious to get home and into bed but decided to stop at his favorite Asian restaurant and take out a container of chicken soup. He wasn't sure he could eat anything, but he thought the soup might help him feel better. Liang drove another two blocks before taking a left on Temple Street. Liang's only worry was losing his job. No work meant no pay, and he needed every dollar he made.

CHAPTER
7

Sam was waiting outside his son's apartment building entrance when Andrea arrived to pick him up the following morning.

"Good morning Andrea. Did you sleep okay?"

"Not really. I cried myself to sleep, as always. I lost Juli, and my daughter now lives with my sister. So, it's not easy for me."

"I'm sorry, Andrea. I understand what you're going through. If I were Burke, I'd temporarily assign you far from here, where you and Micaela could be together and safe."

"That won't work, Sam. The suspects have a way of finding out things. Who would have thought Randell, a state trooper, was a mole for the Imam?"

Sam couldn't find words to relieve her pain. It troubled him knowing that Andrea and her daughter were targets of the suspects. He knew the best way to end the threats was to find and arrest the fugitives and send them to prison for years. Sam was absorbed in doing just that, eliminating Andrea's constant fear and worry.

"I'm sorry, Sam. None of this is your fault, and I shouldn't complain to you. I don't want to lose your friendship."

"That's not going to happen, Andrea. You know I'll do whatever it takes to keep you and Micaela safe."

"I know that, Sam."

"Damn it, Andrea. I intend to find and arrest these guys to end any further risk to you. Hopefully, it will bring life back to normal for you and Micaela. Until that happens, I will be here for you and Micaela. Understood? We'll find these guys, even if I have to do it alone. Now, let's have breakfast, go to headquarters, and find out if there's any news on finding the suspects. If not, let's head to Lynn and wait near Sara Randell's place until she arrives home. Maybe we'll get lucky, and she'll cooperate and talk to us."

After breakfast, they arrived at State Police Headquarters in Framingham. Major Burke was in conference, so Sam followed Andrea to her office until Burke was free to meet them. After Andrea checked her messages, she contacted her sister to see how she and Micaela were doing. Sam was about to call his Hartford office when his cell phone rang. He didn't recognize the number but answered it.

"Agent Caviello, this is Sergeant Michaels at the Boston Correctional Center. I thought you'd want to know that Parnia Jahanbami received a visitor this morning. The woman identified herself as Ada Esfahani."

"Do you have an address for her, Sergeant?"

"She didn't have a driver's license and gave an address in Lawrence. While she visited, I searched for her name and the address she gave in Lawrence but didn't find either one. I planned to confront her when she finished her visit, but she had already left. I didn't see her leave. It was a quick visit on her part."

Sam figured the call didn't provide much help. He had Ada's last name and address, but both were probably fake.

*　　*　　*

Max's phone vibrated. He recognized the number and quickly answered it. "Hey Max, it's Kim. I'm at a diner a few miles from your office and anxious to get home. So, I hope we can get this done soon."

"You picked a good day to show up. I'll leave work and meet you at the diner. Text me the address." Max ended the call and walked to his boss's office.

"Ms. Gibbons, I'm not feeling well. I think my knee might be infected. I need to see my doctor at the Vet's Hospital. I may need the rest of the week off if it's infected. I cleared my desk and locked up."

"Alright, Max. Take care of yourself. Call and let me know how things went with your appointment and when you'll return to work."

* * *

Just before noon, Max entered the diner and searched for his old army buddy. He recognized Kim Kiyoshi, nicknamed KK by their squad leader, waving to him from the rear booth. As Max sauntered to the booth, KK stood up. They hugged and patted each other on the back. They both had served in the same squad together in Afghanistan.

"It's good to see you, KK. It's been a while. So, fill me in on what the rest of the guys are doing now."

"Sparky, Shep, Case, Doc, and I work with Sarge in Tennessee. Beni works for a new hi-tech company that received a sizable contract from the Army. Wess got a job at an ITAR-registered machine parts supplier for the defense industry located only a few miles from where Beni works. The two companies are only twenty minutes apart from each other. Both are paying good wages and benefits, more than you're getting here, Max. You won't believe it, but Sarge started a commune in the same area. It's right up TK's alley. He surrounded himself with a clan of women and hired workers along with Sparky, Shep, Case, Doc, and me. As we all know, Sarge is into guns. They're his favorite toys. Somehow, he started his own business at the compound, assembling guns with parts and making his unique brand of fentanyl. You should join us there. It's not the Taj Mahal, but there's no rent, good food, and all the beer you want, helping his business make loads of money selling his products. Pretty much what we did in the army. The best part is the pay is good, and there's plenty of booze and women around."

"I'm not interested in joining his tribe, KK. Sergeant Trent Killingworth was a warrior on the battlefield, but his psyche is very suspect outside the war zone. He killed whoever he thought was a danger to him, including women and kids. It worked in Afghanistan, but it's not going to work here. He was very erratic and exhibited way too much rage. We didn't give TK the nickname Killer for no reason. But, if TK needs help with his business and the pay's good, I'd be willing to help out, but I'm not bedding down in his little fiefdom."

"The Sarge has calmed down a bit, but he still gets irritated, especially with those who don't do their share of the work at the compound."

"Well, I'm still upset with some of his unpredictable actions against those he saw as the enemy, but I'm putting that behind me. I still get nightmares about the war and the horror we faced. Nevertheless, I have to credit Sarge for what he did to ensure the squad went home alive and not in a box."

"Not to change the subject, Max, but let's move on to the plan at hand so we can leave here and you can start a new life with your buddies."

"It just so happens that today's a good day to put the plan in motion. I'm all packed and ready to move on. I'll go over the details, and then we should be heading south within a few hours."

CHAPTER
8

Wdown at the screen and saw no caller ID. However, he was curious
hile Andrea was still talking with her sister and daughter, Sam went
to the break room to get coffee when he got another call. He looked
and decided to answer the call.

"Yes, who's this?"

"It's Tsarina, Sam?"

"How did you get this number?"

"I have my ways."

Sam had no way to trace the call while standing in the break room.

"Good to know, Tsarina. Why are you calling me?"

"I want to make a deal."

"What do you have in mind?"

"I'm willing to tell you where the Imam and his associates live. But, in exchange, I want your promise that my brother, his wife, and I can leave the country without interference."

"That's unlikely. The Imam, your brother, and Rashid were the leaders responsible for killing many police and federal officers. Besides, the state and federal prosecutors will have the final say in any deal, not me."

"My brother only allowed the Imam and Rashid to use his farm. He was not part of what happened when the police came to attack those at the farm.

My brother and I were miles away from the farm and have never killed or hurt anyone."

"You and your brother gave Rashid and his men a place to hide after shooting a police officer in Boston. Your husband Tucker submitted a false building inspection report. By doing that, you both became a party to what they did and are considered just as guilty. It's called a conspiracy. I'm sure you are familiar with the term. Speaking of your husband, why aren't you including your husband, Tucker, in your request for a deal?"

"He doesn't want to leave America. Besides, Tucker was not part of what happened that morning. He only looked the other way to help my brother get the barn ready for the hired farm help to have a place to live. He also did it so my brother would give his blessing for the marriage. It was a marriage of convenience. Tucker is old, and your government should be lenient with him. Maybe, a small fine for what he did."

"Well, I can't make any deal with you, but I will bring your request to those who can. After that, the prosecutors will make the decision. How can I get back to you?"

"You cannot call me. Tell me how long it will take. Then I will call you."

"I should know something by this time tomorrow." Sam heard nothing in response, only silence. "Hello, are you still there, Tsarina?" Sam realized she had ended the call. He wondered how Tsarina got his cell number and felt uneasy about trusting her. He decided to reach out to Major Burke and AUSA Ranero to fill them in on Tsarina's request.

*   *   *

"That's it," said Max pointing to the black van parked in the back of the apartment building on Worthington Drive. "That's the wheels we'll use for the pickup. Once we have our package, we'll bring the van back like it never left here. I didn't see any obvious pole cams on this street, but to be on the safe side, once we return the van, we don't want you spotted walking away from the apartment. So we have to make it look like you went inside the apartment building from the rear entrance. We'll drop off your SUV right after getting the van. Once we get the package, you'll drop me off to get your SUV, and I'll follow you a distance behind back toward the apartment. You'll return the van to the same parking space. Then, you walk between the two adjacent apartment buildings that you'll see on the slope straight ahead. I'll be waiting for you on the street in front of them. That'll make sure no one sees you leaving after you drop off the van. From there, we head south."

"Simple enough, Max. Let's do it."

"Okay, KK. Drive a short distance down the road and take the first left onto Grove Avenue. Drive until you see the apartment buildings on the left. I'll tell you when to stop. I'll get out and walk between the buildings to the van. I'll drive the van out and meet you where we'll leave your SUV. From there, you drive the van wearing a cap I'll give you."

Max then put on the cap, exited KK's SUV, and carefully snuck between the apartments watching to ensure no one saw him. He then moved down to the black van and unlocked the driver's side door with duplicate keys he made after borrowing them from Liang Wu's maintenance locker. He slid into the driver's seat and started up the van. He slowly backed out of the parking space, placed it into drive, and drove out onto the road.

Minutes later, Max drove to where KK waited in his SUV. KK took over driving the van while Max gave him directions for the short drive to the nearby elementary school. Max directed KK to park across the street from the first school bus in line, waiting for the school day to end and for the kids to come out of the old red-bricked school building. They didn't wait long before Max saw the front doors open, and the kids started piling out. Max left the van and remained a short distance from the first bus with KK behind him. Max kept his head down and wore dark sunglasses. When Max saw her, he yelled out. "Ena, it's Max."

Ena Oshiro heard her name and turned to see Max waving to her. She looked puzzled, seeing him, and wondered why Angie's brother was there.

"Hi, Ena. Angie called me at work because she wasn't feeling well and went to the doctor. She asked me to pick you up because she's not at home waiting for you. I'll call your mom and see if she wants me to bring you to her."

"Okay, Max," said Ena.

Max introduced Ena to his friend. "This is Kim, Ena. He's my friend. We work together, and since I don't have a car, he offered to drive Angie to the doctor and me to pick you up."

"Kon'nichiwa, Ena. Aete ureshīdesu. Kyō no gakkō wa dōdeshita ka?" KK, speaking in Japanese, said it was nice to meet you and asked how school was today.

"Yokattadesu," Ena said, answering that it was good.

Max noticed a teacher eyeballing them and heading in their direction. "Let's get you to your mom, Ena." He grabbed her hand and walked her to the van, keeping his back to the teacher. He helped Ena into a rear seat, secured her with a seat belt, and then slid onto the front passenger seat.

KK, wearing the hat Max gave him, glanced at the teacher calling Ena's name, climbed into the driver's seat, and drove off just as the teacher approached, calling out to Ena.

"That was my teacher. Maybe she wanted me for something," said Ena.

"It's okay, Ena. She can ask you when you see her in school tomorrow," responded Max.

CHAPTER
9

After being briefed about Tsarina's call to Sam, Major Burke was adamant about not agreeing to any deal with Tsarina but agreed to discuss it with the State's Attorney.

Sam followed that up by calling and briefing AUSA Ranero about Tsarina's proposal for a deal. "First, I'm skeptical about trusting her. Second, I'm not in favor of giving her or her brother a pass, but, perhaps, we could give her brother's wife a pass and a promise for a reduced sentence for her and her brother followed by their deportation."

Ranero listened to Sam's proposal. "I'll run it by my boss and the FBI. They might agree on a lesser sentence and deportation, providing Tsarina gives us the whereabouts of all the remaining persons involved, leading to their arrests."

"We need to put an end to this investigation. Jail time and deportation should satisfy everybody. Tsarina will call me back within twenty-four hours for an answer. After that, we should be ready to trace the call. Could you have the FBI ping the cell towers on the call she made to my cell a few minutes ago? It may give us an idea of the area she is calling from."

"Okay, Sam. I have your cell number. I'll call you when I have everything. Thanks for calling me."

"Before you hang up, Donna, Andrea Serrano, and I will attempt to interview Lieutenant Randell's wife when she arrives home from work. I'll call you later to let you know how it went."

*   *   *

Andrea and Sam watched Sara's residence waiting for her to arrive home from work. Andrea kept her conversation centered on the business at hand despite her feelings for Sam. She couldn't stop thinking of him ever since Juli revealed she found her perfect match, her soulmate, in Sam. Juli had described Sam as caring, attentive to her needs, especially when making love, and treated her with respect. Andrea was envious, and after Juli died, she began working as Sam's new partner. She saw for herself the same qualities in Sam as Juli did— respectful, trustful, and caring. She wanted him as her soulmate but worried she would never see him again when he finished his assignment in Boston and returned to Hartford. After Sam had rescued her daughter from the terrorist kidnappers, it cemented her love for him, especially since her daughter, Micaela, also adored Sam. She knew he would make a perfect husband and father. Before he left Boston, she had to convince Sam to stay with her or take her and Micaela with him to Hartford.

It wasn't until nearly seven o'clock that Sara pulled into her residence's driveway. Moments later, lights went on inside the house. Before approaching her, Sam and Andrea agreed to give Sara time to settle in at home. They waited twenty minutes before exiting their car and heading to the front door. Once the doorbell rang, the front outside light came on. Sam saw Sara peeking through the sidelight window before she finally cracked open the door.

"What do you want?" Sara asked in an unfriendly tone.

Andrea first showed her state police identification and badge. "Sara, we would like a few minutes of your time. We have an offer to present that may interest you."

"What kind of offer?"

"It's related to criminal charges affecting your husband and you."

"I have no charges against me. Have you talked to my husband's attorney?"

"We will talk to your husband and his attorney but would like to speak with you first. I believe you will agree that our proposal is fair and beneficial to you and your husband."

"Shouldn't I have the attorney here?"

"That's up to you, Sara. However, our offer doesn't require you to say anything to us, only listen to what we propose. Furthermore, we will not ask any questions about the criminal charges pending against your husband."

Sara thought it might be worthwhile to listen to what they had to say if she didn't have to answer questions. "I will listen to your offer but will have to talk to my husband and his attorney before I respond to your offer."

"We understand."

Sara then opened the door to allow them into her home. She had them follow her to the kitchen table, where she asked that they sit.

Andrea began by mentioning that the federal and state prosecutors agreed to the offer she was about to make. Andrea paused to get Sara's reaction before beginning. "What you may not know, Sara, there were several leaders involved in what happened at the farm when the government arrived with search and arrest warrants. These leaders fled the scene, leaving others to fight their battle against the police. They abandoned their crew and went into hiding. We know who they are and want to find where they are hiding. You may have heard their names, Shahrad Abedini, his wife, and sister Tsarina, and the Imam. We want to locate them and hold them accountable for killing state and federal officers."

Sara became repulsed by who the detective blamed. "It was the police who went on the owner's property to kill these men. The police had no right to go there. They should have left the men alone instead of assaulting them."

Andrea responded quickly. "Sara, an officer saw Rashid and his men holding a young American girl hostage in their van. A police officer followed the van and forced it to pull over. When the officer walked toward the van, Rashid shot the officer and then left the scene in the van. The Imam arranged for Rashid and his men to hide from the police at Abedini's farm, where they held two young women they planned on killing. The police could not allow that to happen and went to the farm to rescue them."

Sara looked surprised that Rashid and his men not only held young women hostages but shot a police officer. No one mentioned that to her when the police arrested her husband. She sat in silence, contemplating all that Andrea had said to her before speaking in a softer tone. "I have not yet heard your offer."

Sam spoke before Andrea outlined their offer. "Sara, we first should mention that the police did not arrest you the night they arrested your husband. However, everyone involved in what these men did that day at the farm, including harboring Rashid Al Madari, will be indicted and arrested. These indictments will also name you and your husband for sheltering a murderer and fugitive in your home."

Sara's face grimaced as her jaw tightened and lines of concern appeared on her forehead.

"I will be arrested?

Sam's knee hit Andrea's, signaling her to answer Sara.

"We will ask you to appear before the court to answer the charges rather than have the police come to your workplace or home to arrest you. The criminal charges of harboring a fugitive are severe and call for many years in prison. However, I think you will agree that it's essential that you consider our offer to reduce the charges against you and your husband in exchange for information that both of you can give us."

Sara responded anxiously. "What information?"

"We want to find Abedini, his wife and sister, and the Imam and his associates who remain hiding from the police. Therefore, we encourage you and your husband to help us find them, and in exchange, the charges against you would get reduced and result in less prison time for your husband."

Sara reflected on their offer. She initially said she would not speak but only listen, but now, she had questions that needed answering. "Will you deport my husband and me?"

Sam looked to Andrea to answer her.

"That will depend on how much you and your husband cooperate. Your husband will certainly lose his job and will likely get deported after serving prison time. However, I don't know if the prosecutor will recommend deporting you."

"Will I lose my job?"

Andrea looked to Sam to answer her question.

"If you and your husband give us the location of the persons we mentioned and we arrest them, we will do our best to help you keep your job."

"If we cannot help you find these people, will I go to jail? As you can see, I am pregnant."

"Right now, I can't answer that. The prosecutor decides that."

Sara's face displayed uneasiness. Her hands trembled, and her eyes watered as she wiped her brow while trying to get comfortable in her chair. Then, unexpectedly, she stood up without making eye contact. "Is there anything else you want to tell me?"

"Only, it is in your best interest and your husband's to help us find those we identified. Sometimes, if we find one, they will cooperate and tell us where the others are hiding. With your help, I believe you will not go to jail, and you can have your baby without worry," said Andrea.

Sam tuned in again. "Also, Sara, the government will not force you to testify against your husband in court if you cooperate."

"This is good to know. If there is nothing else," said Sara, indicating the interview was over. "I will talk to my husband and his attorney. We will consider what you told me." Sara then escorted them to the front door.

At the door, Sam thought to add another suggestion. "One more thing. You and your husband might consider not having the attorney present if you decide to talk to us. I assume the Imam or Abedini arranged for the attorney and are paying him. If so, the attorney could be more loyal to them. So, if you and your husband decide to cooperate, the attorney will certainly communicate this to whoever is paying him."

Sara didn't respond, avoided eye contact, and opened the door for them to leave. On the way to their car, Andrea questioned whether Sara and her husband would talk to them without the attorney.

"I'm not sure, Andrea, but I wanted to plant the seed to give her something to consider. We did our part. It's up to her and her husband now."

*   *   *

"Where are we going, Max? We should be home by now," asked an anxious Ena.

As planned, Max signaled KK, who reached for his cell and made a covert call to Max. Max answered the cell. "Hi, May. Thanks for returning my call. Angie wasn't feeling well, so I brought her to the local hospital. She texted me that the doctor was admitting her for the night. I'll watch Ena until you get home. Uh, what? Max paused, pretending to listen to Ena's mom. "Oh, okay, no problem. I'll see you later tonight. Yep, okay, goodbye."

Max turned to face Ena in the back seat. "That was your mom. She said she was working a double shift tonight. So she won't get home until after midnight. Kim lives several miles from here. He's going to let me borrow his car to take you home. It's going to take a while to get to his place. So, sit back and relax. If you're tired, take a short nap, and I'll wake you when we get you home."

"I'm not tired. It's too early for a nap."

"Okay, do some of your homework or read a story. Then, if you get tired, close your eyes and rest." He glanced at KK, who hunched his shoulders as a sign that Ena might not take a nap and that they would eventually have to deal with her. Max nodded in agreement and remained silent while KK entered the entrance ramp to the Mass Pike for the long trip to Tennessee.

CHAPTER
10

Mayumi worked until past midnight. She didn't have time to call Angie again to have Ena sleepover. So, she would get her in the morning to see her off to school. Mayumi set the alarm for six the following day to get Ena up early enough for breakfast and then walk her to the school bus stop at the end of the street.

When the alarm rang in the morning, Mayumi wanted to hit the snooze button for a few extra minutes of sleep. Instead, she shut the alarm and closed her eyes for seconds before forcing herself to get out of bed, concerned she'd fall back asleep. She was exhausted from the long hours of depressing work at the hospital. She rubbed her eyes to remove the sticky dried-up tears that had often filled her eyes the night before. Finally, Mayumi slowly rolled up and sat on the edge of the bed, thinking of the horrors of working with so many sick, older adults, many of who subsequently died. She showered, put on a robe and a pair of worn sandals, and moseyed over to Angie's apartment next door. After ringing the doorbell, Mayumi waited several minutes before Angie peeked out the nearby window to see who it was and finally opened the door.

"Good morning May. Is everything alright?"

"Yes. I'm sorry if I woke you. I'm here to get Ena."

"What? After we talked yesterday, I got a message from the hospital saying you were leaving early and would pick up Ena at the school."

Mayumi's throat tightened, and her color drained from her face. "I didn't ask anyone to message you." Panic grabbed her words as her voice went dry. "Where is Ena, Angie?"

"I don't know, May. She's not here. Maybe we should call the school. But first, come in the house."

Fear paralyzed Mayumi as she entered Angie's apartment. Her legs wobbled, and her hands became cold and sweaty. When grabbing her phone, Mayumi's hand trembled as she called the school just before seven. The school's phone rang several times before the principal answered it. Mayumi nervously demanded why her daughter had not come home from school. The principal was at a loss for words but said she would immediately get the bus monitoring teachers to her office for an answer. The principal promised she would call back within minutes.

A few minutes later. Mayumi's cell phone rang. Her hand uncontrollably shook when reaching for her phone, causing it to slip out of her hand and onto the floor. Angie bent over, gripped the phone, and handed it to May.

"Hello," said Mayumi apprehensively.

"May, this is Diane Henderson, Ena's teacher. I was one of the teachers monitoring the school bus arrivals as the children left for home. I noticed Ena talking with two men. One of them held her hand as they walked to a black van parked across the street. I didn't see the man's face she walked with, but the driver was an Asian man who wore a hat similar to what horse racing jockeys wear. I called out to her, but she may not have heard me. The guy who held her hand placed Ena in the back seat, and both men got into the van and drove off. I was too far to see the license plate, but it looked like a Mass plate."

"Why didn't you call me? I didn't approve anyone else to pick her up from school other than Angie Lomax and me."

"I did call your number, but it was busy, so I called Angie and only got her voice mail. So I left a message for her to call me back or to have you call me back as soon as possible. Did you talk to Angie yet?"

"I'm with Angie now." Mayumi looked at Angie with panic gripping her face. "Angie, Ena's teacher said she left a message for you to call me. So why didn't you call me?

"She left me a message? Let me check my phone." Angie searched for her phone but couldn't find it. Then, she faced Mayumi with a perplexed expression and shrugged her shoulders. "I can't find it. Maybe you can call me so I can hear the ring."

Anxiety and fear encompassed Mayumi's whole being surrounded by those she thought should have the answers. "Angie can't find her phone, Diane. Does anybody know anything about who took my Ena? What am I going to do now?"

"I'll call the police and tell them what happened here first. Then, I'll request the police to call you. I have your number. I'm so sorry that Ena didn't get home. Please, call me after you talk to the police," said Henderson, who ended the call.

Mayumi stared in space, unsettled, as tears began rolling down her cheeks. Angie asked what the teacher had told her. Mayumi said nothing for a moment. Fear crept up her spine while her eyes darted around the room. Then, abruptly, she felt ill and asked for the bathroom. Angie pointed toward its direction as Mayumi hurried to it, closed the door, kneeled in front of the toilet, and vomited. When it was over, still kneeling before the bowl, Mayumi began to weep.

*   *   *

Thirty minutes later, Mayumi received a call from a Boston police detective who identified himself as Delroy Haywood. He told her he had just finished interviewing Diane Henderson and would like to stop at her place. He wanted a personal description and photograph of Ena and information regarding any special needs, such as medications that her daughter may require and the identity of anyone she may have been comfortable with to get in their vehicle.

Mayumi heard only partial words from the detective, remaining lost within a dazed aura worrying about Ena. Angie snapped her fingers as Mayumi awoke, asking, "What?" The detective repeated he needed her address. She stuttered with Angie's address, and he estimated he'd be there shortly. In the meantime, Angie desperately tried to find her phone without success, so she asked Mayumi again to call her cell number. Mayumi selected Angie's number on her cell and heard it ring seven times before Angie's voicemail came on.

Angie raised her arms and asked, "Well, I don't hear a ring. Did you call the right number?"

"It rang a lot, Angie. Your voicemail just came on asking me to leave a message."

"For chrissake, it didn't ring here. Could I have left it somewhere? I only went to the drugstore down the street. After that, I came home and took a nap for an hour, maybe longer. I remember I didn't get or make any calls after that. I didn't feel that great, so I went to bed early and watched television until about ten before going to sleep."

Not long afterward, Angie's doorbell rang. When she opened the door, the African American man displayed his badge and identified himself as Detective Delroy Haywood. "I'm here to see Angie Lomax and Mayumi Oshiro."

Once the detective entered the apartment, Angie introduced him to Mayumi. Detective Haywood interviewed Mayumi for twenty minutes and obtained a relatively recent photo of her daughter. Mayumi, still in a nervous trance, jumbled her daughter's description, causing the detective to have her repeat it slowly and in detail, including what clothes she wore to school and any special needs or required medications.

"Other than you and Angie, does your daughter feel comfortable going with anyone else she might know? For example, maybe a school friend's parents or a relative of yours," asked Haywood.

"No, no, not here. Ena would only go to my mother, but she lives in New York and hasn't visited here for several months. She wouldn't go with anyone else. I have no other relatives here."

Haywood turned to Angie and asked her the same question.

"I have no relatives other than my brother, Billy. I got a call from the hospital saying May was leaving early and would pick up Ena at the school, so I thought nothing other than Ena was going home with May. However, I can't find my phone now. I could have left it at the drug store yesterday."

"Would you call the drug store when you can?" asked the detective.

"May, let me borrow your phone. I'll call the manager now."

Haywood explained to Mayumi what further investigative steps the police department would take to find her daughter. "We will examine the street and building cameras in the school area. Maybe a camera videoed the van and its license plate. If so, we could identify the owner. We'll interview the teachers and students outside the school that afternoon. In addition, we'll ask residents and business owners in the area if they saw the men in the van pick up your daughter. Here's my card with my cell number on it. Call me if you have any questions."

Angie finished her call to the pharmacy. "They searched for my phone at the pharmacy but didn't find it."

"Please call me if you think of anything else that could be important. Rest assured, we will do everything we can to find your daughter. Call me anytime if you have questions. That goes for you too, Angie," said the detective.

*   *   *

Sam's phone rang. He held it up to see who was calling and saw the No Caller ID on the screen. *Probably Tsarina calling as promised,* Sam thought. "Hello, Tsarina."

"How did you know it was me?" she replied.

"Well, you're the only one who called me with a blocked phone number."

"What did you learn from the prosecutor? Can we get a deal?"

"We can arrange a deal for you and your brother's wife, but not for your brother. The arrangement would require you to tell us where the Imam, his associates, and your brother are staying. We'll then arrest them. If there are no arrests, there is no deal."

"What if I give you more? Can we then include my brother in the deal?"

"What do you mean by giving us more?"

Tsarina wavered for a moment before speaking again. "There are others who are in the area. I can tell you who and where they are."

"You have to tell me what you mean by others and why we'd be interested in them."

"I cannot give you names over the phone. Your government will know them and want to know where they are. Meet me, and I'll give you a list of the names and where you could find them."

"Why would our government be interested in names on a list? Are they radicals who want to harm Americans?"

"Yes. They plan to seek revenge on America and came here without detection."

Sam took his time to consider his next move. "I could meet you somewhere in public where you can give me the list of names and their location. Then, I'll take it to the prosecutor, who will decide if those names are of greater interest to the government than your brother."

"We must meet in a private place of my choosing—just you and me. The names will be of great interest to your government."

Sam chuckled to himself. "Tsarina, I give you my word that no one will arrest you if we meet alone at a place where I feel safe from your people who want to kill me."

"My people? No one knows I called you for a deal. If they knew, they would kill me. I can only meet you where I feel safe. If you cannot do this, I will not call you again. There will be no deal."

"What place do you have in mind for us to meet?"

"I'll call you in about one hour and tell you where to meet me." She then ended the call.

Sam returned to Andrea's car. "How did the trace of her call go?"

"Ranero said the FBI got her phone number and pinged her location near Derry, New Hampshire. Currently, the FBI is tracking her phone near the town of West Hampstead. An FBI tactical team is heading there now."

"Is Major Burke and his team working with the FBI on the surveillance?"

"Yes, I spoke with him minutes before Ranero called me. He and his team are with an FBI team driving to New Hampshire. FBI agents from Manchester, New Hampshire, were alerted and were not far from the area where Tsarina had called."

"Great. Our plan worked to find Tsarina's whereabouts and movement."

Andrea agreed. "Major Burke will keep us informed as to what's happening. He wants to know the place she chooses for us to meet. It could be a setup to kill us. Once Burke knows the location, FBI agents will check it out and get back to us. Burke's instructions are if it appears to be a set-up, they'll take them down."

"Hmm. It may be better to wait for Tsarina's call and listen to what she had to say before our team moves in and arrests them."

Andrea's phone rang. "This is Andrea." Andrea listened and nodded her head a few times before she spoke. "Okay, but Sam feels it might be better to meet with her first." Andrea listened to the caller for a moment before ending the call. "Burke said he'll recommend they wait until she calls before any action occurs. Then, he'll contact us again to work out a plan."

"Okay, Andrea. Let's keep driving and get close to where she may want to meet."

CHAPTER
11

Angie's phone vibrated in Max's pocket. He pulled it out, looked at the phone's screen, and saw it was a call from Mayumi. First, he looked back at Ena to ensure she was still sleeping. Then, he whispered to Kim that it was a call from mom, meaning Mayumi, as he turned and shifted his head toward Ena.

"What are you going to do?" asked Kim.

"I'll call Angie later. I left a burner phone where she wouldn't notice it. She probably has company now, so I'll wait until later tonight to call her and explain the situation."

"What? What if she calls the man in blue? She's friends with the mom, isn't she?"

"She won't call the cops. It's cool, man. Not to worry."

They were hours away from Boston by now. The sedative Max added to the drink he gave Ena did its job of putting her to sleep during the initial long stretch of driving. However, Max was aware that it may become more challenging to keep her calm once she woke up, knowing she was not with her mother yet, and may never see her again.

*   *   *

Andrea's cell rang as she and Sam were only a short distance from West Hampstead. She answered the call from Major Burke, listened to his instructions, and ended the call. "Burke said Tsarina met with five men parked in a small strip mall parking lot. Ten minutes later, the men left her sitting in her car alone. The state police van followed the two vehicles carrying the five men. A few miles past the town of Sandown, the two vehicles turned into a mostly dirt road. One of the officers exited their van and went into the heavy brush to monitor their movement. Hidden in the brush, the officer saw an old abandoned brick building fifty or sixty yards from the main road. He reported someone had shattered most of the worn-downed building's windows. Tall trees and overgrown brush concealed the old building hidden from the road. The officer said the five men first checked out the interior of the building. Then, three men positioned themselves hidden within the surrounding brush on the left side of the building. The other two men drove their vehicles out of sight into a dirt road on the rear right side of the building. He saw both men move into the brush closer to the right side of the building. The officer observed all five men armed with assault weapons. This is definitely a set-up, Sam."

"Did Burke say what they planned to do once Tsarina gets there if she shows up?"

"No. Burke said he'd get back to us."

Sam thought through a couple of scenarios before deciding he wanted input into the decision-making. "I'm calling Burke. I have a couple of ideas for him and the FBI to consider. I want your input on this too, Andrea. What're your thoughts?"

"I don't think we should go into a hornet's nest where five guys with assault weapons will be aiming to kill us."

Sam called Burke to give input on meeting Tsarina

"What's up, Sam?" asked Burke when he answered the call.

"Major, we should wait for Tsarina to call me and listen to what she has to say. It could be her offer is legitimate, and she has a list of foreign radicals in the U.S. that would interest us. Those men hiding in the brush could be there to provide security and prevent her from getting arrested."

"It's too risky. The five men are most likely there to kill you rather than there to protect her."

"That could very well be the case, but I think if she shows up, it's because she wants a face-to-face with me. She could be willing to trade. I'll be extra careful."

There was no immediate response from Major Burke until he voiced his concern. "I still think it's too dangerous for you to go there. However, I'll discuss it with the team and get back to you when Tsarina calls again. We may know a little more, depending on what she says to you. Tell her you are at least an hour away from here when she calls. That gives us time to get more troops to the scene and establish an appropriate plan."

It wasn't long after that Sam's phone rang. He nodded to Andrea to exit the car and call Burke.

Sam waited a few seconds to allow Andrea to move far enough away from the car.

"This is Caviello."

"It's Tsarina. Meet me in one hour."

"Wait. I don't know how long it will take me to get to wherever you send me. Text me the location before you hang up so I can tell you how long it would take to get there."

"Where are you now?"

"I am about twenty minutes away from state police headquarters in Framingham. I'm dropping off my partner. I don't trust you any more than you trust me, so I'm coming alone. I hope you will also be alone.

"I will be alone." Tsarina gave him the name of the road and town and the landmark to find. "Get here in an hour. You are the police. Put on your blue lights and siren." Sam's phone went silent. Tsarina hung up.

Sam called Burke to relay the conversation with Tsarina and repeated his desire to meet with her.

"We'll get back to you once she shows up. But, stay out of sight. You don't want her to see you waiting by the side of the road," said Burke.

CHAPTER

12

FBI Supervisory Agent Dell Haskins' cell rang. He recognized the call from the agent hidden among the heavily overgrown brush facing the front of the abandoned brick building. "Dell, a car just pulled into the dirt road and drove up to the front of the building. My partner will text you the plate number. The driver appears to be on a cell phone. Wait— the car door opened. The driver hasn't yet exited—coming out now. It's a woman— with black hair. She's looking left— wait, I see a light flashing from the inside the brush on her left. She's turning slightly right. Yeah, I see another light flashing. It's a signal of sorts. She's looking around again. She looked our way. We snapped a photo. We'll text it to you. She's on her cell now."

Sam's cell rang. "Caviello."

"Agent, this is Tsarina. Have you found the landmark?"

"Yes, I am here."

"Good." Tsarina then gave him directions to the dirt road to take for the meeting place. "I'll be there in five minutes. I'll see you there shortly." She ended the call.

Sam called Major Burke. "Jack, Tsarina just called, saying she was a few minutes out. She gave me directions to the meeting place. I want to meet with her. I'll be careful. I don't think they'll shoot me on sight. She either wants to deal face-to-face or maybe kill me herself. We need to know for sure."

"Stand by one, Sam." Burke relayed Sam's request to FBI Agent Dell Haskins. "Although risky, I'm with Caviello meeting with her. If you concur, we should put our team on alert and ready for action if all hell breaks out." Haskins concurred and called his team with the plan. When all team members gave the ready sign, Burke spoke to Sam again. "Okay, Sam. We're ready here. Be careful."

"Tell me where I could find you and drop off Andrea before I head to the meeting place." After getting Burke's position, he searched for them while Andrea pleaded with Sam to allow her to go with him.

"Andrea, we've gone over this for some time now. It's too risky. You have a daughter to look after. You're not coming with me. That's final. I'll be okay. Trust me."

Sam found Burke's SUV hidden behind a convenience store and parked adjacent to it. Disappointed, Andrea got out of the car and climbed into Burke's black SUV. Burke slid down his window, and Sam followed suit by lowering his window.

"If things go wrong, use the code word bluebird," yelled out Burke.

"Got it. I'm going in. Have your teams ready. If there's any gunfire, make sure your guys hit their targets, not me. See you later."

Sam drove back onto the main road towards Route 21A, took a left a short distance up the road, and five minutes later, he rounded a sharp curve to the left. He slowed down, looking for the opening among the overgrown brush, and then turned left onto the dirt road. Sam felt apprehension immediately. His stomach felt queasy while he tried focusing on two concerns, finding good cover as he got close to the building and staying alert for gunfire from the surrounding field of brush and trees—one bullet from any direction could end his life.

* * *

Mayumi was back in her apartment. She paced around the kitchen, holding a photo of Ena tight to her heart and praying no one would harm her sweet child. Finally, she decided to call her mother in New York. Tears covered

Mayumi's cheeks, and her words were so uneven and splintered that her mother couldn't understand half of what she was saying.

"May, go slow. I don't know what you say."

"Some strange men took Ena. I feel sick. I don't know what to do. The police are looking for her but haven't found her yet."

"Oi! Please, no. How this happen?" Mayumi's mother became puzzled and upset about why anyone would do such a thing. "I'll come stay with you. I'll take a bus in the morning."

Next door, Angie looked everywhere for her cell phone. She was puzzled about her missing phone and why anyone would take Ena, a young child. She desperately wanted to call her brother Billy. She thought maybe Billy had come home while she took a nap and borrowed her phone, or could she have left it somewhere other than the pharmacy? However, she remembered not leaving the house in the last few days, other than going to the pharmacy. Angie was agitated and could feel her blood pressure rising, making her uneasy. She needed to relax and sat down on the couch. She thought of watching television to take her mind off everything.

*   *   *

Ena sighed as she woke up. She was still drowsy from whatever Max put in her drink. She looked around and was troubled by not seeing the city but open flat land for quite a distance.

"Max, where are we? You said you would take me to my mom."

"It's okay, Ena. Kim got a call from his mom, who said she wasn't feeling good. He's concerned about her, so we'll drive to where she lives to check on her. We figured we had time before your mom got out of work. We want to make sure Kim's mom is okay. While you slept, I spoke to your mom to let her know. She won't get out of work until later. We'll get something to eat, check on Kim's mom, and then get you home."

"I want to call my mom."

"Sweetheart, your mom is very busy. I had to leave a message for her to call me. When she finally called me back, she told me not to call until we got you home. Your mom is helping all the sick people at the hospital. You can call her when we get you home."

Ena didn't believe him. She knew her mom would want to talk to her if she was not home safe, rather than in a car driving somewhere with two men.

CHAPTER
13

Sam's eyes focused left and right as he crept towards what he believed was Tsarina's car parked on the right side of the abandoned brick building. Preplanned mentally, Sam stopped and positioned his car at an angle to her car's right front fender. He figured having her car to his left provided adequate cover from the men hidden in the brush on the left side of the building. Likewise, his car slanted to the left afforded decent protection on his right side. The way he positioned his car, he would exit his car between the two cars giving him cover. Intentionally, he left enough space between his left front bumper and her car's right front bumper to dash in between and sprint the short distance to the entrance on the right side of the building.

After a quick scan of the area, Sam, staying low, rushed to the open entrance and hugged the nearest wall as he entered the building. Sam wore a Level IV ballistic vest with a steel plate on an inside pocket centered over his chest. Sam covered the vest with a shirt and a lightweight blue jacket. In addition, he wore tan combat pants with large pockets on the left and right sides of the thighs. Inside the right pocket was his .40 caliber pistol, and a lightweight five-shot revolver was holstered to his right ankle.

Sam immediately saw Tsarina appear from behind an open passageway leading from an adjacent room about eight yards away. He was astonished and stunned by Tsarina's appearance.

"You're looking very nice, Tsarina. Did you dress elegantly just for me?"

Tsarina stepped toward Sam with a self-assured smirk. "A compliment from you, agent Caviello?

"A genuine compliment. I only hope what you have for me is worth my visit."

Sam guessed Tsarina was of average height, weighing no more than one hundred and twenty-five pounds. She wore a shawl covering the top of her head, showing tads of dark hair in the front and more in the back. Tsarina's wrap circled both shoulders, covering her neck while wearing a designer light blue cotton top and grey striped pants stretching to her angles. Covering her upper body was a long-sleeved, knee-length pink sweater believed to be called a Manteau. She had angle-high pink shoes and carrying a sizeable red tote over her right shoulder. Her light brown-skinned face reflected beauty. Yet, Sam was puzzled at her appearance. She looked more like a magazine model with make-up, perfectly lined eyebrows, and red lipstick. If he saw her shopping in downtown Boston, he would never take her for a trained terrorist.

"I'm just surprised. You look ready for an evening at the theater and an elaborate dinner after the show."

"I may celebrate with champagne and dinner after our meeting. But, unfortunately, I cannot celebrate with the man I love."

"Are you referring to your husband, Tucker?"

"I do not love this man. The man I love is dead."

"I'm sorry."

"Hmm. You are not sorry. Perhaps you remember his name— Rashid Al Madari."

"Wasn't he married to Melika?" Sam said with concern.

"Yes. Their families arranged their marriage, but not for love. I was his only love. But, as you know, Melika is dead too. Your government killed her."

Sam didn't like the way this was going. She sounded like she was here to get retribution instead of making a deal. He needed to get the conversation back on track. "I get it, but you mentioned you had a list of men that would interest my government in exchange for leniency for you and your brother."

"You think I believe your government, or you, can be trusted to allow me and my brother to leave without punishment?"

"I'm here in good faith, Tsarina. If you have something of interest to my government, I will take it to those who decide, and you and I could talk again. I'm here only to get the list you promised."

"Hmm. Well, in that case, I have this for you." Tsarina reached into her red tote bag and pulled out a strip of paper. "This is what you want, so here take it." She held it out toward Sam to take it.

Sam didn't move. He suspected the slip of paper she held was like a piece of cheese on a mousetrap to bait him closer to her. Then, abruptly, his body shuddered with uneasiness. He wasn't sure if it was a sign of pending danger or his adrenaline elevating, knowing something wasn't right with Tsarina's defiant attitude.

"Is there someone else with you in the back room? You said there would only be the two of us," asked Sam.

"There is no one else with me." Tsarina started to step toward Sam, holding the slip of paper. As she walked, she deliberately dropped the slip of paper and waited for Sam to react by moving toward her to retrieve it. When he didn't, Tsarina bent over and turned her body to the right, hiding her tote bag from Sam's view. She reached into the tote bag, stood up, and quickly turned to face Sam. Sam, caught off-guard, had only a second to react.

*　　*　　*

Mayumi felt nauseous, tightness and cramps in her stomach, and her head bore immense pressure. She had vomited twice in the last several minutes. She ultimately crept back to the kitchen table and sat, staring at the wall in a daze with irrational fears she may never see her daughter again.

Unexpectedly, Mayumi's body jerked awake, startled by the ring of her cell phone. The phone sounded abnormally loud as she hurried to find and answer it.

"Hello," she answered nervously.

"Mayumi, this is Detective Haywood. We have identified the van used by the men who drove off with your daughter. We captured it on a pole camera as it left the school. We have the license plate and identified the owner, who is Asian. We found the owner at home and interviewed him. He denies being at the school and having anything to do with your daughter's disappearance. We are holding him for twenty-four hours to investigate his claims that he was home sick in bed during the time in question. Your daughter's teacher, Diane Henderson, got a good look at one of the two men, who she said was Asian and wore a particular type of hat. We found a similar hat on a table in the man's apartment. I called Miss Henderson but only got her voicemail. I will arrange to meet her in the morning to show her an array of photos. Hopefully, she can identify this man as one of the two men."

"You have this man. Who is he? Maybe I know him. Did he say where he took my daughter?"

"I can't release the man's name. We don't have enough evidence to charge him yet. He claims he was not at your daughter's school. He admits it looked like his van and the license plate was his, but it was not him in the van. The man was adamant about it. I will call you tomorrow when we finish our investigation. I think we have our man, but we need further proof."

"Where is my Ena? Please find her. I am so worried about her."

"I promise I will call you as soon as possible, hopefully later today, with better news." The detective hung up.

Mayumi paused to absorb what the detective told her. For a moment, but only a moment, she felt relieved until she realized her daughter was still missing and she might never see her again.

CHAPTER
14

Sam froze, seeing Tsarina with the sneer from her contorted lips. Sam had a second to step back and yell, "Bluebird!" when he saw Tsarina turn and point a gun at him.

He yelled out the distress code in his mic as Tsarina fired two shots that hit him in the chest, plummeting him to the floor. The double blast against his chest was intense, like being pounded with a sledgehammer. Sam closed his eyes tight, holding his breath and biting down hard on his teeth to keep any painful sound from his lips. Tsarina's gratifying smirk lingered before she stepped closer for the final kill. Although in total agony, not wanting his life to end like this, Sam labored stealthily to reach into his side pants pocket for the handle of his gun. He kept his eyes closed as his right hand gripped the gun handle and slid it from his pocket, holding it against his leg to hide it from Tsarina's view.

Tsarina wanted to forever burn the image of her lover's killer in her memory, standing over him and taking aim at the man she despised. She dreamed of this moment to empty her gun of its bullets into Sam's face and decree the words she planned on using so many times.

"You killed Rashid. And now for him, I end your life."

Not paying attention to Tsarina's edict, Sam silently but instantly opened his eyes, swung his right arm up in excruciating pain, and pulled the trigger of his gun. He cranked two non-lethal shots hitting Tsarina's right shoulder. The wounds caused Tsarina to twist right while her right arm fell to her side, maintaining a finger grip on her gun. Still in distress from being shot, Sam struggled to sit upright, steady his aim, and fired a third round, hitting her gun's grip, causing her weapon to launch from her hand a couple of feet away.

Tsarina turned to face Sam with a scowl. "You're supposed to be dead. I shot you two times!"

Sam strained to lift himself from the floor. He was in a world of hurt from the bullets that hit him in his vest. Then, hearing his cover team approaching, Sam used his hidden mic to report the suspect was secure but wounded. He slowly moved close to Tsarina's side. Tsarina swung her left elbow towards Sam's face, but he was ready, turned, and slapped his gun hard against her arm. She yelled out in pain from the bone-cracking sound. Sam turned her body to handcuff her. She screeched in pain when Sam grabbed her right wrist. He saw her right hand was bleeding as he squeezed the cuffs tight, causing her to yell out angry words in Farsi that Sam figured were vulgar curse words.

"You shot me twice, Tsarina. However, I have awoken from the dead just to piss you off and arrest you. Instead of getting deported, you now will spend the rest of your life in prison."

"I knew I could not trust you or your government. You came here only to trick me."

Sam chuckled. "That's funny, Tsarina. Is that why you shot me, and your friends are hiding in the woods to kill me if you failed?"

Suddenly, Sam heard heavy gunfire outside the building. He figured sooner or later, a barrage of bullets would start flying between the FBI and Tsarina's men hiding in the brush.

"Tsarina, Haalet khoobe?" her associate shouted from a backroom window, asking if she was okay.

Sam swiftly cupped Tsarina's mouth and dragged her to the nearest wall for cover. With his free hand, he stuffed his handkerchief into her mouth to silence her as she tried responding. Sam shoved Tsarina down on her butt, then moved to the corner of the passageway separating the front room from the rear. With his gun in hand, he took a quick peek around the open passage and saw the suspect leaning into an open window with a weapon. The suspect saw Sam's glance and fired a volley of several rounds of bullets flying past the passageway corner, chipping away hoards of wood and plaster. Taking a deep breath to steady himself, Sam shifted to a low position, peered around the corner with this gun in hand, and fired four rounds at Tsarina's associate, hitting him in the head. His head drooped momentarily before he collapsed to the ground. Sam heard continued gunfire and rapid footsteps as the agents and police chased whatever suspects remained outside.

Two FBI SWAT members stood just outside the entrance door, calling for Sam. Sam responded, "Everything is under control here. I have the suspect cuffed." The two agents entered the building and took control of Tsarina.

"Everything contained outside?" asked Sam.

One agent responded they chased down the last two who tried escaping through the rear pathway but ran into the agents covering the trail.

"Great," said Sam. He grunted in pain while slowly and carefully taking off his windbreaker jacket and a long-sleeved shirt. He gingerly unsnapped his ballistic vest covering a short-sleeved T-shirt and walked out of the building to gather his composure and get some fresh air. Outside, Sam stood alone, looking at the clear blue sky. He felt discomfort taking in a deep breath. Sam removed the vest, causing the gold chain around his neck to get pulled out onto his white tee shirt. A Saint Michael pendant hung on the chain. Sam rubbed the pendant between his thumb and index finger, whispering his only thoughts as he remained looking at the sky. "Thanks, Michael." Sam was glad to be alive but mumbled to himself words he had said more than once. "I can't keep doing this. I might not be so lucky the next time."

Just then, Sam heard a car approaching that came to a sliding stop. He recognized Major Burke seated in the car. FBI Agent Dell Hawkins, Burke, and Andrea exited the vehicle and marched toward Sam.

"You okay, Sam?" asked Burke.

Sam dropped the vest to the ground and gently lifted his shirt, exposing two sizable bruises just inches below the center of his chest.

"That had to hurt my friend," said agent Hawkins.

Andrea cringed at the bruises and turned to look the other way.

"I was lucky to get my gun out fast enough to hit Tsarina before she shot me in the face. I didn't kill her. She's injured but alive."

"I'm surprised you didn't permanently put her down," Burke said.

"I wanted her alive. There's always a chance she'll decide to give us something worthwhile."

"We'll see, but don't count on it," said Burke as he turned to Andrea. "Andrea, take Sam to the hospital to get checked out. Then, call me with the results. I may want to meet with you both, later

"Yes, sir. I'll take him to Mass General. Come on, Sam."

Once they drove out onto the main road, Andrea glanced at Sam with concern. "Are you okay, Sam? I heard those two shots and then two or three more. I didn't know what to think. I was worried about you. I hope you never have to do that again."

"Yeah. Me too, Andrea. This is the third time someone shot and hit me over the past several months. I shouldn't push my luck. The next time could mean the end for me. Maybe being the boss and sitting behind a desk is not so bad after all."

"I don't want anything to happen to you, Sam. You know how I feel about you."

"Yeah. I have to slow down and not take so many risks." Sam then thought about what he had just said. "But, it's easier said than done."

Even though Andrea used the car's emergency lights and siren, it took an hour to get to the hospital.

At the hospital, Andrea identified herself and mentioned her partner was injured. The hospital staff immediately brought them into an examination room. They waited only a short time before a doctor entered the room. The doctor asked what had happened. After Sam explained the incident, he pulled up his shirt to reveal his bruises.

"Ouch. That looks painful," responded the doctor. "I need to take an x-ray to ensure there's no fractured ribs or other internal issues. If not, I'll prescribe something for the pain. You'll be black and blue for a while. I recommend rest to avoid further interaction involving your chest area."

*   *   *

Thirty minutes later, Sam and Andrea left the hospital knowing there were no severe internal issues other than fractured ribs. The doctor wrapped Sam's torso and gave him sample pain capsules to take with him. The doctor recommended Sam take time off from work and rest.

"You should stay at my apartment so I can look after you," said Andrea.

"I could use the rest and the company. But what about your daughter?"

"Micaela is still with my sister. I'll call Burke to let him know the doctor ordered rest and that you'll call him tomorrow to let him know when you're ready to meet with him."

Sam agreed, but as always, he was anxious to learn what, if anything, Tsarina might be willing to tell them now that she knew she wouldn't be leaving the country anytime soon.

"Oh, Burke mentioned that Randell and his wife, Sara, agreed to listen to our offer. So I'll meet with FBI agents tomorrow morning to prepare for our interview with them."

"Alright. We're getting somewhere now. Let's talk about it at the apartment. This could be the break we're waiting for—to find and arrest Tsarina's brother and the Imam."

CHAPTER
15

The following morning at state police headquarters, a young Asian trooper, Soshi Kojima, knocked on Major Jack Burke's partially opened office door. He reported as ordered at nine sharp. Major Burke had assigned Trooper Kojima to an FBI Asian human trafficking task force (HTTF).

"Come in, Soshi, and have a seat. How are things going in the task force?"

"Fine, sir. There are five ongoing human trafficking investigations in the greater Boston area. The cases involve the kidnapping and interstate trafficking of young Asian girls for prostitution throughout the New England states."

"Has the name Mayumi Oshiro and her missing daughter Ena come up in any investigations you're working on?"

"Yes, sir. Two men, one of whom was Asian, took Ena from her school recently. Ena's teacher got a good look at the Asian guy and the black van he drove. Unfortunately, the teacher didn't get a good look at the other guy, but she believed he was either white or Asian. We captured the van and its license plate number from a pole cam as it drove from the school to an apartment building where the suspect lives. The van's registered owner lives in that apartment building. We identified the owner. He's an Asian guy by the name of Liang Wu. Wu has a conviction of aiding and abetting a Chinese human trafficking organization four years ago. His job was transporting young Asian women within the Boston area and the surrounding states for prostitution. He refused to name the Chinese leaders involved in the trafficking scheme and served eighteen months of a two-year sentence. He got released on probation several months ago. Two FBI agents interviewed Wu. He denied picking up any student from a school several blocks away from his apartment. Wu claimed he stayed home from work on that day because he was sick and stayed in bed most of the day."

"How did he explain that his van was captured on camera driving by the school that afternoon?"

"He couldn't. He claimed somebody must have stolen his license plate or his van. As a result, the FBI prepared an affidavit for a search warrant for his apartment and van. They'll probably charge him and pressure him to cooperate if they find evidence the girl was inside the van during their search."

"Okay, thanks, Soshi. The girl's mother called me yesterday and asked to meet with me. She wants our help because the Boston police detective investigating had told her very little so far, other than they identified the owner of the van but said nothing about her daughter. She'll be here shortly."

*   *   *

Sam felt guilty and bored hanging around the apartment instead of working on the investigation. It was bad enough that he slept late and didn't get out of bed until nearly ten o'clock. Sam took the medication the doctor gave him to ease the pain and skipped showering. Instead, he cleaned himself with a washcloth and soap. In the mirror, Sam stared at the bruise that turned into a dreadful-looking black and blue mark; some refer to it as a 'backface signature,' created on the backside of the body armor after impact. It hurt when Sam took deep breaths, but he dealt with the pain. Sam figured he'd wait until Andrea returned from interviewing Randell and his wife, Sara, and then follow up on what she may have gotten from them. Hopefully, they cooperated and told her and the FBI agent where they could find and arrest the Imam and Tsarina's brother. But, impatient, Sam decided to call Andrea rather than waiting for her call,

The phone rang six times before Andrea answered. "Sam, I can't talk right now. I'll call you when I can." She then hung up.

"Oh, okay, hang up on me. I don't count." Sam indignantly whispered to himself. Frustrated, he sat down after pouring himself a cup of coffee. He thought not all agents question suspects the same, nor do they correctly analyze and interpret what they learn from a suspect. Interviewing a suspect is a science where a trained investigator understands body language, makes it simple, detects truth from lies, and focuses on the objective of the interview—to obtain what's essential to get from the subject. Sam was good at asking the right questions and resolving what's true and what's not true. While sipping coffee, Sam scrambled two eggs, toasted one slice of wheat bread, and then read the headlines in the Boston Globe online. Next, he read the sports page when interrupted by a call from Andrea.

"Hi, Sam. Sorry I couldn't talk with an audience listening. AUSA Ranero, two FBI agents, and I hashed out our strategy for the interview. Specifically, what we could promise and can't, especially for Randell. Things like that. Anyway, we're going to interview them now. We anticipate it'll take a few hours. I'll call you when it's over. Also, Major Burke called and wanted me to meet him at headquarters with the interview details. How are you doing? Is the pain subsiding a bit?"

"A little, but I still feel it. Anyway, call me after the interview while you're driving to headquarters. I'll meet you there."

"Sam, you need to rest. After I meet with Burke, I'll head home and pamper you for the rest of the day. I'll bring dinner and a bottle of wine."

"That's very thoughtful, Andrea, but I'm going stir-crazy here. I need to do something productive, so I'll meet you at headquarters."

"By the way, Randell and Sara decided to meet with us without his attorney present. That's a good sign, don't you think? Maybe they want to make a deal without the attorney knowing about it."

"That's a good sign. If they tell us where the Imam and Abedini are, we may make an arrest soon, and I want in on it. Call me with the details when you can." Sam ended the call.

Sam paced back and forth, thinking about the possibility of arresting the remaining suspects and putting an end to the threats against Andrea and her daughter. Sam worked hard to close the chapter on this investigation and put it behind him. Just thinking about it gave him hope, but unfortunately, it also gave him anxiety that elevated the pain in his chest. Finally, he felt it might calm him and reduce the pain if his son could meet him for lunch. So he called Drew and arranged to meet for lunch in Boston. That immediately made Sam feel better.

CHAPTER
16

Sam waited at the Canal Street Café, a short walking distance from the federal building where Drew worked. When Drew arrived, they bumped fists instead of hugging each other to avoid hurting Sam's chest further. They both sat at the bar. Sam was so proud of Drew for following in his footsteps as a Diplomatic Security Agent with the U.S. State Department. In some ways, Drew was a chip off the old block, as they say. He was a couple of inches taller than his dad and had a similar well-toned body from exercise and healthy eating. Although he had features like his dad, blue eyes, and light brown hair, others claimed he looked more like his mother, but Sam disagreed. Like his dad, Drew was a fast learner, a hard charger, and worked passionately to get the job done right.

Sam asked Drew if he liked his job and what investigations he was currently involved in with his training officer.

"Everything is good so far. Agent Mills and I are currently working on a guy who apparently has a connection to an in-house State Department employee to obtain fictitious passports. We haven't identified the employee yet, but we're watching two that we suspect. It's a good case, and I think we will bring it home for a successful prosecution."

Sam and Drew mainly talked shop while waiting for their burgers. As their sandwiches arrived, Sam's phone vibrated. It was Andrea.

"Hi, Andrea. I hope you have good news for me."

"I'm just leaving the courthouse. I'll give you the short version and fill you in with the rest at headquarters. First, Randell wanted no charges against Sara. He claimed she was not involved with anything he might have done. Regarding the charges against him, Randell will only accept a misdemeanor charge with a reasonable fine but no jail time. He said he may have lacked discretion in helping Radir Semnami and his sister Parnia but didn't divulge anything about the pending raid at the farmhouse to anyone. Randell maintained the meeting with Rashid was at Rashid's request to tell his side of the story before turning himself into Randell as a state police officer. Further, Randell asserted he may have helped fellow Iranians get food and other necessities but didn't know they had kidnapped anyone or were planning to kill Americans. He said he had no idea they planned on killing state officers or federal agents."

"Bullshit. No one will buy that story. I bet that was the strategy Randell's attorney planned on using in court. He knew damn well that Rashid Al Madari was a terrorist, who shot the trooper in Revere, killed state officers and federal agents at the barn, and escaped, yet he harbored him in his home without reporting it. Besides, why would Al Madari reach out to Randell in the first place? Did they know each other, or did someone arrange for the killer to meet with Randell? As Major Burke's assistant, I'm sure Randell had access to the case file, including fingerprints, photos, and the intel related to Rashid. I'm convinced that Randell knew exactly who Rashid was, and I bet he communicated with him before the raid and during Rashid's escape from the farmhouse. I think it was Randell who called Kazmi Baraghani to drop Rashid off on Bowen Court near his home. What did the FBI have to say about Randell's statement?"

"I'll go over that when I see you and Major Burke at headquarters. Are you on your way?"

"I'm having lunch with Drew in Boston. I'll leave here in a few minutes. I should get to headquarters just about the same time as you. Talk to you then."

Sam and Drew discussed having dinner together soon when both were free. They finished eating and left to get back to work. As they walked their separate ways, Sam had a lingering sense of regret for not spending more quality time with his son. He loved his son and was so proud he chose to follow his dad's lead to work in public service. Sam also reflected on his line of work that made parenting difficult, especially after living in separate homes after the divorce from Drew's mom. However, their relationship has bonded much closer since Sam temporarily stayed at Drew's apartment. Thinking of their lunch together, sharing job experiences like friends and colleagues, gave Sam a satisfying grin. He then brushed that aside, wanting to get back to state police headquarters and learn more about Trooper Randell, the inside mole for the terrorist, and his bullshit lies.

*   *   *

When Sam arrived at State police headquarters, Andrea greeted him as he entered. "Major Burke is in a meeting, so I'll go over what the FBI thought of Randell's story."

Andrea took several minutes to summarize Randell's demands, then added the FBI's position. "The FBI firmly felt he was lying, and they will press for the maximum penalties on all the charges he faces."

"Did Randell indicate he knew where the suspects were hiding?"

"He said he wanted guarantees in writing about the charges against him and his wife first before discussing the suspects' whereabouts."

"Well, I agree with the FBI's position on the charges, but if Randell could pinpoint where the Imam, Abedini, and their associates are hiding out, and it leads to their arrests, we should at least consider offering a reduced prison sentence. I should call AUSA Ranero and arrange to meet her to discuss a possible deal for Randell if his information leads to arresting those still at large."

While Sam called Ranero, Mayumi Oshiro arrived and met with Major Burke. She wanted state police help in finding her daughter. Burke introduced

Trooper Kojima, who was involved with her daughter's disappearance, as part of the FBI task force.

"I can tell you that the FBI has identified a suspect who owns the van used in your daughter's abduction. The suspect has denied involvement, but if the search of his van finds evidence that your daughter was inside it, they will likely arrest him.

"I already know that much from the police detective. My concern is finding my daughter."

I assure you that I will keep you informed of any information concerning your daughter's whereabouts." Burke was interrupted by a knock on his door. The door to Burke's office opened part way as Sam peeked in.

"Sorry, Major. I didn't know you were still busy. I just wanted to check in with you regarding Andrea's interview in Boston earlier today. I arranged a meeting with Donna Ranero to negotiate a deal with the suspect. I wanted to get your thoughts on that."

"I'll be done here in a few minutes. So call me on your way, and we'll discuss it."

"Will do." Sam closed the door and headed to his car.

Major Burke planned on convincing Mayumi that the state police, in conjunction with the FBI, were doing everything they could to find her daughter. However, he stopped short of that when he thought about who might help Mayumi more.

"If there is anyone who could find your daughter, it's the man who just knocked on my door. His name is Sam Caviello, and if you hurry, you can catch him before he leaves. Here's my card with my cell number. Please feel free to call me whenever you need to."

Mayumi thanked Burke and hurried out of his office to catch Sam. As she exited the building, she saw Sam at his car door and yelled out to him.

"Mr. Sam! Wait, please." She paused to catch her breath as she approached Sam. "My name is Mayumi Oshiro. My daughter, Ena, was taken by two men from her school. The police have not found her. Mr. Burke said you could help to find Ena. I am worried about her. I can't sleep, and nobody will tell me where she is and why these men took her. Please, could you help me?"

Sam was baffled why Major Burke would tell her he could help find her daughter.

"Ms. Oshiro, if two men took your daughter as you said, then the FBI and the Boston police would be the agencies to help you. Unfortunately, investigating a kidnapping is not my agency's jurisdiction." Sam knew he had gotten involved in the kidnapping of Andrea's daughter by the terrorist, but that was different. Andrea was his partner, and he would do anything to rescue her daughter. Sam preferred not to get involved with another investigation involving a missing kid. Nevertheless, he couldn't help but feel for the woman and what fears her daughter must be experiencing.

"How old is your daughter?"

"She is only eight years old. The police tell me that if they do not find her in two or three days, maybe they will never find her."

"What did Major Burke tell you?"

"He said the FBI found the man who owns the van that took Ena, but the man said he didn't take her. Mr. Burke only said the man might get arrested if they find evidence Ena was in the van."

"I don't know if I can help you." Sam knew he shouldn't get involved and didn't have the time to help. But, knowing it involved a missing kid, Sam thought he could at least get further details before deciding if there was a way to help.

"I have an appointment in Boston very soon and can't be late. But I could meet you later and talk about your daughter and who might have taken her. So give me your number, and I will call you later today."

They exchanged telephone numbers before Sam left for Boston. On his way to Boston, he called Major Burke to discuss getting the U.S. Attorney's office to negotiate a better arrangement for Randell if he cooperated. Burke wasn't sure they should offer Randell any deal, but it depended on his full cooperation in telling the truth. Sam then asked Burke why the Asian woman asked for his help in finding her daughter. Burke answered that the state police were involved in the investigation as part of an FBI human trafficking task force.

"It's a kidnapping case, Sam. We have a trooper assigned to the task force investigating the young girl's abduction. I advised the woman to seek your help because you have shown great insight in finding people. Anyway, I'll transfer you to Trooper Soshi Kojima, so he could fill you in on whatever information that's available to him."

Sam waited for the transfer to go through.

He then listened to Soshi outline all he knew about the task force investigation and answered Sam's questions where he could. Unfortunately, what Sam learned was not very helpful. The more he thought about getting involved, the more he felt he shouldn't have arranged to meet with the Mayumi. Sam didn't want to give her hope if it turned out he couldn't do any more than the FBI to find her daughter. But, again, Sam had a weak spot where young kids were victims of crime. He would honor his agreement to meet Mayumi if not only to find out as much as possible before deciding if he could help. Before ending his call, Sam asked Trooper Kojima to call him if the FBI ended up arresting the van's owner. If they make the arrest, Sam also asked Kojima for whatever background information the FBI had on the suspect.

Sam arrived fifteen minutes early for his appointment with Donna Ranero at the federal courthouse. He first stopped at the cafeteria for coffee for him and Ranero and arrived at U.S. Attorney's office on time. The meeting started with Ranero saying she was impressed with Sam's investigative savvy and intended to support his recommendations where possible. Sam suggested negotiating a better deal for Randell if it led to the arrest of the remaining suspects. Ranero reiterated the FBI's adamant position on Randell receiving the maximum sentence.

"The FBI seized the burner phones used by Randell. Randell made calls to what we know to be the Imam's burner phone the night before the raid. Sam, you had the Imam's burner number from when you and Andrea interviewed the owner of Lugassi's market."

Ranero promised to do what she could to reach a compromise for a lesser sentence only if Randell fully cooperated and gave up the location of the remaining suspects.

After leaving Ranero's office, Sam called Mayumi Oshiro and arranged to meet her. He requested she have available a recent full-face photo of her daughter, a description of what she wore the day of her abduction, the name and address of her daughter's school, and to arrange for him to meet the babysitter who lived next door. Sam told her to expect him in about thirty minutes. Arriving at Mayumi's apartment, Sam snapped photos of her apartment and the adjoining apartment next door, then rang Mayumi's doorbell.

Mayumi opened the door within seconds. She smiled, gave a slight bow to show courtesy and appreciation for Sam's visit, and welcomed him into her apartment. Sam followed her from the small living room into the combination kitchen and dining area. Mayumi introduced Sam to her mother, Honoka, who greeted Sam with a slight bow. Mayumi asked that they sit at the dining table. The kitchen cabinets, stained brown, showed signs of wear and needed updating. Many photos of family members covered the fridge door. Sam noted one small bedroom on one side of the kitchen and a hall most likely leading to another on the opposite side of the kitchen. Although compact, Sam was impressed that the apartment was well kept and clean, with exquisite wall hangings in the living room and the hall. As Sam sat, Mayumi handed him Ena's photo and a note with the name and address of Ena's school.

"Thank you, May. Let's begin by you telling me everything about the day Ena went missing, starting from when she woke up that morning. Was Ena feeling okay? Did she seem worried or concerned about anything at school that day or the day before? Also, tell me how you found out two guys took her from the school and the teacher's name."

Sam listened and took notes as May told him Ena was fine that day. "Ena is shy but a happy child who loves school. She reads a lot and speaks English better than me. She did not have any concerns or worries. I had to work a double shift that day and worked until midnight. I had called Angie to have Ena sleep overnight, and I would get her ready for school in the morning. That afternoon, Ena's teacher, Diane Henderson, called to tell me that two men had taken Ena. I couldn't take the call because I was with patients.

Diane then called Angie and left a message to have me call the school, but Angie lost her phone, and I never got the message. When I went to get Ena the next morning, Angie said she got a phone message from the hospital saying I was leaving work early to pick up Ena at school. I left no message like that with the hospital. I called the hospital, and they told me no one at the hospital had called Angie. Ena has a phone and would have called me if something wasn't right."

Sam saw Mayumi nervously shaking, and her eyes became puffy with tears. Her mom tried to calm her to no avail. Sam wanted to take her hand and say something to calm her down, but he wasn't sure if touching her was appropriate in Japanese culture.

"I'm very sorry and understand your concern, May."

Before Sam was about to continue, Mayumi cut him off. "I want Ena back. The police tell me nothing. Your Mister Burke said the FBI found the man with the van, but the FBI said nothing to me."

"May, the FBI needs solid evidence before making an arrest. So, maybe, the FBI is looking for additional physical evidence before charging the man. When they do, I'm sure someone will contact you. Did you talk to Ena's teacher?"

"Yes. Diane told me two men in a black van took Ena. She said one man was Asian and thought Ena may have known him or maybe he was a relative. Diane did not see the other man as good, only that he was white, maybe Asian."

"May, what was the name of the Boston police officer who contacted you."

Mayumi looked for his business card and found it in her folder. "Here is the card he gave me." She gave Sam a brief rundown on what the detective told her. "He has not called me anymore."

Sam noted that the detective's name was Delroy Howard and put him on his list of those he should contact. At this point, he only had one more line of questioning. "May, who is Ena's father?"

"Ena's father is dead. She never knew him. Why is that important?"

"Well, in a case like this, the father would be the first suspect who may want custody or equal custody of the child, and the wife won't allow it."

Mayumi simply shook her head in disagreement. Sam could tell it was a touchy subject with Mayumi, but he wanted to understand why. Then, Sam heard the doorbell ring as he was about to ask more about Ena's father. Mayumi looked puzzled since she wasn't expecting any visitors. Her mother left the chair to answer the door. When the door opened, Sam heard a woman identify her and her partner as FBI agents looking to speak with Mayumi. As the two agents entered the kitchen, Sam immediately sensed he was in a precarious position.

CHAPTER
17

The female FBI agent approached the kitchen table and saw Mayumi sitting across from Sam. "Mayumi Oshiro, I'm FBI Agent Kiara Rivers with agent Gavin Sloan."

"Yes. First time I hear from you. I understand you found the van's owner, but where is my daughter?"

"Who told you we found the van's owner?" inquired Agent Rivers.

Mayumi remained silent while eyeing Sam.

Sam felt this is where it became uneasy for him knowing Agent Rivers would question why he was interviewing Mayumi in an investigation that clearly falls under the jurisdiction of the FBI. Sam looked straight into the agent's eyes when he spoke.

"The State and Boston Police Detective mentioned it to Ms. Oshiro. They told her the FBI sought a search warrant for the van after its owner denied taking her daughter."

"And who are you, sir?"

"I'm Agent Sam Caviello with ATF. I'm assigned to a state police task force and working closely with AUSA Donna Ranero."

"Oh—you're the ATF agent that worked with our agents at the farmhouse raid near Haverhill."

"That's right, Kiara."

Agent Rivers, a woman of color, about thirty-five years old, dressed in a light blue collared shirt, a black sport coat, and grey trousers, looked rather sternly at Sam.

"So, why is ATF involved in the kidnapping of Ena Oshiro?"

"I asked Sam to help me. I got little information from the police or FBI about my daughter," answered Mayumi.

"I see," said agent Rivers. "Well, we are here to give you the status of our investigation and discuss it 'privately' with you. Your mother can stay, but agent Caviello need not remain. We'll take it from here. We have arrested the person we believe was involved with the taking of your daughter. I assure you that we will work closely with you and keep you informed every step of the way in our investigation."

"I would like Sam to stay," said Mayumi.

Sam knew the FBI agents didn't want his presence, so he felt he should leave. Besides, he had what he wanted from Mayumi and wanted to get the first crack at interviewing Angie Lomax next door before the two FBI agents went there next.

"May, these two need your full attention. I should go. I'll stay in touch with you."

Mayumi frowned before relenting. "Okay, Sam. Thank you for meeting with me."

As Sam walked past the two agents, he appealed to them. "Agent Rivers, Agent Sloan, please find Ena soon and bring her back to her mom." He turned to Mayumi and her mom and gave a slight bow. "Have a good night." He then left the apartment and hurried to Angie Lomax's apartment next door and rang the doorbell.

*　　*　　*

Angie opened the door slightly as Sam displayed his badge to her. "Hi, Angie. Mayumi mentioned that I would stop by to ask you about Ena."

"Yes, okay. Come in."

Angie opened the door wide for Sam to enter. Sam saw that her apartment layout was identical to Mayumi's apartment. However, he noticed the living room was sparsely furnished with a worn grey couch and an adjacent maroon club chair at a slight angle facing a large screen television sitting on a small rustic table. Between the chair and sofa was a small end table that looked hand-painted white. On the table was a lamp with a partially ripped lampshade and a framed photo of a man in an army uniform. The living room walls contained a religious wall hanging and several framed photographs of soldiers in military dress.

"You can sit on the couch," said Angie as she sat on the chair.

Sam took note of Angie's answers to his questions from when Mayumi came to pick up her daughter early the following morning after Ena's abduction from her school. Sam's questions were specific and detailed.

"You told May that you received a message from the hospital informing you that May was leaving work early and would pick up Ena at school. What time did you get the message, and who was it that called you?"

"I don't remember the time. It was sometime after one o'clock, I think. I don't recall if he left a name. I think maybe he was Asian because of the accent he had. After that, I didn't think of calling him back."

"So, it was a man, not a woman, who left the message on your phone."

"Yes, it definitely was a man's voice."

"That's helpful, Angie. You thought you might have left your phone at the drugstore. Did they find it?"

"No. The manager looked at all the phones they had in lost and found."

"How about your brother who lives with you? Might he have borrowed your phone?"

"No, he has his own phone. Plus, he moved that afternoon."

Sam felt it was more than a coincidence that Angie's brother moved the same day her phone went missing. While deciding what to ask Angie next, Sam examined the framed photos on the end table and hanging from the walls.

"Is that your brother in the photo on the table?"

"Yes. That's Billy. He spent six years in the Army and did three tours in Afghanistan. He lost his leg when the Humvee he was in ran over one of those bomb traps they set in the road. He spent time in a VA hospital, where they fit him with a prosthesis. I asked him to come live with me for a while, and he agreed."

"Did Mayumi know or ever meet your brother?"

"No. May moved next door less than a year ago. By then, Billy got a job in the Back Bay and was either still working, hanging out at the VFW, or on his computer in his room when May picked up Ena after work. He left for work early either by bus or Uber, so they never saw each other in the morning. I only watched Ena after school until May picked her up after work. Ena met Billy, though. They got along great. Billy would let her play games on his laptop. Ena called him by his nickname that all his army buddies called him."

"Is that a photo of his army buddies you have hanging on the wall?"

"Yes. They all had nicknames, too. Do you want to see them?"

"Yes, please. Maybe you can tell me a little about your brother's buddies and what nicknames they used."

Sam joined Angie at the photo. Angie first pointed out her brother. "They called my brother Max because our last name is Lomax. Next to Billy is his good friend Kim. They called him KK. I don't remember his last name, though—too many names to remember." Next, Angie pointed to another guy in the photo. "This guy was their sergeant. I remember his name—Trent Killingworth. They called him TK to his face but Killer among themselves."

"Why did they call him Killer?"

"Billy wouldn't tell me everything, only that their sergeant killed more of the bad guys than the rest of the squad."

"So, all these guys in the photo were in the same squad?"

"Yes. All for one and one for all, they said. These guys in the unit were very close. Billy said their squad had the most kills in the company."

"How about the other guys in the photo, Ang?"

Angie couldn't remember the full names of all of them, but she remembered their first names and nicknames. For example, she recollected the name Roger Shepard, who was called Shep, and the guy called Case was Stuart Casey. She also pointed to the guy in the squad who got killed in action.

"His name was Lucas Petersen. They had called him Luke," Angie said.

Just then, they heard a phone ringing.

"Is that your phone, Angie?" asked Sam, knowing she had said her phone was lost.

"What? It doesn't sound like my ring. I looked all over for my phone. Be right back."

Angie rushed to her bedroom to find the phone. She impulsively patted the bed, searching for it, thinking she might have taken it to bed during her nap, but she didn't find it. She had three pillows on the queen size bed. The ringing sounded like it came from the vicinity of the furthermost pillow. She lifted it and heard a thud on the floor as something fell from under the pillow. Angie walked around the bed and spotted a cell phone still ringing on the floor. "Ha, so this is where you were hiding," she bellowed. She instantly grabbed hold of it, but the look and feel of the phone surprised her. *This isn't my phone. How did it get here?* The phone continued ringing, so she answered it.

"Yeah, who's this!" she asked in an upset tone.

"It's me, Angie."

"What? Who? Who's this?"

"It's Billy, Ang."

Knowing the agent might overhear her talking, she began to whisper. "What's going on? Whose phone is this that I found? Do you have my phone?"

"Calm down, Angie. I'll explain everything."

"This doesn't have anything to do with Ena, does it, Billy?"

Her question surprised Max. He wondered if the cops were already investigating and asking questions. "Angie, I already told you once I get settled, I'll send for you. But, wait, hang on a second." Ena's movement got Billy's attention. "Angie, I gotta go. I can't talk now. I'll call you back later. Don't call me."

"Wait!" The phone went silent. Billy had hung up.

While Angie was in her bedroom talking on the phone, Sam took pictures of the framed photos of Billy and his army buddies. He put his phone in his pocket when he noticed Angie returning to him.

"Is everything alright, Angie?" asked Sam.

"This isn't my phone. I've never seen this phone before."

"But you got a call from someone with the phone's number. Why would someone call you on a phone that isn't yours? I assume you know the person who called you?"

"I, uh, don't know who called me. I asked who was calling, but no one answered, and hung up. I've been so confused lately. All the drama that's happening with Ena and my missing phone." Angie appeared distressed and guarded. "I don't feel good now. I'm afraid I can't answer any more questions. My health is not that great. Billy took care of me when he was here. He told me once he gets settled in his new job, he wants me to move in with him."

"Where is that, Angie?"

"I don't know. Billy talked about two or three places close to where some of his army buddies settled." Angie felt uncomfortable answering further questions from the agent. She was puzzled about the phone and Billy calling her on it. The agent seemed suspicious about the call, so she didn't want to say anything else to him until she spoke to her brother.

"I'm exhausted now. I need to rest. I hope you have everything you need from me, Sam."

"Well, just a couple of more questions. You mentioned Billy worked in the Back Bay. Did he leave there because he was unhappy with his job?"

"No, he liked it there working with computers, but his buddies wanted him to join them where they lived. I guess a new company opened there, doing a lot of work for the government. Some of his buddies work there and said the pay and benefits are great."

"Does Billy have a car?"

"No, he didn't drive after his injury."

"Was Billy flying or traveling by bus to his new job?"

"He told me one of his buddies came to help him move."

"Do you remember what buddy came to help him?"

Angie felt she better not say too much. "I don't remember who helped him, but I know he was on the phone a lot with KK. I need to rest now."

"Well, I think I have enough for now. If I need anything else, I'll contact you. Could you call my number on that cell you now have, so I'll have your number if I need to call you again?"

Sam's request put Angie on edge. "I don't know whose phone that is, but it doesn't belong to me. I don't feel right giving out somebody else's phone number." She paused. "I'm beginning to feel lightheaded. I need to lie down. I'm sorry."

"I understand. Thank you, Angie. I hope you get to feel better."

Sam placed his business card on the coffee table and left her apartment. As he walked to his car, Sam knew the first call he'd have to make was to request the military personnel documents of those who served in the squad under Sergeant Trent Killingworth from the U.S Army Record Center in Saint Louis. He sat in his car momentarily, pondering what he had learned during his visit with Angie. When Mayumi had asked Sam for help, his first reaction was not to get involved. However, investigations were like a puzzle, and Sam gained some interesting pieces to the mystery after interviewing Angie. Sam felt if he gathered a few more parts, he might have enough to solve the puzzle regarding Ena's kidnapping. Angie's responses prompted several questions that needed answering first, and Sam knew how and where to get them.

CHAPTER
18

Ena complained when Max stopped at a motel. Max explained they were tired and needed to rest. Ena no longer believed anything Max told her. She was now frightened by Max and his friend, thinking she would never see her mom again. She initially thought Max was a nice man when she first met him at Angie's place. Max had taught her how to play online games on his laptop and how to use the educational homework helper program for kids. Now, she was scared of him. Surprisingly, while spending the night at the motel, Max told Ena he was her father. He was somewhat convincing, saying her mom was tired of working so many hours at the hospital and decided to join a small group of doctors in Nashville. Max said her mom gave the hospital her two-week notice and would soon travel to Nashville to be with them. In the meantime, Angie would join them until her mom arrived. His explanation calmed Ena to some extent, but she still insisted on calling her mom to no avail. Knowing his lies would eventually become apparent, Max swayed Ena to be patient. But, while Ena slept in one bed, Max and KK pushed their bed up against the motel door. Max claimed they didn't feel safe in a strange area and wanted to prevent anyone from breaking into their room at night. Ena, however, knew it was to prevent her from leaving the room and finding help. She cried herself to sleep, thinking only about whether or not she would ever see her mom again.

The following morning, Max stopped at a take-out burger place for breakfast sandwiches and ate while driving straight to Nashville. Ena refused to eat. She was too afraid and cried during most of the ride. KK had a list of apartments for Max to look at in the suburbs near where Max intended to work. When they arrived in Nashville, Max once again tried calming Ena. "Your mom has a lot to deal with at the hospital, gathering all the paperwork she needs for her new job, and arranging a new school for you, Ena. She'll call once she gets all that done."

Ena didn't believe Max was her father. She knew her mom would not have lied that her father was killed during the war. Ena was certain that Max lied about her mom leaving Boston and coming to meet with Max. Ena was afraid she'd end up locked in a room somewhere and never see or talk to her mom.

The first thing Max did in Nashville was to have a real estate agent show him three apartments and a house for rent while KK stayed with Ena in the car. The real estate agent took Max to a furnished home that was available immediately. Then the agent showed him two separate apartments in a large complex that were unavailable for a couple of weeks. Max was anxious to get a place to live right away instead of waiting for availability. It was easy for Max to decide on the house since it was furnished and ready to move into now. In addition, he preferred not to stay in an apartment where Ena might have contact with neighbors.

Max signed off on the rental agreement and paid the security fee and the first month's rent. Then, the real estate agent gave Max the keys to the house and a handshake. Max was pleased that the transaction was quick and easy. KK congratulated Max and recommended he take Max and Ena to meet Trent Killingworth and his other ex-military buddies at the compound.

Max agreed, so KK drove to the compound. On the way, KK pointed to the ranch house he stayed at a mile from TK's community. "You picked a great place to rent, Max. It's probably less than four miles to the TK's place. I'm sure TK will be happy to see you and could use your help even if you only want to work part-time there."

"Well, I talked with my new boss yesterday morning. I sent him all the information he asked for via email. He told me if their security background check on me is good, he'll hire me. So, I plan on calling him tomorrow morning to arrange to meet him. I'll need a few days to paint, fix a few things at the house, and buy another bed for Angie and Ena. If Trent agrees to let me work part-time as my schedule allows, I'll be glad to earn some extra money."

KK drove to the front security gate of the compound. He stopped at the gate while one of the security guys recognized him and opened the gate. Max was surprised at the size of the compound community. KK pointed out the old western-style two-level house centrally located in the commune.

"The previous owner had the original two-story ranch house constructed of brick and stone with metal roofing. Years later, the owner added an addition to the right side of the house. Trent and the guys recently added a similar section on the left side. All the kids bunked in the added open room on the right side of the house, and most of the women slept in the newest addition."

"Where do TK and the men sleep?" asked Max.

"Trent and his so-called trusted buddy, Doc, who are partnered with a woman, live in separate bedrooms on the second level of the house. Of course, Trent gets to pick which woman he wants to bed with on different nights. Pretty good arrangement for him, don't you think, Max? You could be one of those trusted guys if you're lucky."

"No way. I want my own place and my own family. If I find a woman in this place, she'll have to move in with me, not live here at the compound."

"Well, in front of the house is the large canopy covering tables and benches for outside dining in good weather. Then, on the west side is the barn where all the manufacturing occurs. The men's bunkhouse is next to the barn. That's where the men sleep, eat and drink, especially when it rained. Some guys, including me, stay at that ranch I pointed out a mile down the road. The guys who stay there keep watch for any cops coming this way. We store small equipment in the shed between the house and the barn."

"I notice they park most of their vehicles near the bunkhouse and barn. Can we park closer to where the women are under the canopy and have the women watch over Ena while we meet Trent?" asked Max.

"Uh, yeah, but I'll have to get one woman I trust to keep Ena away from the others. We don't want Ena crying about not wanting to stay here. We'll park near the canopy, drop off Ena, and drive to the barn."

KK then parked among the other vehicles near the barn. Max noticed two men sitting outside the entrance of the barn.

"What's the reason for the two outside the barn door?" asked Max.

"Security, man."

"That won't give anyone enough time to prevent the cops from busting in and seizing everything in the barn."

"Maybe not, Max, but once the guys at the ranch house spot the cops, the workers inside the barn get signaled, and the security protocol begins. First, the front barn doors are heavy-duty steel barricaded from the inside. Simultaneously, two big heavy-duty trucks are placed at the front security gate to prevent any accessible entrance to the property. Inside the barn, the workers quickly box up all the products on the work floor and wheel them to the rear of the barn. At the rear, two men unlock a heavy steel door hidden behind a false wall. The steel door gets pushed open, and the boxes slide down a conveyor belt to an underground concrete storage room where the boxes are stacked and stored. Several workers stay in the storage room while the steel door is shut and locked and the false wall gets moved back in position. The remaining workers clean the manufacturing machines, tools, and equipment and sweep the floor. The men transfer the debris into a trash bag, carry it outside the rear door, empty it into a hole, and then cover it with dirt."

"Wow, who drew up that plan? Certainly not Trent," said Max.

"I believe Sparks and Shep brainstormed the idea, diagramed the blueprint, and drafted the protocol."

The security men notified Trent Killingworth that KK and Max were at the barn door. Trent opened the door, greeted Max with a hug, and invited them inside the barn. Trent guided Max to each workstation, where workers, using 3-D printers, designed and made ghost guns and bump stocks.

"The printers make the polymer grip, the frame, and then we add hybrid gun parts like the trigger housing, the slide, and the barrel to complete a fully operable gun that shoots real bullets. The bump stocks replace a rifle's standard stock that a shooter holds against the shoulder. The added stock bumps back and forth while the trigger gets held back, causing the rifle to fire again and again, similar to a machine gun. But, of course, these items are illegal, and you don't want to get caught by the ATF with one; otherwise, you'll be spending a lot of time in prison. The ghost guns don't have serial numbers, so they're untraceable and in great demand. We make a lot of money selling them."

"Let's move into the rear section." Trent guided Max and KK into the rear portion of the barn, where the smaller room was secured and ventilated. "This is where we make our private brand of Fentanyl. Everyone wears protective equipment and works shorter hours, but we pump out loads of pills that sell for big money on the street. We make and sell thousands."

"I'm impressed. You must bring in a ton of dough. As I told KK, I'm up for helping out on a part-time basis, mostly weekends, if that will work for you."

"We could use your help, Max. Whatever hours you could spare to help out would be great. We pay twenty-five dollars an hour plus bonuses. So if you put in sixteen hours each weekend, that's four hundred clear, with no taxes. That's more than you'll earn on any two days working at the local companies, including the one you're planning on working at in the area. So what do you think?"

"I think it's great. I'm in. I'd like to see the rest of the compound and meet everyone."

KK took Max around the complex, pointing out the bunkhouse, the primary residence, general dining, and the meeting area under the canopy. Kim introduced him to the women, including Trent's wife and the guys not currently working in the barn, including three of his former army buddies, Sparks, Shepard, and Casey. It was like old times drinking and joking with the guys he spent so much time with in Afghanistan. While collaborating with his buddies, Max couldn't help noticing an attractive woman who arrived under the canopy.

"KK, can you introduce me to that gal in the short skirt that just showed up? I wouldn't mind getting to know her."

"Forget it, Max. She's with Trent."

"What? Didn't you introduce me to Trent's wife?"

"Yep, I did, but that hot-looking gal is Trent's alternate wife. You have to ask Trent's permission to hook up with any woman in the compound. Remember that, Max."

"I see. I guess I won't be finding anyone here if I need Trent's permission. Let's get Ena and get out of here."

CHAPTER
19

The alarm went off at six-thirty the next morning. Sam turned over in bed and pressed the snooze button. He heard the alarm sounding off once more and reached to hit the snooze button again. Moments later, an alarm still sounded. *That's not mine. It must be Drew's,* Sam thought. Sam figured Drew was getting up for work, so he slipped out of bed to have coffee with him. He first took a quick shower, dressed, and headed to the kitchen to brew coffee. Sam then grabbed his iPad and pressed the link for the Boston Globe. A front-page headline near the bottom of the page read *FBI Arrests Local Man for Abduction of Young Girl.* The article reported that Liang Wu, a twenty-eight-year-old man from Boston, was arrested for kidnapping an eight-year-old girl from her school earlier this week. An FBI spokesperson had no further comment since the investigation was ongoing. The young girl's name was not released. The news story reported Wu previously spent time in prison for transporting young Asian girls across state lines for prostitution. Wu was released on probation ten months ago and currently works for an office maintenance contractor in Boston.

Drew entered the kitchen and walked immediately to get a cup of coffee. "Good morning, dad. You're up bright and early."

"Good morning. What's going on at work to get you up this early? Anything exciting?"

"As I mentioned when we had lunch, Eric Mills and I are working on a passport fraud case. We identified the employee in the passport office selling passports to illegals through a third party. We're getting close to making an arrest. Also, the Vice President is visiting Harvard, and we're helping with his security for the day."

"Well, they're keeping you busy. That's a good thing. You're getting exposed to all the different facets of the job."

"What's up with you? Are you close to ending your temporary stay working with the state police? You must be anxious to get back to your office in Hartford."

"Not really. It's been a real challenge working with the state police. The investigations are high-profile cases. I've never experienced anything like them and probably never will again."

"So, what's up for today?"

"I just read a newspaper article where the FBI arrested a suspect for abducting a young girl. Without getting into any detail, I'm not sure they have the right guy. The kid's mother asked for my help. Again, don't ask me why she did, but I got involved when I shouldn't have. I will do a little more digging into the case before deciding whether I should stay involved."

"I have the answer for you. Leave it to the FBI. It's their jurisdiction, and you're again putting your nose in their business. You won't be making any friends with them that way."

"I hear ya. But, I need to convince myself I can't do more to find the abducted girl than the FBI. That won't happen until I find out if my hunch is wrong."

"Don't say I didn't warn you. Anyway, I have to get to work early. It's going to be a busy day. Take care and avoid getting shot at again."

"Thanks for the warning. I'll keep my head down."

Sam returned to reading the newspaper article and learned that Liang Wu worked at 2034 Columbus Boulevard in the Back Bay at the office building where the largest tenant is the Baumann IT Services Company. That information got Sam thinking back to what Angie had told him—that her brother Billy worked with computers at a company in the city's Back Bay section. So, could it be a coincidence that Billy Lomax and Liang Wu might work in the same building? That's a thought Sam knew needed answering.

While finishing his coffee, Sam pondered his son's warning that he wouldn't make friends with the FBI by sticking his nose in their business. He concluded his son was new to the job, still a novice, but once he is a seasoned veteran, he'll think more like his dad. Sam was sure of it. He unplugged the coffee pot, left Drew's apartment, and headed to the Back Bay.

He found the office building with little problem, but finding a parking space on the street was another matter. Sam circled the neighboring streets but found no place to park. Finally, he decided to park in the office building's side parking lot, disregarding the posted sign saying employees only. He placed a police official business placard on the dashboard and exited his G-ride. The five-story red brick building had a cornerstone with 1968 chiseled into it, recording the date of its construction. He tried the side entrance door, but it required a keycard or token to gain access. Sam walked to the front of the building and entered the main entrance door. A security guard greeted him at the desk in the small lobby. The lobby had an oversized couch and two cushioned chairs between large indoor plants to his right. He spotted three elevators straight ahead behind the security desk.

Sam displayed his official identification and asked to speak to a supervisor from the IT Services Company. The security guard called that office and told Sam someone would be down to meet him momentarily. Several minutes later, the elevator door opened, and a woman Sam guessed was in her fifties walked toward him.

"Hi, I'm Helen Gibbons, the supervising manager for Baumann IT Services. How may I help you?"

Sam showed her his identification. "I'm Special Agent Sam Caviello. I understand you have Billy Lomax working for your company. I'm investigating a missing child, and Billy may have information about the suspect. I'm hoping he has information that may help in the investigation. Is he here working today?"

"No. Bill is on leave. He was experiencing a problem with his knee that needed a doctor's attention."

"Could you confirm the date and time when he left work that day?"

"Let's go to my office so I can be sure of my answer."

They rode the elevator to the fourth floor. Sam noticed the directory in the elevator, which showed the IT Services Company encompassed the second, third, and fourth floors. When the elevator door opened, Gibbons showed Sam to her office. Gibbons pulled out Lomax's employment folder and studied her notes inside it before speaking.

"Just as I thought. It was this past Tuesday. He came into my office not long after he arrived for work. I jotted down the time—eleven-twenty-five that morning. He wasn't feeling well and wanted to see his doctor. So I excused him for the rest of the day. He promised to call and let me know the outcome of his visit with the doctor."

"That was Tuesday. Did he call you after seeing his doctor?"

"No, but he did say he might need a week of rest. I thought I'd hear from him by now, but perhaps he was admitted. He's not in any trouble, is he?"

"That's not why I'm here. It's just a background check."

"Has Billy applied for a job with the government?"

"I'm sorry. I'm not allowed to answer that question."

Sam asked Gibbons if she had a photo of Lomax. She did and showed him a face and shoulder photo. He took a picture of it with his cell. In addition, Sam asked and received his employment dates, how he got along with her and others, and how she rated his overall performance. Her answers were primarily positive about Lomax.

Sam then stood from his chair and thanked Gibbons for her cooperation. He started to leave her office but stopped to ask about office maintenance.

"Do you know Liang Wu, who works maintenance in the building?"

"I know who he is, but not personally. I know he works in the building cleaning our office spaces. He seemed nice and friendly, and he did a good job cleaning. None of the workers complained about him."

"Is there a maintenance office manager in the building that I could talk to about Wu?"

"Yes, there is an office on the basement level. There's a sign outside the office door. The manager is Wil Adkins. In case you,"— Gibbons paused momentarily, wondering if she should say more about Wu. "Are you aware the FBI arrested Wu? The Globe reported his arrest in this morning's paper."

"Yes, I'm aware. Thank you again for everything, Miss Gibbons. Have a good day."

Sam took the elevator to the basement floor and walked to the end of the hall, where he found the maintenance unit. He knocked and walked into the office. He walked past a locker room on his left before entering the main office room, where an older African American gentleman sat at his desk.

Sam showed his badge and identification. "Are you Wil Adkins?"

"I am. What can I do for you?"

"I understand Liang Wu worked for you in maintenance."

"He did, but he's not here and may not be coming back to work."

"I assume you know the FBI arrested him."

"I do know. Li was a good guy. He was my best worker. Li always showed up on time, worked hard, and nobody ever complained about his work. It's too bad he got in trouble. I liked him."

"You call him Li, short for Liang. Is that the name everyone called here in maintenance?"

"Just about. I think everyone in the upstairs offices called him Wu, as far as I know."

"When was the last time he worked here?"

"He went home sick on Tuesday. But, he did a good part of his shift and promised he'd make up the hour or two he didn't finish. I could tell he was sick. He looked like crap and needed to go home and get in bed."

"What time did he leave that day?"

"He came in early and took no lunch or morning break. I didn't have him punch out but remember he left close to one."

"Do you have his employment record here?"

"No, sir. You have to talk to the company's owner, Clay Meeks." Wil reached inside his desk drawer and handed Meeks' business card with the address and telephone number. "He'll give you what you want to know."

"Thank you, Wil. Nice to meet you. I noticed the locker room as I walked in. Did Li and the other maintenance workers use the locker room?"

"Yes, the lockers are used by the maintenance workers. There's a men's and ladies' facility in the rear."

"Does anyone besides your crew have access to the locker room or bathroom?"

Wil thought for a moment before answering. "Well, sometimes someone from upstairs may come in with a cleaning request and might need to use the bathroom. But, they don't have access to the lockers."

"Are all the lockers locked?"

"Maybe a few but not all of them."

"Did Li have a lock on his locker?"

"No. I checked it myself when I read he got arrested."

"Do you know Billy Lomax? He works up on the third floor. He has a prosthesis on one of his legs."

"Yeah, I know, Max."

"You call him Max. Is that the name he uses?"

"I don't know, but I call him Max.

"Has Max visited your office in the past week or two?"

Wil paused to think back if Max had visited recently. "Uh, yeah, Max came in and asked for a rug cleaner. He spilled coffee on his sister's rug and needed to clean it up before she saw it."

"Did you give him the cleaner?"

"Yeah. I gave Max a container and tol' him to bring back what he didn't use."

"I don't see any cleaners here. Do you have a storage area where you keep your supplies?"

Wil nodded yes and pointed to the back area where Sam saw a door that he assumed led into a storage room.

"Did Max get the cleaner, or did you?"

"Oh, I did. Nobody's allowed in the room unless they work here."

"So you went to get the cleaner, and Max waited out here."

"Yep. I don't move like I used to, getting old, you know, but it didn't take me too long." Wil snickered. "If I recall, Max had to pee while I got the cleaner."

"You mean Max wasn't waiting by your desk when you returned to your office?"

"That's it. I called out to him when I heard the toilet flush. He came back here and said he had to pee. Ha. I remember that part."

"Well, maybe you don't move as fast anymore, but you have a great memory. Thanks for your help, Wil. I'll call Mr. Meeks when I leave here. I noticed there is a side door just outside your office. Do I need a keycard to go out that way?"

"No, sir. You can go out but can't come back in without the security card."

Sam left the office and exited the side door into the parking lot where he had parked. While sitting in his car, he thought about what he had learned from Gibbons and Willy. Sam would love to get what the FBI had on Wu but knew there was no chance of getting it. So he had to find a way to go around them. If his hunch was correct, which he believed it was, what he'd do next was what his son warned him he shouldn't do—end up not making any friends at the FBI.

CHAPTER
20

S am's next stop was at the Boston PD's communication center. He identified himself by displaying his federal badge and asked to view the pole cameras from School Street to Worthington Drive. The woman at the police desk directed Sam to a police technician. When Sam asked what he wanted to view, the technician told him the FBI agents had already studied them.

"I'm aware of that, but I believe we may have missed seeing footage before and after the segments they observed."

Sam directed the technician to start with the times the FBI had already viewed. The technician took out the notes he maintained on the date and times on the video recorder he had copied for the FBI. He then stopped the video when he reached the starting time on that date. Sam asked the technician to begin. It took only a few seconds for him to spot the black van driving up School Street, take a right on West Street, left on Worthington, and right on Pearl Street. The van drove into the parking lot behind the apartment where Liang Wu lived. Sam took some notes and then asked the technician to stay on that scene for several minutes. He wanted to ensure there was no further activity by the driver or movement of the van. There was none. It would appear to anyone viewing the video that the driver, presumably Wu, entered the apartment building from the rear entrance.

Sam then asked the technician to go back two hours to view any activity near the apartment building before returning to the present scene. While screening the past hours, Sam asked the technician to stop each time a vehicle drove toward the apartment. The first three vehicles that went past the apartment didn't pique Sam's attention, but the fourth vehicle did. Sam was intrigued by the light-colored SUV that stopped just before the apartment parking lot entrance and remained there for about two minutes before moving and taking a left onto a street a short distance past the apartment building. Sam had the officer close in on the SUV's license plate and noted the out-of-state plate number. Sam then asked if the technician had a street map which he did. Studying the map, Sam saw that the street the SUV turned onto was Grove Street. The technician then mentioned there was no pole camera facing that street.

Sam reflected on what he had seen so far. He speculated different possibilities for why the SUV stopped near the apartment before driving off and turning onto the next street. Finally, he asked the officer to return to the initial time sequence when they viewed the black van driving from School Street to Wu's apartment building. Sam had the officer stop the video when the van first entered the video sequence.

"Would you rewind the video to about ten minutes before the van took a right onto Pearl Street and then play it back at normal speed?" Sam watched as many vehicles drove by on Worthington.

"Stop it right there," said Sam. He closely studied the light-colored SUV that appeared on the screen. "Can we get a close-up on the license plate of the SUV?" Sam didn't say anything but noted the plate number.

"Is that the same SUV we saw stop at the apartment building earlier?" asked the technician.

"It appears so. Let's follow where the SUV goes next?" asked Sam.

The operator started the video as Sam watched the SUV drive past Pearl Street and turn right on the next street that paralleled Pearl Street.

"I'll check if there's a security camera facing that street which is—uh, Maple Street." The technician took several minutes. "Sorry, no pole camera there, so we can't follow the SUV down Maple Street."

Sam looked at the street map again and saw that Grove Street was the next street around the corner on Maple Street. "Okay, let's see if the SUV comes back out of Maple or Pearl Street," said Sam.

They waited several minutes with no sight of the SUV.

"Do you want me to continue waiting?" asked the operator.

"Yes. Let's stay with it for a few more minutes."

As Sam expected, the video captured the SUV returning to the corner of Maple and Worthington. Then, it took a left on Worthington and drove past Pearl Street. "Can you back it up and stop the video where you can zoom in for a close-up view of the passengers in the front seats?"

The operator backed up the video to get the best view, paused it, and zoomed in on the vehicle's windshield.

Unfortunately, the faces of the two persons in the front seats were a little out of focus. "Any way you can bring the driver and passenger into focus?" requested Sam.

The operator made a contrast adjustment for clarity. The adjustment allowed Sam to see that the driver was Asian and wearing a hat similar to what the driver of the black van wore earlier in the video sequence. As to the passenger, Sam studied his face, which looked familiar.

"Could you start the video again in slow motion?" said Sam.

The technician started the video in slow motion and paused it when Sam asked him to stop. Next, Sam asked the tech guy to zoom in on the vehicle. It was apparent that there was a person in the back seat, but Sam couldn't distinguish the person's identity facing away from the window.

Sam then asked the technician to follow the SUV as far as possible. The operator followed the SUV on Worthington until it turned onto Prospect. Not long later, it was on River Street, crossing the Charles River Bridge and exiting onto Soldiers Field Road. From there, the vehicle entered the ramp for the Mass Pike, heading west.

"We can follow it on the Mass Pike until it leaves the Pike or the State," said the technician.

"No, I think I got all that I need for now. I noted the beginning and ending sequence times we reviewed. If I give you those times, could you copy that timeframe on a flash drive?"

The operator confirmed he could and took several minutes to provide Sam with a copy. Sam thanked the operator and left the department.

Once back in his car, Sam drove toward the federal courthouse. He first called the Boston ATF office and asked to speak to Debbie, the TECS (Treasury Enforcement Communications System) operator. Sam requested she check the SUV's license plate through the system to identify the owner and if there were any wants or warrants on the owner. Debbie told him she had three others to do first and would call him back shortly. Next, Sam called Donna Ranero's cell when he arrived at the courthouse.

"Hi, Sam. I can't talk. I'm in court for most of the day," said Ranero.

"Is that the arraignment for Liang Wu?

"No, can I call you later?"

"I'm in the courthouse. I just need to ask about the Liang Wu arraignment. What court are you in?"

"I'll only have a few minutes, so you'll have to make it quick." Ranero gave Sam the courtroom number.

Sam entered the courtroom within minutes. Ranero saw him enter and walked to meet him away from the prosecutor's desk. "Make it short, Sam."

"I just left the Boston PD and viewed the pole-cam videos of Wu's black van used to abduct Ena Oshiro from her school. Based on what I saw, I believe Wu had nothing to do with the abduction. Within a day or two, I should know who the two men were who took her."

"Sam, I can't deal with that right now. However, I can call the FBI and have their case agent contact you. You could then tell them what you have."

"No. You don't have to call on my behalf. I know what agent is involved in their investigation. I'll call her myself. Any chance I could interview Wu?"

"Not without going through the FBI. Besides, the public defender assigned to the case didn't want anyone talking to Wu until he discovered the evidence against his client."

"Okay. I'll call you later in the day. Thanks, Donna. Good luck with your court case."

"Sam, why are you digging into this case? It's clearly FBI jurisdiction."

"The girl's mother asked for my help. I just want to ensure the girl is found safe without wasting time targeting the wrong suspect, which will delay finding her. She could be in danger."

"Well, get what you have to the FBI quickly. And Sam, please tread carefully on another agency's turf."

Sam left the courtroom and searched his wallet for the FBI agent's business card. When he found it, he called Agent Kiara Rivers. Her phone rang several times before going to voicemail. He left a message to call him regarding the Ena Oshiro abduction case. Once in his car, he drove back to Cambridge. He wanted to talk to Angie Lomax again. It was a short drive to West Street as the crow flies, but this was greater Boston, and nothing is a short drive here. Boston, often called Beantown, was an old city with eighteen-century row houses and a mix of historic and modern office buildings. Although not huge in area, Boston has over 400 high-rise buildings, including the Prudential and the John Hancock skyscrapers in the Back Bay District. Water makes up one-quarter of the total Boston landscape, including Boston Harbor, a part of the Atlantic Ocean on the east, and the Charles River on the north. In addition, the city has some of the most prestige's colleges in the U.S., including MIT and Harvard University. It's also the home of Fenway Park, the oldest professional major league baseball field in operation for the Boston Red Sox. It's a remarkable city to visit, but very expensive to live there. And since the city's population is nearly seven hundred thousand people, it's no wonder traffic is a bear.

Sam parked in front of Angie's apartment once he arrived on West Street. He rang the doorbell twice with no answer. Sam paced back and forth, wondering why it took so long for her to come to the door. Now anxious, he decided to peer into the living room window just to the right of the door. His face cringed when seeing the apartment was empty. All the framed photographs of Angie's brother and army buddies were gone.

Frustrated, he called Mayumi as he climbed back into his car. When she answered the call, Sam asked if Angie had moved.

"What? I don't know. Why?"

"I'm outside her apartment. She didn't answer the door, so I looked through the window. The apartment is empty."

"I know she once told me her brother was planning to move and wanted her to go with him, but she never mentioned anything further about it."

"Does Angie have the same landlord as you?"

"Yes."

"Can you text me the landlord's name and number to call?"

"Okay. Do you have anything on Ena, Sam?"

"Sorry, May, I don't, but I'll call you if I find anything. I promise."

While Sam waited for the text message from Mayumi, he called Clay Meeks, the owner of the maintenance company where Liang Wu worked.

"Meeks Professional Cleaning Services, can I help you?" answered Clay Meeks.

"This is federal agent Sam Caviello."

"Yes, sir. What can I do for you?"

"I'm calling about Liang Wu. I assume you heard about his arrest, and I wanted to get your thoughts on Liang's character and performance on the job."

"I already got a call this morning from you guys. They're coming to see me in about an hour."

Sam figured it was the FBI who was meeting with Meeks. He first thought about how to respond and then came up with the answer. "Mr. Meeks, I'm with the state police task force. We also are involved in the investigation of the missing young student. I just need a few minutes before you meet with the FBI. I'm only five minutes from you."

Meeks agreed to meet with Sam. While driving to Meeks' apartment, he received a text from Mayumi with the name and number of Angie's landlord. He called the number that rang several times before going to voicemail. *Doesn't anyone answer their phone anymore?* Sam thought. He left a message to call him back. Moments later, Sam arrived at Meeks' apartment.

Sam walked into the small front entrance hall of the apartment building. He spotted the mailbox with Meeks' name and pressed the call button to his apartment. He heard the buzzer and the inner door's clicking sound to unlock it, allowing Sam to enter. Meeks was waiting at his open door and let Sam into his apartment.

"Thanks for seeing me. Clay. I'd like you to describe Liang's character— what kind of employee was he? Also, how would you describe him as a neighbor here in the building?"

"Liang is a good guy. When released from jail, he told me many times he would never do anything against the law again because he did not want to go back to prison. He was one of my most reliable workers and did a great job. He's a very quiet young man, very polite, and sometimes would help me clean vacated apartments and move furniture and stuff in the apartments."

"Did you see or talk to him the Tuesday he left work early because he felt ill?"

"Yes, I saw him come in the parking lot. I was out back, throwing garbage into the trash bin. He told me he came home early because he was sick and needed to go to bed. He didn't look good. He was white as a ghost and slumped over. As he walked to the back door, he vomited. He turned to me and said he was sorry and would clean it up later. I told him I'd take care of it. That's the last time I saw him."

"If you know, did Liang leave any time after he went into his apartment?"

"I didn't see him leave. I doubt that he would. He looked in bad shape. Oh, I did call him a few hours later to see how he was doing. It took a while for him to answer. I must have woken him. Lee said he wasn't feeling too good and would stay in bed until morning and ended the call. He certainly didn't sound good."

Sam didn't have any further questions and decided to leave. He didn't want to be seen at the apartment building by the FBI agents as they arrived to interview Meeks. Sam thanked Meeks for his perspective on Wu and left the apartment building. As he drove off, Sam called Major Burke and asked to arrange a meeting with Trooper Soshi Kojima, who Burke had assigned to the FBI task force.

"You're in luck, Sam. Trooper Kojima is here at headquarters. Are you on your way here?"

"Yes. I should be there in about thirty minutes, depending on the traffic."

Seconds after hanging up, Sam answered a call. "This is Agent Caviello."

"Agent, this is Tim Reed, the property manager for Angie Lomax's apartment."

"Thanks for calling back, Tim. I stopped to see Angie several minutes ago, and she didn't answer the door. So I looked into the front window and noticed the place was empty."

"Yeah, Angie called two days ago and said she was moving south. So I stopped by the same day to see her and inspect the apartment. She already had a moving company at her place for storing her furniture until she got to where she was moving."

"Did she leave a forwarding address?"

"No. Angie said she doesn't have an address yet, but we're holding her mail until she settles."

"Do you know the name of the moving company she used?"

"I could text it to you once I get back to the office."

"Thanks, Tim. I appreciate it. Any issues with Angie before she left."

"No. Angie was a good tenant, and we'll use the security deposit she made to cover the remaining days in the month."

Sam was now more confident than ever that his hunch was on the money. His decision on whether or not to get involved in the search for the abducted girl just got made. He intended to find her and bring her back to her mom before it was too late.

CHAPTER
21

Sam met with Major Burke at state police headquarters and summarized what he learned from viewing the pole cameras on the day two men abducted Ena. He also briefed him on what he gathered from Helen Gibbons, Willy Adkins, and Angie Lomax's property manager.

"For the short time we've worked together, I'm impressed how you could put together so many pieces of an investigative puzzle in such a short time working alone," said Burke. "It doesn't surprise me anymore. I've come to expect as much from you, Sam. So is that why you want to talk to Trooper Kojima."

"I wanted Soshi to fill me in on what the FBI has so far in their investigation. The more information I have, the more the pieces fit together."

Burke then called Trooper Soshi Kojima to his office. While waiting for Soshi to enter the office, Sam received a text from Angie Lomax's property manager with the moving company's name, address, and telephone number. Sam promptly called the moving company and spoke to the manager. Sam took notes and ended the call when he had what he needed. Now assured, Sam informed Burke he believed that Liang Wu played no part in the school girl's abduction.

"Did you get the plate number on the SUV?" asked Burke?"

"Yes, I received the registration owner's information as I arrived here." Sam gave the particulars to Burke. "I called the FBI agent working the case but only got her voicemail. When she returns my call, I'll give her what I learned today. But, first, I wanted your approval to follow up on the case as a task force member. There's a young girl terrified of the two guys who took her. Ena could end up harmed or scarred for life if not found soon. I'm close to finding out where she is and don't want to wait until another agency decides they have the wrong suspect. I'm ready to go and intend on finding her before something bad happens to her, physically or emotionally."

Trooper Soshi Kojima knocked on Burke's door and peeked in, allowing Major Burke to see it was him.

"Come in, Soshi and have a seat," said Burke. "You remember Sam Caviello. He's here to ask you to fill him in on everything the FBI has on Ena Oshiro's kidnapping investigation."

Soshi outlined all that he knew about the FBI investigation. But unfortunately, Sam didn't learn more than he already knew. They ended the discussion when Soshi got a call from the FBI asking him to report to the task force office. Soshi excused himself and left the room.

"Have you identified the other guy in the SUV?" asked Burke.

"I know who the driver is and where he lives. At this point, I only have a gut feeling about who the other guy might be, but I'll contact the ATF office where I suspect they have taken Ena and request their help to find the two men. I'm certain these two men served together in the military, and a search of their military records would confirm it. I need your permission and funding to travel to where I believe the two men have her."

"Hmm. We've done this once already when we rescued Andrea's daughter. I'm a believer that you have a way of tracking people down. If you tell me you believe you know where her abductors have her held, I'll approve whatever you need to bring her back here safely."

"Thanks, Jack. I hope you don't mind me calling you by your first name."

"I don't when we're alone, but among the troopers, let's stick with decorum."

"Will do. Not to change the subject, but how is Detective Andrea Serrano doing in her temporary assignments?"

"She's not happy, Sam. She wants to be close to her sister and daughter. She's adamant that she could look out for herself and her daughter. She wants to come back to headquarters."

"I think we're close to getting cooperation from Randell or his wife, Sara. If they help us locate and arrest the remaining suspects, we can close the case, and it will be safe for Andrea to come back without worry."

"Our D.A. called this morning to tell me the feds are meeting with Randell today with another offer to cooperate."

"If Randell doesn't, I'd like to take another crack at his wife, Sara. She has a lot to lose and may be willing to help us. We gave her a great deal, but her husband balked at what the U.S. Attorney offered him."

Just then, Burke's cell phone rang. He answered and listened for several minutes before speaking. "That's great, Andrea. Sam is here in my office. Okay, let me know what you two decide to do." Burke handed the phone to Sam. "Andrea wants to talk to you, Sam."

Sam took the phone and listened to Andrea.

"I just got a call from the CI, Joram Haddad. He told me Imam's assistant asked for help to bring supplies up to New Hampshire. Joram agreed and traveled with him to a secluded house near Durham. When they got to the house, Joram helped carry boxes and bags of supplies, mainly food, into the back hall entrance. When Joram brought the last container and dropped them on the hall floor, the Imam's aide came out the kitchen door. Joram glanced into the kitchen and saw the Imam and another man he thought was Abedini. The Imam's aide closed the door quickly and told Joram to wait in the van. When the aide came out to the van, they drove back to Lynn. When they got to the Mosque, the aide gave Joram twenty dollars for his help and told him he didn't see a thing and to keep his mouth shut."

"Oh man, that's great, Andrea. Let's act on it immediately. I'll discuss it with Major Burke."

"Sam, let Burke know I want to come back and help confirm the location."

"I'll let him know. We'll call you back. Thanks. Good job, Andrea." Sam ended the call and handed the phone back to Burke. "I think we ought to act on this now, and Andrea wants to be in on it. After we meet with Joram, we could have him take us to where he saw the Imam and confirm the location and description of the house for an affidavit to search the place. However, don't tell Andrea I said this, but I think she shouldn't expose herself to these creeps during any arrest. I don't want her to get targeted by any of the Imam's unknown associates as payback."

"I agree, Sam, but it goes for you too. Let's keep both of you out of any take-down this time."

"I'd like to be in on busting these two creeps, but I support your decision. Plus, it would minimize Andrea's bad feelings if she knew I was left out too. So, will you contact Donna Ranero or the FBI once we confirm the location?"

"I'd prefer to do it in-house when making the arrests."

"Just a suggestion. As a courtesy, you might want to appraise Ranero when you're ready to hit the place and request a couple of FBI agents to assist in the raid. They lost agents too and would have hard feelings if they were left out."

"I'll discuss it with my team, but you're right about inviting them to assist. How fast can you and Andrea confirm the address and description of the house?"

"We'll arrange to meet with the CI today. We'll take him to New Hampshire and have him point out the house. We'll call you with the address and the description when we have it. Let's let Andrea know. It'll make her day."

Sam was ecstatic about tracking down the location of the suspects. Arresting them would finally end the threats against Andrea and her daughter and put an end to the investigation. That would cause him to celebrate big-time.

*   *   *

Sam left the state police headquarters and called Andrea. She had already set up a meeting with Joram in two hours at the same hotel parking lot where they had previously met. Sam had an hour or more to kill. He was hungry, so he stopped for coffee and a light sandwich at a diner. While having coffee, he called Alli Gaynor, the reporter who once worked in Hartford and covered the serial killer investigation that Sam worked on jointly with the city detectives. Unfortunately, Sam's investigation got leaked to the suspect's father, a politically influential businessman. To protect his son, the father, with the help of political insiders, concocted a scheme to have Sam arrested and jailed for murder. However, Gaynor's balanced and honest reporting supported Sam by questioning the sparse evidence against a highly respected agent.

Meanwhile, Sam's ATF colleagues in Hartford quickly developed overwhelming proof that the murder never happened. Sam was released from jail and exonerated by a federal judge. He rejoined the local police and found the evidence to arrest the businessman's son and his cousin, two serial killers. The arrests became a huge national news story, resulting in several follow-up interviews between Alli and Sam that evolved into more than a friendship. However, when a major national news network offered Alli a big job in D.C, the long distance separating them affected their ongoing romance.

Nevertheless, it didn't affect their remaining feelings for each other. Sam continued to stay in touch to discreetly provide her with inside information on significant investigations that helped her rise from a local news reporter, then a national field reporter, to the weekend news anchor for a national broadcasting company. Sam called to inform her that the search to find and arrest the remaining terrorist leaders was imminent.

CHAPTER
22

Sam met Andrea near her East Boston apartment. He climbed into the passenger seat of her sedan, and they drove to the hotel parking lot. After parking in the designated area and waiting for Joram to show up, Sam sensed Andrea's glaring eyes on him but said nothing.

"I miss you, Sam. Even Micaela always asks about you."

"I know, Andrea. I miss you guys too, but you know how I feel about a romantic relationship so soon after Juli's death. We can be best friends for now. I can't promise anything more than that, uh, other than having dinner together after we finish with Joram tonight."

"I'd love that, Sam. Could you spend the night at the apartment? No funny business, just talk, I promise. It's something that I miss."

"Hey, is that Joram entering the parking lot?" Sam quickly changed the subject, not wanting to spend the night at Andrea's place.

It was Joram, so Andrea flashed her headlights and had him follow her to the back area of the lot. Joram parked adjacent to Andrea's car, exited his vehicle, and climbed into the back seat of Andrea's sedan.

Sam greeted and shook hands with Joram before getting down to business. "Joram, do you remember the address where Imam's assistant took you to in New Hampshire?

Joram reached into his coat pocket for a folded piece of paper. He unfolded it and read the address he had jotted down at the New Hampshire house. "I'm not sure of the town, but I saw the number on the mailbox in front of the driveway, and when we left, I looked for the street sign and remembered it."

"If we take a ride up there now, do you think you will remember how to get to the house?" asked Andrea.

"I think so, yes. I watched as Amir drove there. We didn't take too many roads or turns other than on the street the house was on."

"Okay, Joram, we will drive to New Hampshire now. As we get close, point out the directions, okay?"

With the heavy traffic, it took more than an hour to cross into New Hampshire on I-95. As they drove, Joram pointed out directions until he asked her to go slower as she approached route 52 near a body of water. Andrea slowed to a crawl as Joram studied the streets as they passed. After some time, while closely watching the roads they passed, Joram shouted and pointed. "There. That is the street."

Andrea slowly turned onto the road and eased her foot off the gas pedal. The street sign indicated no outlet meaning it was a dead end. Andrea crawled along, waiting for Joram to point out the house. Unfortunately, it was a heavily treed area with few homes, none of which were close together.

"There's the mailbox," said Joram.

Scanning the property, Sam could only see a portion of the house visible at the end of the long driveway. The driveway curved left toward a garage on the right side of the house with an SUV parked facing the garage.

"Andrea, I'm going to jump out and go on foot. I'll try to get an angle on the vehicle to take a photo of the plate and the house. While I do that, drive down the road a short distance, turn around and slowly drive back to pick me up. I'll get a photo of the mailbox too. It should only take a couple of minutes to get what I need."

Sam scuttled down the edge of the driveway until he was in a position to snap a few photos of the SUV and the house. He then moved back to the road while studying the property for security devices. Sam took a snapshot of the mailbox marked 19 as Andrea arrived a short distance past the house. He slid into the front passenger seat as Andrea lightly stepped on the gas and left the neighborhood.

Sam turned to face Joram in the back seat. "Joram, are you sure that was the house where you saw the Imam and possibly Abedini inside?"

"Yes, I am certain. That is the same mailbox and long driveway to the house."

"Okay. You did good."

*   *   *

Andrea parked adjacent to Joram's vehicle when they arrived at the East Boston hotel parking lot.

Sam handed Joram a fifty-dollar bill and told him he would get another fifty if the police found the Imam in the house. "Don't say anything about what we did tonight or where the Imam is staying to anyone. Understood, Joram?"

Joram agreed and headed back to his vehicle. While waiting for Joram to exit the hotel parking lot, Sam called Major Burke to relay the town's name and the house address. He added the SUV's make, model, and plate number parked in the driveway. Sam then sent the photos he took to Burke's cell phone with a message, 'All confirmed.'

"Now that we got that done, let's get a take-out and eat back at the apartment," said Andrea.

Andrea drove to the restaurant along the Mystic River with a great city view. It was a lovely evening, so Sam suggested they eat on the restaurant's outside deck and admire the spectacular setting. Once seated, they both stared at the Boston skyline, beautifully lit up in the evening sky. The moon was nearly full, illuminating the river with the lights of the city skyscrapers reflecting off its slow-moving current.

"I love it, Sam. It's so beautiful. I'm glad you thought of eating here. It's very romantic."

"It is, isn't it? I remember when we ate here with Juli, your sister, and Micaela. It seems like only days ago. Anyway, I can't dwell on that. It hurts to talk about the past. Let's order something good, have a glass of champagne to celebrate finding those creeps, and top it off with a fat dessert."

"That's what I like about you, Sam. You pick romantic places to dine at and enjoy good food." Then with a suggestive smile, she added, "But that's not all I like about you."

Sam chuckled, knowing what she probably meant, but he didn't want to respond to it. Instead, he only wanted to enjoy the evening before getting some sleep without Andrea bringing up relationship issues again.

CHAPTER
23

Sam's phone rang several times before he reached over to answer it. He was still a little tired, not getting a comfortable sleep on Andrea's couch. "Morning, this is Caviello."

"I didn't wake you, did I, Sam?" asked Agent Aliyah Mayfield of the Nashville, Tennessee ATF office.

"Uh, I was just getting out of bed." Sam pretended as he sat up. "Did you already get the records from the Army's Records Center?"

"Ha, you must be kidding. Nothing moves that fast in government. But you already know that. I'm calling because Kiyoshi has no record, but he's connected to the main suspect in our ongoing firearms investigation. The main shady character in our investigation is Trent Killingworth. He operates a small commune just south of Nashville, and we believe he's manufacturing ghost guns and kits to convert assault weapons to fire fully automatic. We're working with the Nashville police and the Tennessee Bureau of Investigations. We believe Killingworth is also illegally manufacturing fentanyl laced with a deadly substance."

"Any information on William Lomax?"

"Negative, so far, but we have a BOLO on him."

"Let me know immediately if your lookout confirms Kiyoshi or Lomax is in the area. If they are, I want to fly out and meet with you and a local detective for more info on the commune and its residents." Sam ended the call, got off the couch, and hurried to the bedroom shower. Andrea yelled out when he turned on the water, asking if she could join him.

"No, Andrea. You promised."

"Okay, okay, I'm just teasing."

But, when Sam finished and reached for a towel outside the shower curtain, Andrea stood nearby, totally naked.

"I was just waiting for you to finish so I could take a shower."

Seeing Andrea naked reminded Sam of Juli. Both Juli and Andrea could pass for look-alike sisters. Both were about the same height, weighing around one hundred and fifteen pounds, give or take a pound or two. They were captivating women with gorgeous model-like figures. If Sam only looked from her neck down, he wouldn't know if it was Juli or Andrea. *Amazing*, he thought.

Sam avoided looking at her as he stepped out of the shower wrapped in a towel. As he tried walking past her, Andrea moved in his way, causing him to look at her.

"Andrea, you don't have to do this. I know you're beautiful and—well, you know."

"Sexy, Sam?"

Without acknowledging what she asked, Sam hurried out of the bathroom. He dressed in seconds, watching to ensure Andrea didn't follow him. It didn't take occurrences like this to convince Sam that Andrea had strong feelings for him and continued in her attempt to seduce him to sleep with her. Sam was still emotionally hurt by Juli's loss and refused to start a romantic relationship with Andrea, Juli's best friend. Although he committed to supporting Andrea as a friend, he refused to bed down with her. Sam stepped into the kitchen and searched for the coffee K-Cup pods to place in the Keurig. While the coffee dripped into his coffee cup, he scrambled four eggs and put wheat bread in the toaster.

It was only minutes before Andrea entered the living room wearing only a short, moist clingy white t-shirt showing more than Sam wanted to see. Sam abstained from eying her while poring coffee and dividing the eggs onto two plates with the toast. He placed a coffee and a dish in front of Andrea.

"Thanks, Sam. I'm glad you stayed the night, but you could have used the bed instead of that couch."

Andrea's cell phone rang before Sam responded. *Good timing for that call*, Sam thought. Andrea hurried to get her phone on the bedroom's end table. While she answered the phone, Sam gulped down his breakfast before she returned. When she did, she said the call was from Major Burke.

"They have search and arrest warrants for the Imam and Abedini, and the swat team is prepared to raid their house within the hour. I asked that they wait for us, but he said it would be better if we were not involved. He said you agreed with him on that. Why, Sam?"

"For your safety. I felt it better the suspects didn't see you as part of the arresting team. I didn't want you at risk again for them to seek revenge against you or your family. I want the threat of retaliation against you, your daughter, and your sister to end now. Their arrest should allow Burke to bring you back to working at headquarters. Your safety and Micaela's were the only reason Burke and I felt you should not participate in the arrest."

Andrea just stood staring at Sam. Her eyes watered. She quickly wiped them with her shirt sleeve before they rolled down her cheeks. A warm, appreciative glow then emitted from her face. Andrea understood Sam's concern for her to be safe from retaliation.

"Thanks, Sam, for caring about us. You know Micaela and I care about you. I hope you'll never forget that."

"I won't forget, Andrea. You and Micaela will always have a special place in my heart, no matter what. But, not to change the subject, I'm still on the task force and recently got involved with an eight-year-old girl's kidnapping. If my hunch is right, the abductors took her to Tennessee. Major Burke has authorized me to travel there to find and bring her back to her mom in Boston."

"I want to go with you."

"Not a chance, Andrea. You should get your life back to normal with Micaela and your job. You once told me why you decided on forensics instead of the more hazardous field assignments was because of Micaela. As I see it, the investigation in Tennessee is a risky assignment, so you should stay safe here with your daughter and back at headquarters working forensics."

Andrea knew Sam was right and felt better knowing he cared about her and Micaela. However, her feelings for Sam remained deep-seated. She couldn't just turn them off. Instead, she hoped time heals the blame and hurt Sam felt over Juli's death, and that he will once again yearn for love. When that happens, she'll be there to give him all the love he needs.

"I know you'll find that young girl and bring her home to her mom just like you brought Micaela back to me when those monsters abducted her. When you bring that girl back, can we—you, me, and Micaela celebrate the occasion?"

"You can count on it. I have to go. Tell Micaela I asked for her, and I'll see her when I get back." Sam kissed Andrea's cheek and left the apartment. Once in his vehicle, Sam called ATF Agent Mayfield and told her he planned on traveling to Nashville in the morning. *I'm going to find Ena and bring her home,* Sam promised himself.

CHAPTER
24

The Mass State Police tactical team, state detectives from Massachusetts and New Hampshire, and four FBI agents positioned themselves to effect search and arrest warrants at the home where the Imam and his associates isolated themselves from capture. Not far from the scene was Allison Gaynor, the news reporter Sam had tipped off about the pending raid.

All the officers waited for the 'go' signal to charge into the home and arrest the suspects who had killed state police officers and agents during a previous FBI raid. All were ready and prepared for potential hostility when they entered the house. They waited a long time to arrest these guys and anxiously awaited to hear the order to proceed. Then, seconds later, they got the word from the tactical commander.

"On my three count."

The second the tactical leader counted to three, the back and front doors of the house were slammed open, and tactical officers swarmed into the home, shouting police. Multiple sounds of gunfire resonated inside shortly afterward. It lasted for less than a minute. When all became quiet, the Imam, Abedini, and two associates lay dead on the floor, clutching weapons. The tactical leader radioed that all suspects were secured and asked the search team technicians to enter. Not long after the search began, a state police officer escorted Major Jack Burke, FBI supervisor Dell Haskins, and AUSA Donna Ranero into the house.

As Burke, Haskins, and Ranero scrutinized the scene, the tactical team leader advised that they immediately took fire from the suspects when they entered and had no choice but to put them down. Also, police detectives searching the premises found multiple weapons, improvised explosive devices (IUDs), and written plans for kidnapping yet unidentified persons in Massachusetts using only code numbers instead of names.

Burke, Haskins, and Ranero conferred for several minutes before they agreed on calling in the coroner's office and additional help to search every corner of the premise, determine who owned the property and conduct interviews with the owner and the surrounding neighbors.

A local police officer assigned for outside security entered the house and interrupted Burke and the others. "Major, sorry to interrupt, but a news reporter is outside asking to speak to whoever was in charge."

"Oh crap, just what we need now," moaned Burke. "Tell him we'll be out in a few minutes."

"It's a she, sir."

* * *

Early next morning, Sam was waiting to board the plane to fly to Nashville when he got a call from ATF agent Aliyah Mayfield.

"Good morning, Sam. I can't meet you when you land here, but a Nashville detective will meet you at the airport. I'll get together with you later at the PD. Have a safe trip."

When the call ended, Sam called Andrea to get the latest on the state police raid on the New Hampshire house. Andrea told him the tactical team had to take down everyone inside, including the Imam and Abedini, who opened fire on the team as they entered the house.

"Sounds like they were ready for the raid. Maybe they had a device monitoring the outside. Any officers hit?"

"No. SWAT surprised them, but they must have had their weapons nearby and ready. The tactical team entered the place with four detectives and three FBI agents. Major Burke, an FBI supervisor, and believe it or not, the federal DA, Ranero, were outside to supervise the operation. They found weapons, IUDs, and plans for further attacks. Burke and the FBI ordered an internal investigation to justify what happened there."

Sam deliberated for a moment before responding. "I'm sure the officers had no choice in what they did. Fortunately, none of them were injured. In some way, I had hoped we'd arrest them, have a jury convict them for multiple murders, and send them to prison for the rest of their lives. But, on the other hand, this should end any further threats against you and Micaela. That's the good thing. Even better, there's no further need to negotiate a deal with Randell and his wife. They could now take their chances at trial for their part in the conspiracy. I don't wish them well."

*　*　*

The flight from Boston took about two hours and forty-five minutes to land at the Nashville International Airport. Sam disembarked the plane carrying a backpack and wheeling a carry-on suitcase as he walked toward the airport exit. A small group of drivers or chauffeurs greeted travelers coming off the plane with name posters to get their attention. Unfortunately, Sam didn't see his name on any of the posters. He thought there might have been a slip-up in having someone at the airport to greet him. Sam studied the posters, swirling around to ensure he didn't miss his name. Not seeing any, he walked toward the exit doors when he heard his name called out from behind. He turned and saw an African American woman dressed in a pair of casual tight blue jeans, torn in both knees, a black V-neck top, and a waist-length, lightweight maroon jacket. Adorned on her head was a black Gatsby-type octagonal cap. She also had a black cross-body bucket bag hanging by her right side. She had her Covid mask lowered to her chin. Sam debated how this woman knew his name, but he was about to find out as she sauntered toward him.

"Agent Sam Caviello?" she asked. She put out her hand to shake his. "I'm Detective Gabbi Walters, Nashville PD."

A welcome surprise, thought Sam as he shook her hand. "Hi, Gabbi. Nice to meet you."

"I'm your local police partner to help you find your way around. My car is right outside the door."

Sam followed her to her detective's sedan parked curbside with its emergency blue lights flashing.

Once in the car, Gabbi drove them through the busy airport traffic like she was responding to an emergency. "I hate driving around the airport— too many lost drivers not paying attention to the road."

Sam's reaction to Gabbi was amazement. He thought she was one hot-looking woman before responding. "Oh, I'm sorry you had to come to the airport to pick me up. ATF agent Mayfield was supposed to, but..."

"Yeah, I know. ATF operates the joint task force, and she's helping out with a warrant this morning. I'm looking forward to working with you. I understand you're here to find a little girl kidnapped from Boston. Aliyah mentioned you might know who took her. We just have to find out where they're staying. She said the guy might be an army buddy with some of the guys at the commune. We're sure there's a lot of suspicious stuff goin' on there."

"If the commune is close by, I'd like to take a cursory look at it without being seen."

"It's not on the way. Besides, the Captain told me to first take you to headquarters, where he wants to meet you. Aliyah contacted me as I arrived at the airport and said the warrant was a success, and she'll probably meet us in the captain's office by the time we got there. It's about a twenty-minute ride depending on traffic."

Sam enjoyed the view as they drove closer to the city. Gabbi acted as a guide, proudly describing Nashville as the capital of Tennessee and known as the Music City where the Grand Ole Opry, famous for country music, is located. As they crossed the Stillman Evans Bridge over the Cumberland River on I-24, Sam asked Gabbi for a quick tour of the historic sections of

Nashville, especially the Grand Ole Opry, so that he could have a lasting image of it and the city.

"Glad to do it, but it'll have to be quick."

Sam was impressed with the city's blend of a modern-day metropolis, with its skyscrapers, renovated historic buildings, museums, and theaters. The city's mix of new and old reminded Sam of Boston. Gabbi depicted the city with its colorful lights brightening the city streets at night and the music in all genres as the heart and soul of the city filled with musicians, artists, and wannabes. But, she surprised Sam when revealing that gangs were prevalent in the city's low-income areas. Sam's perception of city gangs was unique to the northeast cities like New York and Boston and the gold coast cities of LA and San Francisco. Instead, Sam had pictured the southern cities filled with church-going, hard-working people with cultural dialects and customs who loved southern-style cuisine and country music.

Thirty-five minutes later, Sam followed Detective Gabbi Walters into the Nashville PD's detective's squad room and Captain James Walters' office. Gabbi introduced Sam to the captain, who asked Sam to brief him on his investigation and how the PD could help. Sam gave a run-down on the abduction of Ena Oshiro and who he believed took her, and why to Nashville. He added the two suspects had a connection to Trent Killingworth. At that moment, ATF Agents Aliyah Mayfield and Rafael Torres entered the captain's office and introduced themselves to Sam.

Aliyah, the supervisor for one of the ATF groups in Nashville, acquainted Sam with ATF's gun task force with the city and state investigators.

"The Nashville PD and the TBI have an officer assigned to the task force focusing on street violence involving local gangs and drug dealers. Our current focus is on ghost guns recovered at crime scenes, and the growing number of deaths among fentanyl users, both of which we believe came from the commune operated by Killingworth. We previously obtained Killingworth's military record and expedited your request for the military records of the squad members under Killingworth's leadership in Afghanistan. Our Saint Louis office has established protocol with the records commander for in-person review and acquisition of records in special cases, of which this was one of them. So hopefully, we should have all the documents by tomorrow."

"Sounds great, Aliyah. Detective Walters and I brainstormed how we might find Billy Lomax, one of Killingworth's squad members," said Sam. "Detective Walters suggested we check with the commune residents under the guise we're looking to find a missing child. By showing the missing kid's photo among the women at the commune, they might recognize her or know where Lomax lives and works."

"Well, I'm not sure they would welcome you there, and we don't want to give them any indication we're looking at them. We don't want anything to interfere with us gathering enough PC to hit the place with a search warrant," answered Aliyah.

Gabbi Walters thought differently. "Well, our agencies have worked this case and watched Killingworth and his minions for weeks, resulting in nothing close to gathering enough probable cause for any warrants. In addition, none of our informants have access to the commune or a connection to anyone there. So let's try a different approach with Sam and me showing up and asking for their help. I'll identify myself as a detective and Sam as my partner, not an ATF agent. It's a long shot, but maybe some of the commune women who have young kids might feel for the abducted child and help us. Even if they tell us to get lost, we'll get an up-close look at the place and maybe see something we haven't recognized before."

Aliyah looked at the captain for his thoughts. He simply shrugged his shoulders and nodded affirmatively, indicating it may work.

"We wouldn't be able to cover you. The commune security has spotters along the road to the commune. So you'll be on your own."

"We could deal with that. If we have a problem, we'll text you a code 99."

CHAPTER
25

When the meeting broke up, Gabbi suggested to Sam that they head out toward the commune so he could get a sense of the area. While walking out to the police parking lot, Gabbi proposed getting a room close by the commune's location for their search for Ena and Max. They found Gabbi's sedan and drove to the city's rural section.

"I know a couple of decent hotels not too far from the commune. We could get a room, have dinner, hunker down at a hotel after showing you the area, and get an early start the next day."

"When you say we could get a room, I assume you mean two separate rooms, right?"

Gabbi laughed at Sam's assumption and decided to joke around to loosen him up. "Yeah, they have two double beds in rooms unless you prefer a king-size bed to share." Gabbi glanced over at Sam to catch the puzzled look on his face. "It's cheaper to have one room than to pay for two rooms, no? I get the bathroom first in the morning, of course."

"Uh, won't that create a lot of talk in the squad room if your colleagues found out? I don't think Captain Walters would like the idea of us sleeping in the same room."

"Maybe, Sam, but wouldn't it be fun." Gabbi enjoyed toying with her new partner. She was immediately attracted to Sam when spotting him at the airport. She was a fun-loving, spirited, and playful woman who loved to tease friends in an innocent light-hearted way.

Sam's forehead crunched with squinting eyes and tightened lips, not knowing what to say next. Gabbi's eyes widened when she saw his uncomfortable expression and began laughing uncontrollably.

"Oh, I guess I bought that hook and sinker, didn't I."

"Sorry, Sam, You looked so—I don't know, quiet, tense, and out of place here in the south, or is it me you're uptight about? I'm just trying to get you to relax and talk to me as your partner, not a stranger. Have you worked with women partners before, Sam? Don't be shy. I don't bite." Gabbi glanced at him. "Oh, look at you, I see a little bitty smile, nevertheless it's a smile."

Sam widened his smile and sat up from a slouched position. "You're right, Gabbi. You got me good. I confess I haven't talked much, but I've got a lot on my mind. I'm always thinking ahead about what to do next and how best to do it. My sole mission here is to find the young girl, probably terrified about her situation. I'll try loosening up. I sense I have the right partner to help me do that and enjoy the southern hospitality."

"You can count on me for that, Sam." Gabbi never worked with or had the pleasure of being with a 'Yankee' from the north, as they called them. So, she decided to have a little fun with her northern partner. Gabbi always heard that northerners were workaholics, always in a hurry, and not as carefree as southerners. So, she planned on putting that rumor to the test with Sam.

"In regards to your question, have I worked with female partners? The answer is yes, many times with several exceptional investigators."

"Good to know. You'll have to tell me about yourself and the cases you've worked on, and I'll do the same."

It took nearly thirty minutes for Gabbi to stop at the road leading to the commune. "This road is a little over a mile long. There are only three small ranch-style houses along the way. Two are abandoned and broken down. The other is where four workers from the commune live. Their job is to signal any unwanted traffic heading toward the commune. We suspect that two of them work at the commune on twelve-hour shifts and the other two the other twelve. The entrance to the commune is heavily gated, so any vehicles approaching have to stop and be checked in by their security crew. An eight-foot-high fence with barbed wire at the top surrounds the compound like a prison."

"I don't see a street sign with the road's name," said Sam.

"It was Jenkins Farm Road named after the original owner of the entire area leading to the commune. Killingworth had the town change the road's name to Warriors Way, but the sign mysteriously disappeared after the town put one up."

Gabbi stopped at the Holiday Inn and booked two adjoining rooms not far from the road leading to the compound. Sam graciously covered the cost for both rooms. Once settled, they opened the doors between their rooms for accessible communication in planning the next day's schedule. Next, Gabbi selected a small family restaurant two miles from the hotel. Once there and seated in a booth, Gabbi started with her questions.

"Okay, let's get to know each other, Sam. How long have you been with ATF, and what kind of cases have you worked? Are you married, have kids, what do you like to do outside of work, you know, like what do you do for fun since you seem so tense and serious?"

Sam had to chuckle at Gabbi's enthusiasm to know more about him. He liked her down-to-earth attitude, pleasant personality, and especially her looks. Sam also wanted to learn more about her, so he first answered her questions, or some of them anyway. He told her he was divorced and had one son who worked for the State Department. He's been with ATF for nearly twenty years and currently assigned to a state police task force working on an investigation targeting terrorists. Sam purposely didn't mention his supervisory position with ATF in Connecticut. He didn't want any confusion about her equal standing in their partnership. Sam noticed how attentive Gabbi listened to his every word. She had a likable charm that captivated him. *They sent the right person to be my partner,* Sam thought.

"Now, it's your turn to tell me a little about you," said Sam.

"Right after you answer what you do outside of work and what you do for fun?"

"Hmm. I often work out at a gym, love good healthy food and good company."

"What do you mean by good company, specifically?"

That stopped Sam in his tracks, unsure what she had in mind. "Well, good company means spending fun times doing things you have in common with someone you respect and like. Is that what you meant?"

Sam's answer opened the door for Gabbi to press him for specifics. "What fun do you enjoy the most with this person you respect and like?"

Sam studied Gabbi momentarily, noting how pretty she was but wondered what she was trying to pry out of him.

"Hmm, I'll keep that a mystery to answer at another time."

Gabbi responded with a silly giggle that Sam took as an embarrassing one, but maybe it was her having fun with him.

"Your turn, Gabriela."

Gabbi tilted her head back with a broad smile showing her perfectly aligned white teeth.

"I'm divorced with no children, but I would love to have a bus load." She giggled again. "My parents taught me the importance of a good education. I graduated first in my criminal justice graduating class at the University of Tennessee. I worked patrol for eight years before being promoted to detective. The first black female detective, I might add. I solved two significant cases during my first two years, one an unsolved assault case and the other resulting in the arrest of a mid-level drug dealer. I've worked undercover twice, once buying cocaine and the other a stolen gun. I also exercise at a local gym to stay fit and love eating out at great restaurants."

"And what do you enjoy doing for fun, Gabriela?"

"You like calling me Gabriela."

"I do. It's a beautiful name for a beautiful woman."

Sam's remark elicited a bubbly reaction from Gabbi, showing a widened smile and radiant eyes. "Wow, Sam. I wasn't expecting that."

"I hope I didn't offend you. But, if I did, I"—

"No, no, of course not," she interrupted. "I just haven't had anyone say that to me that way. Say it anytime you'd like."

"So, back to my question. What is it that you do that's the most fun?"

"Oh— I'll tell you my secret if you tell me yours."

"Good answer. We'll have to work on that."

The waitress brought their meals—glazed salmon for Gabbi and Hawaiian sunfish for Sam, each with mixed vegetables and a side salad. They decided to share a large Banana Crème Pie Pudding Cup for dessert. They got along like they had known each other as friends for years. Sam felt very comfortable being with her and sensed the chemistry growing between them. When finished, Sam picked up the tab and then drove back to the hotel. Once settled in their rooms, Gabbi knocked on the adjoining room door and peeked into Sam's room, only wearing a fitted silk short-sleeve sleepshirt.

"Sorry, Sam, but the water in my bathroom shower won't get hot. Can I try yours?"

"Knock yourself out."

She threw her phone on the edge of Sam's bed, meandered into the bathroom, and turned on the shower. Then, Gabbi called out to him. "Hey, it's getting hot, Sam. I'm going to jump in."

When she did, Gabbi began to sing a sweet southern lullaby that impressed Sam with her talent. Sam lay on his bed and closed his eyes to relax while listening to Gabbi hitting some high notes that impressed him. While in a dream-like state listening to her singing, his cell phone ring startled him. He quickly straightened up and slid to the side of the bed. He reached for his phone on the end table. He recognized the number and answered the call from Boston FBI agent Kiara Rivers.

"Agent Caviello, I got your message about extending the pole camera video review and taking note of the SUV you mentioned. First, I appreciate the head's up, but at the same time, I have to question why you felt the need to check on what we did at police headquarters."

"Well, after gathering information from Ms. Oshiro and her babysitter, I wasn't convinced your agency arrested the right guy."

There was silence for a moment before Rivers spoke again. "You could have come to me in person instead of leaving a message on the phone. Where are you, Caviello?"

"Why is that important? You want to meet and scold me in person?"

"No. I want to know where you are to determine if you're still involved with our investigation."

"If I'm anywhere important to your investigation, don't you think that's where you should be right now?" Sam wasn't happy with Rivers' tone, so he ended the call.

He placed his phone back on the end table and lowered his head back down on the pillow, exasperated by Rivers' admonishment. Then, still sulking, he heard Gabbi yell out to him.

"Sam, I forget to bring a towel. I don't see one here in the bathroom. Can you find one for me, please?"

Sam slid off the bed and entered the bathroom to get her a towel. He didn't see any towels on the towel rack or the vanity, so he opened the vanity double doors and saw two towels.

"I found one, Gabbi."

Gabbi then slid open the curtain wider than intended, revealing more than she should have to Sam. Embarrassed, she quickly grabbed the towel, thanked him, and closed the curtain. Sam smirked regarding the incredible view he had gotten and strolled back to the bed with an added bounce in his step. Gabbi soon entered the bedroom, covered only with the towel, and carrying her sleep shirt.

"Thanks, Sam. I'll replace your towel with one of mine."

Sam didn't answer or look up at her. Somewhat taken aback, Gabbi entered her room and returned seconds later with a fresh towel wearing the silk sleep shirt, only wet in spots, leaving less to one's imagination. Seeing her like that, Sam hid his face behind the book and didn't respond to her.

"What? Everything all right, Sam?"

"Uh, huh."

"I'm replacing the towel I borrowed."

"I heard you."

"What's with you, Sam? What's wrong?"

"I'm answering you, just not looking."

"Why? Is my hair messy or—wait, because of what I'm wearing? It's just a sleepwear shirt?"

"I know, but … ."

"What?" Gabbi looked down at her shirt and saw it was wet in spots from her damp skin. "Oh, shit, sorry. I'll change and be right back." As she moved toward her room, her phone on Sam's bed rang.

With her arms crossed against her wet shirt, hiding what was revealing, Gabbi dashed to answer the call. She sat on the edge of Sam's bed with her back to him, listened to and agreed with the instructions the caller gave her, then ended the call.

Gabbi then turned to Sam. "That was Captain Walters warning us of a huge impending storm heading our way. He wanted us back in the city where there are appropriate shelters. I told him where we were, and he said he would call back with information on shelters in this area, if any. What do you think we should do, Sam?"

"Did he give a time when the storm will hit our area?"

"They're predicting between nine and noon tomorrow."

"We should get up early and get an update on it in the morning and then decide. If the weather update prediction doesn't change, it gives us a few hours to find out what we can about the possible whereabouts of Lomax and the girl. We should get to the commune right after breakfast, and if we strike out there, head for a shelter."

"Sounds good. I'm sure the Captain will call us with an update in the morning."

"You keep calling him Captain Walters, but isn't he related to you?"

"Uh, yes, he is. He's my father, but he and I agreed to keep our relationship formal in-house." Gabbi then sighed. "Sam, Are we good? Did I embarrass you prancing around with only a towel and the sleep shirt?" She chuckled at herself. "I'm just a fun-loving gal trying to get you out of deep thought about who knows what. I'll try to be on my best behavior from now on. I'll leave and let you get back to your book. Wake-up in the morning is still at six, right?"

"Let's make it five-thirty so we don't have to rush through breakfast."

Gabbi purposely walked with a swagger toward her room before turning to Sam to see if he was watching. Seeing that he was, she asked again. "Are we good, Sam?"

He didn't say anything.

"Okay, okay, I'm leaving. Goodnight."

"Gabbi," Sam bellowed. "I love the way you are. I'm glad we're working together. Get a good night's sleep—we're good, and I shouldn't say it, but you can prance around wearing whatever you want. It's fine with me."

Gabbi closed the door between the two rooms and pranced to her bed with a satisfying smile. Sam put his book down, shut the light off, and puffed up his pillow. As he relaxed, his first thought was how alluring and daring Gabbi was, but she also had a charismatic charm and glamorous side that intrigued him. Her manners and how she moved absorbed his thoughts before quickly brushing away any seductive notions. He quickly shifted his attention to why he was there—to find Ena. He intended to do just that tomorrow, storm or no storm on the way.

CHAPTER
26

Sam and Gabbi ate breakfast at the same restaurant they had visited the night before. During their meal, Gabbi was fixated on Sam as they planned their approach to the commune. While they ate, Sam was deep in thought and hardly spoke. Once they finished eating and finalized their strategy, Sam left cash for the bill while he smiled back at Gabbi and asked her, "What's up with the look you've been giving me?"

"What look?" Gabbi questioned. "Loosen up, Sam. You've been very tense all morning."

Once they got back into her car, she glanced at Sam again, wanting to say something supportive. "I'm glad we're working together, Sam. We make a good team."

"I already know that, partner." They both gave genuine smiles back at each other.

Before driving off, Gabbi got another call from her dad. She took note of what he said, then ended the call. "That was the Captain— my dad, who said we're in the storm's direct path, and the weather experts say it has all the makings of a whopping tornado. He gave me the name and directions of an old church with an approved basement shelter about three miles from here. I know that church and how to get there. He also called the church Pastor to expect us. My father didn't ask but ordered us to the shelter as soon as we finished what we had to get done this morning and nothing else. They predict the storm will hit this area between nine and ten. Regarding Killingworth, my dad said he's at city hall with his attorney this morning trying to obtain a working farm tax exemption for the commune."

"What's Killingworth claiming he's planting crops of fentanyl and gun parts at the farm?"

Gabbi chuckled and added, "Well, they grow vegetables there but don't sell any."

"Well, let's get to the commune and get this done before the storm reaches here."

Gabbi started the car and peeled out of the restaurant parking lot speeding west toward the commune. On the way, Sam asks how long has her department and ATF had an ongoing investigation on Killingworth and the commune. Gabbi answered for about four months.

It only took ten minutes to get to Warrior's Way. Gabby turned onto the road and drove past the small ranch house where Killingworth's men lived.

"That ranch house on the left is connected to the commune. The men living there act as the recon team that signals the commune when strangers drive toward it."

Sam noted a truck parked at the ranch house. As they approached the commune, Gabbi pointed out a pickup truck inside the commune racing toward the security entrance gate. A man and a woman exited and stood waiting at the gate when they arrived. Gabbi parked up close to the entrance.

"We should snoop around in there if they let us in," said Sam

"I'm not sure they'll let us in, let alone allow us to snoop around. Whatever you do, Sam, don't get confrontational with anyone. Let me do the talking."

"You got the lead."

"Wow, that was easy. When I'm with the all-male detectives, they always tell me not to say anything, just to listen and key on them."

"Well, we're equal partners. I'm counting on you since you're more familiar than me with the people and territory here."

Gabbi and Sam exited the car. Sam scanned the commune, capturing the layout of the old farm converted into a commune, and admired the brilliant sun rising in the east on a clear day with a golden glow stretching what seemed for miles. The sun began warming up the cool air. The land was flat and very open, without many trees other than those that surrounded the ranch house they had passed a moment ago. Sam thought he enjoyed visiting cities, but he'd take open space where you can see further than across the street any day. Gabbi and Sam approached the two standing guard inside the gate. One was a woman.

The imposing, heavily built, gruff-looking guy abrasively yelled out to them. "What's your business here? You're on private property."

As agreed, Gabbi did the initial talking. "I'm Detective Gabbi Walters, Nashville, PD, with my partner Sam Caviello. We're trying to find a missing young girl that may be in the area. We're hoping the residents here may have seen her and could help us find her. I just want a few minutes to show the girl's photo to the women."

"Nobody here knows anything about any missing girl. The residents live and work here and rarely travel outside." The husky brute moved within inches of Gabbi and forcefully spouted, "No one is allowed in here, especially the police. You're on private land, so get on your way."

"Hmm. I know you. It's Otis, right? Otis Riggins. We have your photo posted on our bulletin board. There's an outstanding warrant for your arrest for a no-show at your last court appearance."

"That charge was bullshit."

"Bullshit or not, all I have to do is call this in, and a team of police officers will be here in minutes and take you downtown." Gabbi let that sink in before negotiating. "Let us show the photo around, and I'll forget I saw you here."

"Yeah, right. I let you in and do your thing, and then you'll call the cops as you leave."

The woman with Riggins stepped forward. "Riggs, we don't want any cops coming here. I'll handle this. It won't hurt to take them around to show the photo. It'll only take a few minutes. I'll stay with them."

"That's not how TK set up the rules, Amy."

"I know, Riggs, but this is to help find a little girl. Besides, you need to get everyone prepared for the storm. That's your priority now. So you should work on that while I handle things here."

Riggs grunted in disapproval, shaking his head while walking toward the outside canopy. Sam was studying the layout of the commune as Gabbi negotiated with the two inside the gate.

"I'm Amy. I'll let you in and show the photo around, and then you'll have to leave. They're predicting a big storm coming this way."

"Thank you, Amy. We'll do this as quickly as we can and leave. We know about the storm and need to get to a nearby shelter too."

Amy punched in a security code, opened the gate, and had Gabbi and Sam follow her to the canopy where several women and children were eating. Riggs remained close by under the shaded tent to watch the unwelcome visitors. Amy stayed close to Gabbi as she displayed Ena's photo to the women, who shook their heads no to recognizing her.

"Okay, you two. Nobody knows nothing, so out you go," shouted Riggs.

"Riggs, get my two girls over here. I want them near me when we head to the shelter," said Amy.

"What about these two? They need to go, now!"

"I'll take them out. Get my kids over here, and then get some of these women and their kids to the shelter."

Not happy being told what to do by Amy, Riggs drifted away from her, whispering, "Bitch," under his breath. Then, irritated, he yelled and waved his hand to Amy's two daughters for them to come to him. "You two girls over there with your mom."

Amy, slender, maybe thirtyish, not much taller than five feet and weighing a hundred pounds soaking wet, softly whispered to Gabbi. "I've seen that girl. I'll tell you more and where you might find her if you take my girls and me with you."

Gabbi nodded okay, and they began to walk toward the gate. Amy put her arms around her two girls and whispered for them to stay close as she escorted the visitors toward the exit. Watching behind them was Riggs. He didn't like cops and wondered why Amy bent the rules and cooperated with the police. Suspicious that Amy wanted her daughters with her, Riggs started to follow her to the gate to ensure the intruders got bounced from the inner sanctum of the commune without further whispering between them and Amy.

"Do you know where the missing girl is, Amy?" asks Sam while nearing the gate.

"One of our residents showed up with Billy Lomax with the girl. I overheard Max say he rented a house not too far from here. He said it was on the same street where he was going to work. I don't recall the street's name, but I know where that company opened. I can show you."

"Why are you helping us?"

"The commune has limited shelter space, and Riggs doesn't like me. He has his favorites he will protect at the expense of my kids and me. There are other reasons I won't mention. I don't want my daughters here. Would you take us with you to the shelter?"

"We'll take you with us, Amy, but we'll try finding the girl before heading to the shelter," said Sam. "Detective Walters and I will walk to the car after you open the gate. Walters will open the rear passenger door, get in the driver's seat, and start the car. You and your daughters move quickly to the car and get in the back seat. Close the gate as you leave."

Amy glanced behind them. "Riggs is heading this way. Let's move!"

Seeing the detective's car with the rear door open and Amy pushing her girls out the gate, Riggs picked up his pace to head them off, shouting, "Hold up there, Amy!"

CHAPTER
27

The phone rang six times before Mayumi quickly answered the call from the hospital. Teresa Perez, the hospital administrator, knew Mayumi was distraught over her daughter's kidnapping, but the hospital was in dire need of her help because of the ongoing pandemic.

"Hi, May. The staff and I are so sorry about Ena. We all pray that she is returned to you safely and unharmed. I know you are in pain, and your attention is on getting Ena back, but it may help alleviate the anguish and despair you're feeling by focusing on helping those in need at the hospital. We miss you dearly, and the patients need you. So please come in, if only for a few hours a day. You will find support from the staff and gratitude and love from the patients.

Mayumi listened to Teresa while staring at the framed photo of Ena on the living room end table. Her face showed sadness, puffiness around her swollen eyes from crying, and ruddiness in the crimson-colored cheeks. Her lips, typically curved up in a happy smile, were turned down in a sad frown.

"May, I can hear you breathing. Please, say something. It would help if you didn't stay home alone. You need a circle of friends around you for support."

Mayumi sniffled and wiped away a tear before responding. "I'll try."

Still tentative about her usefulness in a hospital setting, Mayumi realized loneliness and depression are unhealthy and that she needed to remain a part of something meaningful. As a doctor, she felt duty-bound to provide care for patients. It was Mayumi's dream for a career that helped those in need. She continued to believe Ena was alive and would return to her, but she was alone in a dark place of hopelessness. As a doctor, she knew the importance of not being alone in desperation but being surrounded by those who cared and would provide support.

"Okay, Teresa. I will come in for a few hours today. I have to shower first and could be there in an hour."

*   *   *

Back at the Nashville PD, Captain James Walters was glued to the television in his office, waiting for the commercials to end to hear the latest weather report. When the forecast came on, it reported that a colossal tornado had developed east of Jackson, creating devastation to the area and heading toward Nashville. Moreover, the report predicted the storm would hit Tennessee's capital by ten in the morning, increasing in size and predicting severe damage to whatever was in its path. Walters reached for his cell phone and called his daughter to warn her to get to a shelter immediately.

Gabbi's call from her father went unanswered. She was too involved in getting Amy and her kids out of the commune. She rushed to her car, opened the door for Amy and her daughters to jump in while she got behind the wheel, and started the car. As Amy screamed instructions to her kids to get in the car, Riggs opened the gate, rushing toward the car and yelling obscenities at Amy. "You're going to pay for this, bitch! We'll find you no matter where you hide!"

As the car doors shut, Gabbi spun her wheels on the turf and raced down the road. Riggs grabbed his phone and called the ranch house about a mile down the road to block the car heading their way. But, when someone answered his call, he abruptly realized that forcing the police car to stop might bring trouble to the commune. Peeved, he hung up the call. Riggs' face crumpled like discarded paper as he sulked, shuffling back to close the gate.

As Gabbi sped past the ranch house, Sam wanted Amy to start giving directions to the company where she believed Lomax worked. Amy instructed Gabbi to take a right at the first intersection and drive straight ahead for a mile. Amy kept a close eye on the streets they passed before she said to take the next left. Gabbi then went close to a mile before coming to a four-corner intersection. Gabbi stopped waiting for Amy to tell her which direction to continue. Amy studied the area as Gabbi's phone rang. She answered the call from her father.

"Gabbi, Where are you? I called you ten minutes ago. An enormous tornado is heading our way. It crossed into Tennessee and increased its speed in our direction. They predicted it would hit us directly within an hour. I want you to get to the shelter I mentioned, and I mean now!"

Gabbi took a look at the time and saw it was nine-fifteen. "Okay, dad, we'll start heading there in a few minutes. We have only one quick stop to make, and the church is not far from here."

"Gabbi, this thing is shattering everything in its path. Get to the shelter, now, for chrissake."

Gabbi couldn't waste time talking further, "We're on our way, dad. Talk to you later." and ended the call. "Amy, we have to move quickly. Where to next?"

"I thought this was the street, but I remember there was a sign at the intersection pointing toward the new company. So it's probably the next street up on the left."

"I hope so, Amy. Unfortunately, we don't have a lot of time for guesswork."

Gabbi drove to the next intersection, but it wasn't the street. Gabbi and Sam turned to face Amy with impatient faces.

"Sorry. When we made the first stop, I think we had to go straight through to the next intersection."

Gabby circled the intersection and headed back to the first cross streets. She glanced over at Sam's worried look, knowing he felt disappointed.

When reaching the original junction, Gabbi turned right and drove to the next stop sign.

"Oh, I see the street sign. I remember now," cried out Amy. "It's Rosewood Drive. I didn't notice it before. It's the right street. Now, when we get to the next stop sign, we should see the company sign, and I'm pretty sure that is the street where Max rented a house."

Gabbi gazed at Sam again and saw a more hopeful look as he smiled back at Gabbi. Gabbi hit the brakes at the next intersection and looked at the row of houses straight ahead.

"This is it. There's the company sign across the way," said Amy.

"Yikes. All the houses look the same. You have any idea what house it is, Amy?" asked Gabbi.

"Sorry, Max never mentioned the house number or the color."

Sam wasn't as concerned as Gabbi. He counted ten similar houses on the right. All the homes were modest dilapidated older ranch houses, painted different colors, and likely a low-rent housing project supported by the town. A neighborhood park surrounded by trees took in nearly all the land on the opposite side of the street.

Sam reached into his pocket and felt Ena's favorite bracelet given to her by her 'baba.' "Let's drive by the row of houses. Maybe we will see something that points to a particular home," said Sam, hoping the gift from Ena's grandmother would bring him luck.

Studying the row of similar homes again, Gabbi couldn't see how driving by them would help find what house Billy Lomax rented. She studied each house before peeking at the time. It was almost nine-thirty. Gabbi figured she only had time to drive by the homes, then turn around and race to the shelter with her police emergency lights flashing. She stepped on the gas, passing the first house on the right.

"Slow down, Gabbi. I want to inspect each house as we crawl past each one." As they crept passed the fourth house, Sam's upper torso shuddered while his right arm trembled, enough that Gabbi noticed. Nonetheless, the sensation Sam felt lasted only a few seconds as they continued past each house.

"I'm going to turn around at the last house and race to the shelter. It's nine-thirty, and it's a ten or fifteen-minute ride to the church."

After passing the last house, Gabby made a U-turn and hit the gas hard. Sam quickly told her to slow down and stop in front of the yellow house.

Gabbi pulled over and stopped in front of the residence. "Why are we stopping here?"

Sam quickly made up whatever came to him. "I saw something in the window. Amy, you and the kids, stay put while we check out this house. Let's go, Gabbi."

Gabbi slowly exited the car and pondered what Sam could have seen that caused him to think this might be the house. She had to quicken her pace to catch up as Sam raced to the front door.

At the door, Sam whispered to Gabbi. "You knock on the door," as he hid to the right with his back against the house, "She'll recognize me."

"Who'll recognize you?" she whispered back.

"ID yourself and tell her you're informing everyone in the neighborhood to head to a shelter immediately."

Puzzled, Gabbi looked at Sam with her hands flaring in confusion. "How do you know this is the house?"

"Just knock, hurry."

Exasperated, Gabbi hit the door several times, thinking Sam might be losing it. No one came to the door. She looked at Sam again, frowning with a questioning look. Sam ignored her stare and motioned toward the door with his head, signaling to knock again. She pressed her lips tightly together while her eyes squinted and raised her fist to strike again. When she did, the door finally opened a crack. A woman peeked out, only saying, "Can I help you."

CHAPTER
28

Gabbi stood speechless for a second, staring at the woman who peeked from the door.

Gabbi glanced at Sam before speaking. "I'm Detective Walters. I'm warning the neighborhood residents that a tornado is heading this way and that you and any family members should immediately seek shelter."

"I know. My brother just texted me. I'm about to go where he works down the road. They have a shelter there."

"Are you alone?"

"No. My daughter is here with me."

"I don't see a car here. I can give you a ride?"

"No, I already called an Uber."

Sam glanced around the door frame to get a look at the woman. He made a closed fist, then stepped in front of the door, nearly knocking Gabbi over.

"Hey, Angie. It's Agent Caviello. I think you know why I'm here. Tell me where Ena is so I can take her back to her mother."

Horrified, Angie attempted to close the door, but Sam shoved it open, knocking Angie back and nearly causing her to fall.

Sam stepped inside and began calling out Ena's name. "Ena, this is the police! We're here to take you back to your mom in Boston! Where are you? Call out to me!"

No answer.

Sam then walked to a closed door and turned the doorknob to enter, but it wouldn't open.

He knocked on the door. "Ena, are you in there?"

A soft squeaky voice sounded. "Yes."

"Could you open the door, Ena?"

"I can't. It's locked, and Angie won't let me come out."

Sam swiped the top door frame ledge, searching for the key but found nothing.

"Angie, where's the key?"

"I don't know where it is."

Gabbi stood by Angie, stunned, knowing Sam had chosen the right house.

Angie's lie angered Sam. "Ena, back away from the door. I'm going to break it open."

He waited a few seconds, then pushed hard, stepped back, and slammed his left shoulder hard into the door as it popped open. Inside, he saw Ena staring at him, probably wondering if he was indeed the police.

Nervously trembling, Ena didn't move. Sam pulled out the little heart-shaped stone on the necklace Ena's grandma had given her as a good luck charm. "Your mom gave me this to give you. She misses you. I promised her I'd find you and bring you back to her."

Ena stared at the necklace momentarily as a tear rolled down her cheek. Then, with a slight smile and tear-filled eyes, Ena stared up at Sam like he was her savior. Sam held out his hand for her to grab it. But, instead, she moseyed up to him, took the lucky charm from him first, and then grasped his hand.

"We're leaving here. Is there anything you want to take with you?"

Ena shook her head, no. "I want to go home to my mom."

Sam walked Ena into the front living room, where Gabbi held Angie's arm. Gabbi was dumbfounded and speechless that they had found the missing girl.

"Angie, you're under arrest for aiding and abetting the kidnapping of Ena. Gabbi, would you handcuff her?"

Sam's shout got Gabbi out of her trance. She handcuffed Angie, who tried pleading her case. "I'm only helping my brother babysit his daughter."

That assertion took Sam entirely by surprise. He took a deep breath debating if he should refute Angie's claim, but there was no time.

"Sam, let's lock up here and get to the shelter," said Gabbi.

"That's my phone," softly said Ena while pointing to it on the table. Sam saw two phones on the table, grabbed both, then locked and shut the front door as they left the house.

Sam had Angie squeeze into the back seat with Amy and her daughters.

"I'll drive," said Sam. He put Ena in the middle of the front seat and slid behind the wheel.

"Ena, this is my friend, police detective Gabbi Walters. She helped find you."

"Hi, Gabbi. Thank you for finding me," softly said Ena.

"You're welcome, sweetheart. It's nice to meet you."

Sam put the car in gear and quickly drove to the stop sign. He switched on the emergency light and siren and raced toward the church as a phone began to ring.

"That's my phone ringing," said Angie. "Could you answer it, please? It's probably my brother. I'm supposed to meet him at his company. They have a shelter there."

Sam reached into his pocket for the phone, remembered the incoming caller's number, and then put it back in his pocket. Then, with a worried look, Gabbi pointed to the black sky and the enormous twisting mass of wind up ahead. It caused the tree tops to sway wildly, with branches breaking off and flung in all directions.

"Jesus, Sam. Let's move! That thing is close. The church should be just up the road a bit. I hope." Gabbi's concern mirrored Sam's as he floored the gas pedal. The police sedan's speedometer hit seventy miles per hour in a thirty-five-mile-an-hour zone.

"There's the church on the right, shouted Gabbi. "My dad said the basement entrance is in the back." As they approached the church, Gabbi gave directions. "The parking lot is on the far side of the church."

Sam turned into the parking lot, where he estimated there were twenty or more cars and three motorcycles. Gabbi was disappointed when she saw the motorcycles. She recognized they belonged to members of the Renegades outlaw gang.

Rather than parking among the other vehicles, Sam drove onto the grass and around to the back of the church. He stopped at the basement entrance pointing to the basement stairwell.

"Everybody out, including you, Gabbi. Get everybody down the stairs and bang on the door. I'll drive the car to the other side of the church, away from the tornado's direct hit. Hopefully, with luck, it will save our ride back to the PD. We don't want it flying away in the wind."

"What about you, Sam?" asked Gabbi as she exited the car.

"I'll get back here before the basement door opens. Count on it."

Gabbi held Ena's hand while directing Amy, her daughters, and Angie down the stairs to the basement door. Gabbi carried Ena down the stairs and started pounding on the door.

Sam parked tight to the other side of the church building, exited the car, and ran to the back of the church, where he joined Gabbi and Ena. He slammed the door with his fist for someone to open it.

The rumble and swirling sound of the tornado winds whipped through the church parking lot. Sam and the others heard loud clashing and banging sounds from the lot's direction. Ena, Amy, and her daughters were terrified, shaking nervously, fearing they would get whirled into the storm's wind.

"Shit. I forgot to take case files with me. I can't lose them. Keep the door open for me." said Gabbi as she ascended the stairs.

"What? No way!" yelled Sam over the roaring sound of the tornado. As she reached the top of the stairs, Sam grabbed the belt around her waist and pulled her back into his arms.

"Let me go, Sam!"

While at that very moment, one of the motorcycles, lifted by the tornado, slammed into the corner of the stair embankment where Gabbi had just stood, sending metal parts everywhere. One part nearly hit Sam's left arm that held Gabbi, and several pieces scattered over everybody's head, hitting the church building above the basement door. The wind sucked in the bike and flew it into the trees across the way. Gabbi's eyes stayed glued to the top of the stairs, still held by Sam's arm, knowing she would have been crushed against the building when hit by the flying machine. *Shit, I'd be*—she was too numb to finish her thought of being dead as the basement door creaked open.

Amy pushed her daughters and Ena into the basement. Angie stumbled through the doorway while Sam steered Gabbi inside. Once all were inside, the tremendous wind pressure forced the door inward as the Pastor couldn't push it shut. Sam quickly got behind the door to help close it, shoving it halfway but no further. The tornado's strength widened the open gap, causing Sam's feet to slide back. Losing the battle against the door, Sam began screaming at the others. "Everybody, help us push!"

*   *   *

At the Dwyer-Sloan IT Enterprise Company, a security staff member announced the instructions for all employees to proceed to the main administration building basement level in preparation for the impending storm. Working on the second level of the adjacent warehouse and office building, Max, concerned Angie didn't answer his call, listened to the announcement to proceed to the shelter. But, before leaving, he quickly called his friend, Kim Kiyoshi.

The phone rang six times before KK answered it. "Kim, we just got word a tornado is heading our way. Get your ass to a shelter, like now."

"I'm in the barn working. Nobody said anything to me about it. When is it supposed to hit here?"

"Man, it's only minutes away from here. Get your ass to the shelter."

"The barn only has a small underground basement. Right now, it's filled with all the products. If everybody squeezed in together, there's only room for maybe ten people."

"What about the house?"

"It's an old house with only a crawl space underneath. The shed has a basement with a tunnel built in case TK had to escape from the cops. It's not too big either. TK reserved the shed's basement for all his women and kids. Maybe a couple of his most trusted friends."

"Well, buddy, you better find out where you can fit in there, and I mean now. If they're not going to have space for you, get the hell out of there and find shelter at a school or someplace. We have one here in the basement of the admin building if you can make it here. I gotta go. The alarm is sounding off here."

Lomax left his desk and ran down the stairs, wondering if maybe Angie had arrived with Ena. As he exited the office building, he searched the front entrance of the admin building for them but didn't see them anywhere. He called her cell again, but it went straight to voicemail.

"Angie, where the hell are you? Call me. I could hear the damn wind from the tornado from here. Get here now."

CHAPTER
29

Sam's shout for help triggered Gabbi and Amy to rush to the church basement door, adding more strength against the door. Even Amy's daughters squeezed in between the others for whatever it was worth. Their combined effort moved the door inch by inch until it was close to shutting inside the doorframe.

"Push it shut while I place the security bar across the door!" shouted the Pastor.

The intensity of the wind picked up, forcing the door back open a foot while Sam and the others continued to push with all their strength to close it tight. Finally, two young guys in their twenties appeared from the large shelter room to help force the door shut while the Pastor lifted the security bar in place, securing it. Those who helped secure the door exhaled a breath of relief.

"I have to go to the bathroom," complained Angie. Suddenly Angie and the others quickly cringed as they heard a booming sound as another motorcycle and a compact car from the parking lot got carried into the tornado's wind cyclone and crashed into the side of the church. Deafening sounds of thunder and the whirling wind roared, causing the old church to creak and emit popping sounds. Angie began crying and begged Sam to remove her handcuffs so she could go to the bathroom.

"I gotta go bad. I'm about to pee my pants."

"I gotta go too," said Amy's two daughters in unison.

"The restroom is down the hall on the right," said the Pastor.

Sam requested Gabbi to escort Angie and the two young girls to the restroom.

Sam thanked the two guys who helped secure the basement door. Then, exhausted from his efforts at the door, Sam took a moment to scan his surroundings in the shelter. A floor-to-ceiling wooden wall separated the large basement room where shelter seekers gathered. The barrier created a hallway that led to the restroom and the Pastor's basement office at the end of the hall. Candles and battery-powered lamps brightened the dark basement.

Sam asked the Pastor if there was a phone available.

"There's a phone in the office at the end of the hall, but the power is out. Oh, and call me Em."

"Thanks, uh, Em. I guess I'm in the dark about the power being out," said Sam fatuously. "Can Ena and I use your office for a few minutes?"

"By all means. You are a guest here in God's house. Make yourself at home."

Trembling, Ena leaned against Sam with her arms around him. Sam picked her up and walked to the office. The office had an old wooden desk and a sizeable worn-out, fading black leather swivel desk chair. The desktop was clear of church business papers, only containing a desk blotter, a telephone, a cup holding several pens, and an empty in and out tray. Sam placed Ena on top of the desk.

"Do you have to go to the bathroom, Ena?"

Ena shook her head no. "I'm scared and want to call my mom."

"I know. I'm scared too, but we're going to be alright. The storm will be over soon. Unfortunately, the phones aren't working because the storm knocked out the power. We'll call your mom when the power comes back on after the storm ends. Okay?"

Ena nodded yes, then abruptly grabbed hold of Sam, hearing another roar from the tornado as it shredded and flung church roof shingles and shattered its windows.

"Hold me, Sam," cried Ena as the desk vibrated while a tremor throughout the church emerged. She held out her arms for Sam to hold her. Sam didn't hesitate to grab hold of her and embrace her in his arms. Ena was about to ask Sam something when they heard voices behind them. They turned to see Gabbi returning with Amy, her two daughters, and Angie, now handcuffed in the front with a sweater covering her hands. The Pastor also entered the office and walked to open a door leading to a stairwell to the upstairs church floor.

"I'm going up to check on the damage and pray," Em quietly said. "You're welcome to stay in the office, but most church parishioners are in the larger room. There's food and water there if you are hungry or thirsty. Please help yourself."

Pray for us all, thought Sam.

"I'm hungry and could use some food," said Gabbi. "Let's all go in and see what's left."

The group followed Gabbi into the large basement room, except for Sam and Ena. Sam wanted Ena to finish asking her question that was interrupted. But, it only turned out that Ena just wanted to know if her mom knew she was found and coming home.

"Can I go home after the storm?" asked Ena.

"We'll have to check if the airport is open first. Because of the storm, it could be closed for a while."

While Sam and Ena talked, Gabbi and her group grabbed a slice of cold pizza and a bottle of water, then picked an open spot to stand against the wooden partition. Gabbi put her head back against the wall and closed her eyes. The sounds of the whirling wind and debris colliding against the church's walls suddenly stopped, and there was only silence. Gabbi opened her eyes, thinking the storm was over. She glanced around the room, detecting expressions of joy and relief from those in the shelter. Unfortunately, her eyes met those of the three gang thugs whispering to each other as they stared at her. She wondered what their twisted minds were thinking to do next.

Unexpectedly, the whole building rumbled again. Gabbi's eyes popped wide open as she leaned back against the wall to steady herself. A massive boom sounded from the tornado as the thunderous cyclonic wind regenerated. The storm's eye had passed, which caused the few minutes of silence everyone had experienced. The deafening sound reverberated throughout the basement, mimicking a Mack truck slamming into the side of the church. Then an enormous tree crashed onto the church's roof with an explosive bang like the sound of two jet planes colliding. The tree caused tree branches to sway and squeal along the roof tiles. Sounds of glass-breaking, wood, and concrete collapsing on the upper floor, gave off a sensation that the church was about to crumble. Fear covered the faces of everyone in the shelter. Amy's kids buried their faces in their mother's chest as she held them tight. Angie hid her head under the sweater covering her hands. Gabbi's heart pulsated rapidly while her whole body shuddered in panic, and anxiety swelled in her chest. Suddenly, the basement became pitch black, as if the tornado gave a ferocious puff that blew out all the candles. Everyone shuttered in fear and hung onto something or someone, wondering if the instantaneous darkness was a sign something dreadful was about to happen. Seconds later, there was complete silence as the storm left its torrential mark, shifting northeast to assert additional misery elsewhere before calming down to a more gentle breeze.

Everyone in the shelter could hear the air from their held breath, expelled in relief. Even Sam, holding Ena close to his chest, hiding under the office desk, breathed a sigh of relief.

Gabbi looked up, thanking the Lord in prayer and thinking how much worry her father must have about her. *I hope that's the end of the storm now,* she thought. Ultimately, she glanced around the room in darkness as many shelter dwellers lit their cell phone flashlights. Some went around with cigarette lighters to relight the blown-out candles to illuminate the room. Gabbi then saw the three gang members advancing toward her as the room brightened. She smirked, knowing their motorcycles were now piled up in some junkyard heap somewhere far from the church.

One of the three gang members walked up close to Gabbi with an antagonistic smile that concerned her. He wore raggedy-worn blues jeans like his two comrades and a stained long greyish t-shirt extended below the brown leather vest worn over it. Gabbi guessed he was in his mid-forties, with long brown but greying hair, unshaven, and in less than decent shape. The other two, similarly dressed and a few years younger, had longish unkempt hair, one unshaven and in good condition, the other bearded and pudgy.

"You look familiar. Did we have fun together one night?" said the guy breathing in her face.

Gabbi said nothing. The guy looked down at Angie sitting on the floor. He reached down and removed the sweater covering Angie's handcuffed wrists.

"I thought so. What did this innocent-looking gal do? Walk across the street against the walk signal?"

Gabbi still didn't speak but maintained eye-to-eye contact with the thug.

"Ah.—Well, looky here, guys. Now I remember this bitch. You were with that black officer who pulled me over and arrested me for no good reason."

"You were arrested for driving under the influence and found guilty, as I remember."

"Bullshit. The only reason your partner pulled me over was because of the jacket I wore."

Gabbi remained silent, not wanting to debate with him any further.

"Have to say, though, sweetheart. You look much nicer out of uniform." He then turned to his buddies. "I bet she would look even better without anything on, wouldn't you say, guys?"

The other two thugs agreed and whistled.

The guy moved within inches of Gabbi's face while wagging his tongue at her. "Yeah, it's coming to me now. You're Officer Waters, right?"

"My name is Detective Walters, not Waters, asshole. Now, move away from me. Your breath stinks, Lenny."

"Woooh! This little sweetheart remembers my name. She must have a thing for me, right, babe?"

"In your dreams, Lenny Nelson, aka, Pitbull, or is it Pissfull. Your ugly mug hangs on the wanted person bulletin board at the PD."

"Gee, I must be a famous guy around your office. Since you know me so well and me being such a note-worthy guy, maybe you'd like to offer my friends and me a little fun after we leave here."

"The only fun I'd have is putting the cuffs on you and your buddies and throwing away the key. Now, get away from me." Gabbi pushed him hard away from her.

Pitbull smiled at first, but it pissed him off that she pushed him in front of his gang buddies. He moved closer to her, pulled a knife out of his back pocket, and shoved the blade to her throat. "That wasn't very nice of you, Walters. So, I think me and my friends will take you for a ride, and I mean a ride you'll never forget, sweetheart."

Gabbi spat in his face and shoved him even harder, causing him to lose his balance. His face crumpled in anger. Pitbull growled in rage and rushed back at her, pressing her against the wall. He pushed his weight against her as she tried reaching for her gun in the small of her back. He raised the point of his knife into her neck, cutting a speck of skin and triggering a pinch of blood to seep from the cut.

"Hey, man, leave her alone!" shouted the two young guys who helped close the basement door earlier. Pitbull's two friends faced the two young guys, one yelling back at them with a knife in his hand, "Why don't you two come over here and do something about it!"

The young guys backed off, not wanting to get into a knife fight.

Just then, Sam walked into the room, holding Ena's hand. Sam stopped in his tracks when he spotted the guy with a knife at Gabbi's throat. He backtracked to the office with Ena and asked her to wait until he returned momentarily. Then, with his gun at his side, Sam moved impulsively toward the guy with a knife holding Gabbi. When he got real close, Sam aimed his pistol at the guy's face and yelled out an order.

"Move away from her and drop the knife, or you're a dead man!"

Pitbull glanced over at Sam, who positioned himself only a few feet away with his gun pointing at Pitbull's face. Now livid, Pitbull turned to his buddies signaling with a nod to attack Sam. His two buddies stood at a standstill for seconds until Gabbi's eyes nervously shifted at Sam.

"Sam, on your right!" she cried out.

CHAPTER
30

oncerned about his daughter, Captain James Walters drove cautiously around tons of debris along the roadways driving his SUV cruiser toward the church. A second marked police vehicle followed behind him. The streets were like an obstacle course with telephone poles and wires lying halfway across some roads. Trees were down everywhere, some clinging to larger adjacent ones. Tipped-over trash cans lined the road; roof shingles, broken window glass, bricks from chimneys, and even turned-over cars created multiple hazards to avoid. It took nearly an hour to travel the usual twenty to thirty-minute ride. Communication towers were down. When Walters and his crew approached the church, he couldn't comprehend the damage he saw on the way there.

* * *

Sam swiftly turned right with his gun still up and ready and saw Pitbull's crony with a knife in hand about to stab him. Sam instinctively pulled the trigger. The bullet hit the assailant in the forehead, dropping him dead to the floor like a two-hundred-pound dumbbell.

Seeing his comrade lying dead on the floor, with Sam's gun now pointing directly at his face, Pitbull lowered the blade from Gabbi's neck. His eyes widened, his face nervously turned white with fear, and perspiration beads formed on his forehead. He realized Gabbi's partner was dead serious and feared Sam might shoot him next.

"This is the last time I'll tell you. Move away from her and drop the knife, or you'll hit the floor dead harder than your friend."

"Okay, man. Take it easy," Pitbull responded in a timid voice. He backed away from Gabbi and dropped the knife to the floor.

Sam then pointed his gun at Pitbull's other associate and ordered both on their knees and lay flat on the floor with their hands behind their back.

"Gabbi, let's cuff them." Once they cuffed the two thugs, Sam searched them, finding a knife on Pitbull's companion. Only touching the tip of each blade, Sam secured them by wrapping both into his handkerchief to avoid his fingerprints on them. He then asked Amy to take her kids to the office, keep an eye on Ena, and have the Pastor bring four large envelopes to him if he had them. Sam asked for the envelopes to hold the evidence collected from the three gang members and the items secured from Angie earlier at her house.

With the perps secured, Sam turned to Gabbi, concerned about the ordeal she had faced. "Are you okay, Gabbi?"

Gabbi, still shaken from the incident, nodded yes.

*   *   *

Captain Walters was apprehensive about his daughter's safety as he arrived and witnessed the devastation surrounding the church. He agonized over Gabbi's well-being. Although he treated her as a rookie detective like any other new officer within the unit of seasoned investigators, he loved her and wanted to see with his own eyes that she was safe. He drove up the curb in the road to avoid the turned-over car blocking the entrance of the parking lot. He exited his cruiser and carefully stepped around the debris left by the tornado until he found the rear stairway to the basement shelter. He soberly stepped down the steps and hammered his fist against the basement door.

"Police, open the door," shrieked Captain Walters. He aggressively pounded again and again, desperate to enter and find his daughter unhurt. When the door finally opened, the captain pushed aside whoever stood in his way to search the shelter's dimly lit room for Gabbi. When he saw three men lying on the floor, his anxiety rose to a level he hadn't experienced in a long time. His heart banged against his chest so loud he could feel it. His eyes shifted in the dim light until he caught Sam standing guard over the three men on the floor. Not seeing Gabbi with Sam caused the captain's lips to tense and be drawn in panic.

Recognizing Captain Walters' fierce look in his direction, Sam turned to Gabbi and pointed at her father. Gabbi leaned away from the wall, moved forward, and saw her dad standing there. Her father's eyes closed in prayer as he glanced up to the Lord, releasing a heavy sigh of relief. Then a peaceful smile appeared as he quickly paced toward his daughter. When he got close, he stopped and stood before her, beaming with a wide relieving smile wanting to hold her tight. He restrained himself from hugging her in front of his fellow officers. But Gabbi didn't—she practically attacked him, wrapping her arms tightly around him. Then, without hesitation, he returned the embrace.

"I was worried sick about you, girl. Are you alright? "

"Yes, I'm fine."

"What the hell happened here?"

Sam answered before Gabbi did. "These three punks became violent, and Gabbi and I had to put them down. Gabbi taught'em a lesson. We'll explain in detail when we get back to the PD."

Recognizing who the punks were, Captain Walters understood. He ordered the three officers behind him to identify and take statements from those in the room, contact the coroner, and then request transport for the prisoners to the lock-up when done.

While directing the captain to the office away from the onlookers, Gabbi and Sam first introduced Ena. The Captain was astonished they had the kidnapped girl. Gabbi then took her dad aside to introduce Amy Norwood, who helped locate Ena and pointed to Lomax's sister, Angie, who they had arrested.

"I'm impressed, Gabbi," said her father. "I can't even fathom how you managed to get into the commune, finding the girl, plus handling these three punks. It's mind-blowing. I'm proud of you, girl, just so proud."

"It wasn't just me, Dad. It was Sam and me."

"Yeah, of course. I meant Sam too. You both took care of business. That's all I'm saying."

Captain Walters recognized Sam with a nod of approval. "Outstanding, both of you." He turned his attention back to Gabbi. "From the look of the damage in the parking lot, I assume you, Sam, and the others will need a ride back to headquarters. I'll call for another car."

"Maybe not, Captain," said Sam. "We parked the car around the other side of the church, trying to protect it from the tornado. I'll run out there and see if it's drivable or even if it's still there in one piece."

"I wanna come with you, Sam," said Ena. "I wanna stay with you."

Sam felt a warm glow inside from Ena's words, like she saw him as her protector. "Okay, Ena. Take my hand and when we get outside, watch where you step."

Ena took Sam's hand, and they both strolled out of the church. Outside, they stopped to gawk at the damage to the landscape surrounding them. All the cars initially parked in the church lot were either turned over, rammed into each other, or missing. All three bikes were gone. Sam glanced from left to right, amazed at the number of large trees uprooted; some whirled against the church, others uprooted on the ground or leaning against other trees. He was astonished to see the amount of debris piled on the church grounds that resembled a junkyard. Looking up at the sky, Sam studied the brightening blue sky, with a light wind shoving the dark, whirling clouds to the northeast. *I've never seen anything like this, ever*, thought Sam, shaking his head in disbelief. Sam and Ena then carefully maneuvered around the debris, turning the corner of the church building and finding that Gabbi's sedan was still there, although slightly damaged. Sam unlocked the door and tried to start her up.

"Yeah!" Sam shouted. "We're in luck, Ena. The car is good to go. Let's get Gabbi and the others and get out of this place. Maybe we could get something to eat on the way, like ice cream. What do you think? Want to?"

"Yeah, ice cream, Sam."

Sam and Ena reentered the church and reported the car had a dent in the trunk and a cracked rear window, but it was good to go. Captain Walters instructed Gabbi to take Ena, Amy Norwood, and her daughters back to the station, and he'd arrange for the prisoners to get locked up. "I'll meet you back at the squad room when finished here. Be careful driving back. It's an obstacle course out there."

Once back in Gabbi's car, Sam requested they search for a place open on the way for sandwiches and ice cream to take with them.

"Good luck with that, Sam. I doubt we'll find anyplace that's open," said Gabbi.

As she drove, Gabbi saw that her dad was right about the drive back. The streets were a disaster. The ride downtown was like going through a minefield, causing Gabbi to steer around obstacles every few yards, like downed poles and trees, cable satellite dishes, and debris of all kinds. It became worse once on the city streets. Gabbi had to avoid so many large sections of broken glass torn from buildings they passed. When nearing an intersection, Sam pointed out a deli that appeared open on the next street on the right. Surprised, Gabbi steered around a large garbage container to turn onto the road and stopped in front of the deli. An 'open' sign blinked in the front window. They could hear the roar of a generator noisily roaring from the alleyway. Sam entered the deli, where he purchased twelve subs, six large bottles of Coke, four quarts of ice cream, and a bag full of plastic spoons, paper cups, and napkins. Sam had one of the deli workers help him carry everything to the car. From the deli, it was a short ride to the PD.

Gabbi's anxiety diminished once she entered the police department's parking lot and shut off the ignition. She felt not only relief but emotional exhaustion. She sat there momentarily, looking at Sam, studying his reaction.

Sam nodded, whispering, "We made it. We can relax now."

Gabbi rested her forehead on the steering wheel while flexing her fingers after releasing the tight grip she maintained on the steering wheel.

Inside the PD, Gabbi guided everyone to her dad's office, where they set up chairs around the desk for all to sit and enjoy the delicacies from the deli. Gabbi then searched and found a large spoon to scoop ice cream into paper cups for the kids. While Gabbi's hand trembled, scooping small chunks of ice cream for Sam and Amy, her puffy eyes glared at Sam as if beckoning for a hug.

Sensing Gabbi's need for support, he grabbed Gabbi's wrist, giving her an acknowledging gesture that everything was fine, and whispered, "Let's step outside the room for a moment."

He recognized the fright she had experienced at the church, not only the fear from the tornado but the terrifying knife attack from the gang member. *I wanted to flatten that piece of crap with my fist.* Sam impulsively thought. Gabbi followed Sam into an empty office across the hall. Sam closed the door and wrapped his arms around her. "You're one gutsy woman. Like your dad, I'm proud of you."

Gabbi tightened her squeeze around Sam. She didn't want him to let go. "Thanks, Sam. I feel so safe when you're nearby."

To calm her with a bit of humor, Sam responded. "I also feel safe around you, making sure I'm safe and not all tensed up."

Gabbi cracked a smile, knowing he was comforting her by being funny. But, at that moment, she wanted more of him and couldn't wait to get him alone somewhere private.

Back in the captain's office, Sam downed the ice cream while tensely planning their next move. He glanced at his watch for the time. He was anxious to get a written statement from Amy, but in the meantime, his first concern was to find and arrest Max and Kiyoshi for abducting Ena. So Sam asked Gabbi if they had any unique emergency phones that might work so they could try calling Max.

"We have a few satellite phones we could try using, but we have to use them outside to connect to a satellite."

"See if you can get your hands on one. I got Max's number when he tried calling Angie on our way to the church."

Ten minutes later, Gabbi returned with a satellite phone.

"Let's go outside, and Gabbi, you call him," said Sam. "I think he'd be less suspicious about getting the call from a female officer. Explain that the police went door to door to warn residents of the impending storm, and since his sister had no transportation, you arranged to bring her to the station's shelter. Ask him to come to the station to get his sister and daughter."

Outside, Gabbi dialed Max's cell number. The sky was clear, with the sun peeking out from the shifting white clouds.

"Yeah, who's this?"

"Max, this is Officer Gabbi Walters, Nashville PD. Police officers went through the neighborhoods to warn people of the incoming tornado and took many of them to the shelter here at the PD. Unfortunately, cell phones are not working in the city. So I'm calling on a satellite police phone. Your sister and Ena are safe and sound. You could come to pick up your family members here. Just ask for Officer Gabbi Walters, and I'll take you to them."

"Oh, thank God. I've been calling my sister but got no answer. I'm glad they're safe. I'm new in the area, so can you tell me how I get there?"

Gabbi provided directions and ended the call. "It worked, Sam. You're a genius."

Back inside the station, Sam and Gabbi planned their interview with Amy Norwood while the kids enjoyed ice cream and drinks. Amy's two daughters kept Ena occupied and talking. Sam took a moment to think about how he'd interview Billy Lomax when he arrived at the station. He originally had hoped to interview Kiyoshi before Lomax. Sam figured Kim, who faces charges for his role in taking Ena, would benefit by cooperating against Lomax. Sam deliberated on how he could make that happen until he came up with the solution.

CHAPTER
31

When Max left the shelter to return to his office, he felt fortunate that the area where he worked lucked out from the horrific damage caused by the tornado not that far north from where he stood. The admin building had a working generator that allowed the workers in the basement shelter, including Max, to listen to the ongoing news that reported massive damage and injury from west-central Tennessee east through Nashville and north. However, the same reports described how the areas south of Nashville received sparse destruction compared to the heavy damage suffered a few miles north.

When outside, Max noticed a few uprooted trees, debris of all kinds and shapes cluttering the site, and glass fragments from four or five shattered windows from the two buildings, but the damage was minor compared to the areas north of his company. Then looking toward the parking lot, Max's facial impression showed anger seeing a few cars slammed into each other. He stood there with his eyelids tightening, a wrinkled-up nose, and tight lips when noticing his friend's car was part of the fender-benders. He whispered obscenities, knowing his ride to the Nashville PD would be a problem now.

"Lomax!" yelled his boss. "Get back to the office. We have some cleaning up to do."

Max hesitated, thinking of his sister Angie and Ena stuck at the Nashville PD. He questioned why Angie never made it to his company's shelter. But then, he figured maybe the police showed up at the house before she arranged for a ride to his company. He was sure she worried about the storm and took the quickest way to get her and Ena to safety. But, on second thought, it bothered him that the police might have received a missing person's bulletin for Ena or possibly wanted posters for him and his buddy, Kim. Thinking of KK, he needed to find out if he had found shelter and was okay. Max felt that if KK had found refuge and was good to go, he could drive Max to the police department. Hearing his boss call out his name again, Max followed him to survey the damage in his building. While looking over the damage, Max told his boss he was concerned about his sister and daughter and needed to check on them to ensure they were okay. The damage was lighter than Max's boss anticipated.

"Okay, Lomax, you can leave for an hour or so to check on your family. Then, if everything is alright with them, get back here to help clean up this mess. We'll need everybody to get this place back to normal. Call me if you can't make it back because something is not right back at home."

Figuring his work friend wouldn't leave work to give him a ride to the Nashville police department under the circumstances, he had no choice but to call KK and hope he made it through the storm okay. Max hurried outside and called KK's cell number, murmuring, "Please answer, buddy."

"Hey, Max," answered KK.

"Hey, you're okay, buddy. You found shelter?"

"Yeah, that prick Riggins let me in at the last second before the storm hit here."

"What's the damage there?"

"The older section of the house was heavily damaged. The canopy got sailed away by the tornado, and the old storage shack at the other end of the property broke apart with a section shoved into the fencing, causing it to lean halfway to the ground. Unfortunately, it affected the gate from opening. The reinforced sections of the barn are still standing, but the damage was less than in the other buildings. The rebuilt shed is leaning and could collapse any minute now. There were some minor injuries to the residents but nothing fatal. I parked my SUV in front of the barn since Trent had steel reinforcements in the barn's backside. It has minor dents and scratches on the fenders, hood, and roof, but it's drivable. I'm not happy with the damage, but it could have disappeared as some did by the tornado north of here. I hear Nashville got hammered. How about where you are, Max?"

"We're further south than the compound, so we didn't get hit as hard here either. I'm glad you're okay. I need a big favor. I was hoping you could pick me up at work and drive me to Nashville."

"Nashville. Why do you want to go there? The city is supposed to be in bad shape, man. I don't even know if we could get there."

"Angie and Ena never made it here to the shelter. I tried calling her, but she never answered. Sorry to say, I got a call from the Nashville police telling me they went to the houses in my neighborhood warning of the storm, and since Angie had no car, they brought her and Ena to the police station, where they have a shelter. I'm a little worried about going there, though. What if the cops know about Ena, or they know we took her."

"Oh shit, man. We can't go there. The cops could arrest us."

Max felt he had to find out one way or another. "Maybe the cops don't know anything. Besides, I can't just leave Angie and Ena hanging there without a ride back home. I have to find out, and I don't have wheels. I need your help. Would you take me there? You could wait out in the car. The cops may not know about us. If they do, we'll concoct a story on the way. Maybe, we say that Mayumi wouldn't let me visit my daughter, and Ena preferred to be with me."

"Max, Ena might have said something to the cops. It's too risky."

"Maybe. But Angie knows not to let anyone talk to Ena. So come on, buddy, just drop me off there. If there's a problem, I'll say it was only me who took Ena, and you didn't know anything other than I asked you to drive my daughter and me to Nashville."

Kim thought about what Max had said but didn't think the cops would buy it. Nevertheless, he agreed to drive Max to Nashville but would wait somewhere away from the police station until he heard back from Max.

*   *   *

"Sam, I could tell you're thinking ahead about something right now. So, what is it?"

"Max said he'd show up to get his sister and Ena. As I remember, Max doesn't have a car, so I just thought maybe Kiyoshi might drive him here. If he does, I would prefer to interview him first since he has a lot to lose. Maybe we could convince him to cooperate and give up Max. Unless Max is an idiot, he will not fess up about kidnapping Ena. So our best chance is to have Kim on our side. What do you think?"

"I agree. But, if Kiyoshi isn't with him, we won't have much choice but to interview Max."

"Yeah. But Kiyoshi drove to Boston to help Max take Ena to Tennessee. They must be close friends. It's a good chance he'll bring Max here, but he probably wouldn't come into the PD with him. We know what Kiyoshi drives and have his plate number. Let's assign an officer out front in a patrol car. If Kiyoshi drops Max off in front and waits outside, have the officer bring him for questioning as a person of interest."

"It might work. I'll set it up."

CHAPTER
32

abbi called the desk officer to have an available female officer watch three kids while she conducted an interview. When the officer arrived, Sam asked her if the phones were working yet. The officer said a crew was on their way to repair their towers, but she didn't know how long it would take. The officer then escorted Ena and Amy's daughters to an adjoining room while Gabbi and Sam interviewed Amy.

Once alone, Gabbi informed Amy that they wanted to know everything about the operation at the commune regarding guns and fentanyl.

"Before we begin, I want to thank you both for getting my kids and me out of the compound to safety. I'll answer your questions, but I want a guarantee that you'll protect my kids and me from Trent Killingworth and his crew. I'm sure he'll try to get back at me for leaving the compound and talking to the police. I also want your promise that I won't face any charges."

"I can only promise we will do all we can to ensure nothing happens to you and your daughters. We'll have the DA talk to you further about the options available for your protection," said Gabbi.

"We'll also have the U.S. Attorney talk to you about protecting you and your kids. Gabbi and I will do all we can to convince the prosecutor not to charge you with anything. However, the prosecutors will have the final say. I want to make that clear upfront," said Sam.

"So, what do you want to know?" said Amy.

Sam began with the questions. "Is there any other reason you wanted to leave the compound with us rather than remain there?"

Amy took her time to answer. "Trent wants to have children with more than one woman, and he likes to choose them young."

"How young do you mean?" asked Gabbi.

"He considers fifteen or sixteen as ready to bear children. My daughter Krissy will be fifteen in five months. Trent has been paying particular attention to her for weeks now. I don't want my daughters to be part of Trent's baby congregation. So I told Trent that Krissy was off-limits to childbearing at her age. He wasn't too happy about it. It got me worried. There's limited shelter space at the compound, and I wasn't going to take any chance that he would not have room in the shelter for me."

"Why did you join him at the compound?" asked Sam.

"An acquaintance suggested I join Trent's group with her since Trent provided work in exchange for room and board and for education and medical care for the children."

"What kind of work did to do at the compound?"

"Help with cooking, cleaning, food shopping, and homeschooling for the children. Once you've been there for a while and earned Trent's trust, he allowed others to work in the barn. You'd get paid for working there. When I first met Trent, he seemed like a good man who helped those going through bad times and needing support. I liked him, and chemistry developed between us. I worked hard and never complained, unlike other women at the commune. Trent eventually allowed me to work in the barn and made me third in command behind him and Doc. Doc is Tony Percey, the army medic who was Trent's closest friend in Afghanistan."

"Impressive," said Sam. "Was not complaining like the other women the sole reason he gave you clout over others?"

Amy's face blushed in apparent embarrassment. She thought momentarily before answering. "I made him happy in bed. Trent likes to play rough, and I was willing to deal with it since my ex-husband had similar sadistic tendencies. Trent didn't hit me or anything like that, but he did things I prefer not to repeat. Trent was a lot like my ex, and I didn't want my daughters ever to experience such behavior."

Sam recognized Amy got quite emotional talking about her relationship with Trent and her ex-husband, so he changed the subject. "What kind of work were you doing in the barn?"

"At first, I was allowed to bring meals to the workers inside, bandage any minor cuts or bring a cell phone to them if they had to make a call. Trent had a rule that no cell phones or alcohol were allowed inside the barn while working. I also had to provide certain rewards to those who finished and delivered the products on time. That's all I'll say about that, other than it led me to have contempt for the man."

"Understood, Amy," interjected Gabbi. "Let's focus on the products that you mentioned. What did the men make inside the barn?"

Amy didn't know where to start since the workers made more than one product. "Well, first, I should mention Trent had the barn inside divided into two work sections. He had the smaller rear section separated by a floor-to-ceiling plastic curtain. The larger front section had two different work areas. One area made 3-D computer parts for pistols and some to change guns to fire like machine guns. In another area in the front room, they made what they called bump stocks to make long guns shoot like a machine gun."

"Quite an operation," said Sam. "What did they make in the back room?"

"I wasn't allowed in that section, but all the workers talked about the fentanyl. Some workers used it and even gave it to the woman they wanted to bed with at night. One of the women got hooked on it and got very sick. Her condition worried me about the dangers of taking the drug. She no longer lives at the compound. Doc took her to the hospital for treatment, so he told me, but she never returned."

"What kind of security do they have at the barn, and did Trent set up any escape routes in situations where they might get raided by the police?" asked Sam.

"I only know Trent had two big guys, including Otis Riggins, who you met yesterday at the compound, stand guard at the entrance. Next to the barn, there used to be a shed for the lawn tractor and tools. Trent had the men tear it down. He then hired a company to rebuild it with enough support for a tunnel underneath. Inside the shed, which is always locked, there's a trap door with steps leading into the tunnel. Trent decided to do this after that big tornado hit Kentucky and devastated an area miles long. It also added more shelter space for the residents. I never paid much attention to their work at the shed and never was in it, but I overheard the men talk about the tunnel underneath it. Trent also, uh, what is the word I'm looking for—you know, to make the barn stronger in case of a tornado?"

"To reinforce it?" said Sam.

"Yeah. I think Trent had a company reinforce some of the barn walls with steel. The barn didn't have a basement, so he also added an underground basement section near the rear of the barn. I heard that the door leading to the basement is hidden and has multiple locks with an alarm system. Trent wanted a secure room to keep the fentanyl and guns before getting delivered to whoever he sold them to. He thought it could be used as another shelter too. According to KK, that's Kim Kiyoshi, Trent also used the basement to store military weapons they smuggled from Afghanistan."

After finishing her statement, Amy sketched the structures at the compound and the purposes of each. She also furnished the names of the residents, including the children. Finally, Gabbi had her recorded statement transcribed into a typed account for Amy to sign. Sam then escorted Amy back to where her daughters and Ena were secured.

Next, Gabbi and Sam were about to interview Angie when Nashville ATF agents Aliyah Mayfield and Rafael Torres arrived at the police station. They joined Gabbi and Sam in Captain Walters' office.

Aliyah pulled out several files from her brown leather bag. "We received the military files on those in Trent Killingworth's squad in Afghanistan. Despite the fact the files report top-level enemy kills by Killingworth's crew, it also chronicled claims of him defying orders, conducting unsanctioned kills, theft, and unlawful drug dealing by him and those in his squad."

Agent Torres passed copies of a telephonic interview with Killingworth's company commander and his platoon leader, Lieutenant Allen Chandler. "Chandler repeatedly questioned Killingworth's reports on enemy kills, specifically, killing non-combatants that Killingworth claimed were soldiers. He reported Killingworth twice for disobeying his direct orders but was overruled by the company commander, who only cared about the squad's success in killing or capturing the enemy. Chandler maintained that Killingworth and his crew operated a theft and drug-selling ring but lacked indisputable proof of wrongdoing. Killingworth and his men were good at covering their tracts with lies and threats made to witnesses."

Gabbi and Sam studied the personnel files. The Army couldn't substantiate any violation contrary to military law or policy for use against Killingworth and his men. As a result, they all received honorable discharges. A total of ten men served within the squad led by Sergeant Trent Killingworth. Other than Lucas Petersen, killed in action, and two severely wounded members, most worked with Killingworth at the compound. From his interview with Angie Lomax in Boston, Sam recognized some of the names and nicknames Killingworth gave to his men.

"Does anybody know when the power will come back on? I need to make a few phone calls," asked Sam.

"I saw men working on the communication towers on the PD's roof. So I called out to them, asking if everything was working. They said things should be back to normal in about a half-hour." answered Aliyah.

"Great, that's good news. Aliyah, you and Raffy should read Amy Norwood's statement. When we visited the compound to show Ena's photo to the women, Amy said she could help us find Ena in exchange for getting her and her two daughters to a shelter away from Killingworth. She gave us enough probable cause to get a search warrant at the compound. In return, she wants guarantees that she wouldn't get charged with any crime and receive protection from Killingworth and his crew. You may want to get additional information from her and register her as a confidential informant."

"Why aren't you or Gabbi registering her as a CI?" asked Aliyah.

"I'm heading back to Boston and will probably never see Norwood again. Plus, the feds should provide her with the protection she needs and the guarantee from prosecution, which Gabbi and I highly recommend. It's your federal case now. I'm leaving after the raid on the compound. Just make sure Gabbi gets credited for all her work on this case."

Aliyah agreed. "Thanks to both of you for the work you did for us. We've only been trying to get enough PC to raid that place for months. I should also congratulate you both for rescuing the young girl. Great job. You made two solid cases in one day. I'd also like to meet the young girl, Ena."

Gabbi corrected Aliyah. "We actually arrested three, well, two, motorcycle gang members today. So make it three criminal cases we accomplished today."

"What? You have to fill me in on that arrest."

"Gabbi and I have to interview the woman who held the abducted kid for her brother. And we anticipate that her brother will arrive at the PD shortly. When we finish with the interviews, we'll have you meet Ena."

A little while later, Gabbi and Sam had Angie brought her into a private room to get her statement. Gabbi read Angie her right to refuse to answer questions and have an attorney appointed without cost if she couldn't afford one. When asked if she would answer their questions, Angie felt she didn't do anything wrong, so she agreed to answer questions. The interview went better than Sam expected.

Angie detailed the aftermath of her involvement when her brother abducted Ena in Boston. Angie maintained she did not know that her brother had taken Ena from her school and then to Tennessee with the help of his army buddy, Kim Kiyoshi. It wasn't until her brother called and told her that he was Ena's father and wanted her to fly to Tennessee to look after Ena while he worked at his new job there. Angie only knew what her brother told her—that Kiyoshi introduced him and his army buddies to Mayumi while on R&R in London. Her brother said he had an affair with Mayumi and later learned she was pregnant. Angie denied knowing anything about that until after her brother took Ena. When the interview ended, Angie agreed to sign a written statement.

"Let's take a break while I call Ena's mom with the good news that Ena will soon be home," said Sam.

"Call her Facetime," said Gabbi. "I want to be in the room to see the expression on her mom's face."

"Okay, let's do it."

"Detective Walters," announced the PD's desk officer over the intercom system. "You have a visitor. Billy Lomax is here to see you."

"Oh, no. What timing," said Gabbi.

"Better now than later, Gabbi. Let's get this done before he decides to bolt."

CHAPTER
33

fter the tornado moved out of the Nashville area, Trent Killingworth was distraught over the damage there as he navigated around a challenging obstacle course driving back to the compound. He had no choice but to remain overnight in a city shelter following his appearance in court. His drive back to the commune was arduous, avoiding garbage containers, fence sections, and piles of vehicles sprawled along the streets. Seeing the heavy damage in the city, TK, as they all called him at the compound, expected the commune to be in shambles. However, when he arrived at the gate, he was surprised to see not as much damage as anticipated. When he approached the compound, TK was understandably disappointed that the house, old shack, and newly built shed were damaged but astonished that the barn still stood firm. However, he slammed his open hand against his truck's steering wheel seeing the security gate was leaning halfway to the ground and couldn't open. TK exited his truck and began yelling at the four men sitting outside the barn, doing nothing except joking around.

"What are you guys doing standing around doing nothing? Get your asses over here and fix this fucking gate!"

Surprised by TK's arrival, the men ran to the entrance gate and began trying to lift the entrance gate section. The four men struggled since about six yards of fencing on each side of the gate also leaned and weighed it down.

Trent watched in disgust at the incompetence of the men. "That's not going to work!" he screamed. "Get me heavy-duty chain sections about ten feet long to attach to the pickup over by the barn. Bring two sections for the fence, and we'll have the truck's motorized winch yank it up from inside."

TK remained upset, watching the two men moseying toward the shed. "Move your asses, damn it. I don't have all day to stand out here! One of you others get Doc to come over here."

While TK impatiently waited for someone to bring the chains, Anthony Percey, the former army medic referred to as Doc, scrambled to where Trent waited.

"Welcome back, Sarge."

"Yeah, yeah. Bring me up-to-date on the situation in the barn. Any equipment or product damage, structural issues to the barn, injuries or whatever?"

"We lucked out having the barn walls reinforced. The roof on the far side needs fixing, as do two small windows. We secured the equipment the best we could, and everything worked okay. All the products got stored in the basement before the storm hit. So, we're all good there, and only minor cuts and bruises to those working inside the barn. I have the equipment pumping out the product as fast as designed, and we're already finishing up the next batch of the fenys."

"I knew I could count on you, Doc. We need to finish up what we have for distribution and get it out of here. Because of the storm, the police will have limited staff working, and those on duty will be busy dealing with looters and chaperoning repair trucks throughout the city. Do we have an entire team working, or has anyone left the property?

Doc hesitated to answer until he considered what men were there working. He looked over at the guys helping with the fence and saw Kiyoshi. "Everybody is here, but KK said he had to leave to give Max a ride to get his sister and daughter from a shelter. He said he'd come back to help."

Kiyoshi spoke up. "It should only take a couple of hours, and I'll get back as soon as possible."

"Okay. The cops will have limited patrols on the roads, so we'll have less to worry about distributing what we have in storage. Let's plan to have everything loaded and ready to distribute by sunrise."

* * *

A uniformed officer waited outside the front of the PD in an unmarked car. He didn't have to wait long when he recognized Kiyoshi's SUV pull up at the police headquarters entrance. After a male passenger exited the vehicle and walked into the PD, the SUV drove off, made a U-turn a short distance up the road, drove back toward the PD, and parked twenty yards in the back of the unmarked police car.

The officer called Detective Gabbi Walters and informed her of the SUV parked behind him.

Gabbi instructed the officer to approach and identify the driver. "If it's Kim Kiyoshi, bring him to me in the detectives unit."

When Gabbi ended the call, she had the desk officer bring Billy Lomax to the detective's unit. She didn't want Max to see the officer take Kiyoshi into the station. When an officer escorted Max to Gabbi, she brought him into a vacant room and asked him to wait there until she could get someone to bring his sister and daughter up from the shelter.

Gabbi then contacted the officer to usher Kiyoshi to her in the detectives' unit. Once Kiyoshi was delivered, Gabbi and Sam led him into a separate room for questioning. Since Sam knew more about the abduction of Ena, he took the lead in questioning Kim.

After identifying himself, Sam began the interrogation. "Kim, have you ever been to Boston?"

Kim, not expecting that question, immediately became anxious. *Did Max already confess about taking Ena?* He thought. He answered with what he thought was innocent enough. "Uh, I might have once visited a friend there but didn't stay long. What's this about, anyway?"

"I'm going to show you a copy of a video from the Boston Police Department exposing two guys abducting a young student from her school."

Next, Sam began the pole camera videos of Kim's SUV, stopping to study Liang Wu's black van parked in the rear of Wu's apartment building.

"That's your SUV where you and your friend Billy Lomax planned to borrow that black van to kidnap Ena Oshiro." Then, Sam began an additional video sequence. "That's you driving the van and returning it to the apartment where you borrowed it. A few minutes later, your SUV, driven by Max with Ena in the back seat, drives by the street where you returned the van. Max took the next right and drove to where he picked you up after you left the van, walked up between other apartments, and joined Max in your SUV. Next, your SUV came out of a parallel street and turned left. I'll stop the video here for a close-up of the occupants. As you can see, that's you and Max. Last, this is the sequence of you driving your SUV with Ena in the backseat to the Interstate turnpike heading east on your way to Tennessee."

KK looked stunned with his eyes glaring and his mouth open in awe.

Sam closed the iPad cover. "We have Max's sister, Angie, and Ena here in the police station. Angie already gave us her statement that Max and you took Ena from her school and crossed state lines bringing her to Tennessee, which is a federal offense. You could get sent to prison for twenty years to life for kidnapping. We know you only wanted to help your friend, Max. He's the guy we want more than you. Tell us how Max planned the abduction, and we'll help you."

Still staggered from watching the video, KK remained speechless with what the pole camera caught. He was upset, thinking back to when Max had claimed there were no pole cameras on the streets from the school to the apartment complex.

"To add to your prison time, we know you are involved with the illegal sale of guns and fentanyl made at Trent Killingworth's compound. A poisonous powder laced the fentanyl tablets you helped make that killed two people so far. That's murder, man. That's life in prison with the possibility of getting the death penalty," said Sam, numbing KK even more. So for your sake, help us, not only against Max but against Killingworth's illegal operation. We can help to reduce the charges against you, but it's a one-time offer. If you decide not to talk right now, we will walk out of here and make no further offers to help you."

Kim's eyes watered as he squirmed in his chair, nervously shaking. "I only tried helping my friend. Ena is his daughter, and her mother wouldn't let him see her. He wants his daughter in his life, and Ena wants to be with him, not her mother."

"That's not true, Kim. Max lived with his sister, Angie, next door to Ena and her mother. Angie babysat for Ena while her mother worked as a doctor in a Boston hospital. Ena only knew Max as Angie's brother, not her father. And she doesn't want to be with Max. She's terrified of him and wants to return to be with her mom in Boston. Max lied to you and got you so deep in shit that you may never breathe fresh air outside a prison fence again."

Kim slumped over in the chair with his hands covering his face. His stomach stirred with anxiety. His head tightened with intensive pressure to the point it felt like bursting. Sam let him contemplate his options for a moment.

"Kim. Look at me," directed Sam. "What makes Max think he is Ena's father?"

Kim shrugged his shoulders while pressing his lips together before saying, "I only know what Max told me."

"Which is what?"

Kim took in a deep breath before answering. "When our army squad took an R&R in London, the guys wanted to go out drinking. I don't mind having one or two drinks, but these guys drink until they pass out. Instead, I went to a nearby coffee shop. I sat alone at a table for two when Mayumi came in and couldn't find an empty table, so I offered her to sit at mine. We're both Japanese and hit it off by talking Japanese, not English. She told me she was attending medical school in London and worried about not having enough money to continue. She was on a partial scholarship but had little extra money for food and school expenses. I felt bad for her. To make it short, we ended up sleeping together that night. I felt sorry for her and gave her money. I had more than I needed. She refused to take the money and began crying. I shouldn't have done what I did next, but I wanted to help her, so I told her my friends had a lot of money and would pay her if she slept with them. Mayumi said no, she was not like that, but when I started to leave, she changed her mind."

Kim paused and took another deep breath before continuing. "I convinced my buddies to visit her and help her by paying her what I did for—you know."

"How much was enough for her to change her mind?"

"I gave her a thousand that night. I told my friends it was what she charged, but it wasn't true. She didn't charge me anything. I gave her the money on my own. I know some guys who met her gave her a thousand, but I don't know if they all did.

"Did Max and all the other guys visit her?"

"Yes. All eight did once, except Max met with her twice."

"I thought there were ten guys in your squad."

"There were, but Luke Petersen got killed in action just before our R&R, and TK didn't visit her."

"So why does Max think he got her pregnant out of all the guys who slept with her?"

"Mayumi required everyone to use protection. Max told me long after our time in London that he tricked her and didn't use protection the second time he saw her."

Disgusted, Gabbi frowned and said, "What an asshole."

Max's trickery repulsed Sam too. Sam had encountered other slime balls in his career and had always enjoyed handcuffing and getting them time in jail, where they might get the same treatment from the inmates. Knowing Max was a scumbag, Sam couldn't wait to arrest him and recommend a long stretch in prison where the inmates might play the same trick on him.

"Kim, Max isn't worth defending if it's going to result in you spending a long stretch in prison. So, what will it be? Talk to us. Tell us Max's plan to kidnap Ena. I think Max made up the story that Ena was his daughter," said Sam.

Kim straightened up in his chair. He wiped away a tear from his puffy water-filled eyes. "I don't want to spend my life in jail. I have family, my mom and dad, and my sisters. Are you serious that you will help me?"

"Yes, Kim, we can help you, but you must cooperate and help us nail Max and Killingworth. They're the bad guy here. If you cooperate, we will inform the prosecutor that you helped us get Max, Killingworth, and others at the compound. Your cooperation will go a long way to convince the prosecutor to recommend less charges against you."

Kim recognized his cooperation would be his best chance for a deal but felt guilt-ridden about turning on his friends. He had no choice. "Okay. I'll help you, but TK will try to get back at me. He's dangerous when he gets pissed off. My army buddies and I think he's bipolar. Can you guys promise he won't know that I talked?"

"We'll tell the prosecutors that Killingworth, or TK as you call him, may seek revenge if he finds out you helped us. After that, it'll be up to the attorney whether or not to disclose your cooperation. If that's not possible for him to keep your cooperation a secret, we'll request the DA's office to maintain tight security around you and away from TK and his associates."

With that, Kim recapped how Max requested his help to take his daughter, who Max said wanted to be with him, not her mother. Max's plan involved borrowing a van temporarily from a maintenance guy at work, so the focus of the abduction would point to him. Regarding gun and drug-making, Kim described TK's illegal manufacturing operation, the hidden security door leading to the storage basement, and the product distribution arrangements. He also disclosed TK's plan to escape through a tunnel under the shed if the police raided them.

"Tell me about the tunnel. How far does it go, and where does it lead? Does he have a car stored at the end of the tunnel?"

"I don't know. I've never been in the tunnel. I only saw the excavation of a trench dug by the construction workers, maybe thirty, forty yards from the back of the shed. The tunnel stopped at a huge boulder on the other side of the fence. When the concrete truck poured cement for the tunnel walls, they also placed a round exit hatch near the boulder that looked like a sewer cover."

Gabbi cut in to ask a couple of questions. "Does TK own the land where he had the tunnel dug? Also, is there a path he could use that leads to another road for him to escape?"

"I don't know. Trent keeps a lot to himself, but all the guys in the squad know he plans for all contingencies."

KK confirmed the details that Amy Norwood had provided. Before continuing the questioning, Sam asked Gabbi if she had any additional questions. She didn't, so Sam pondered what further information Kim might have that was important to know.

"Describe everything TK stores in the basement."

"TK calls everything we make, the gun parts and fentanyl, his product. We package the product according to what the buyers order. It could be small packages of fentanyl for street sellers or large containers for guns and gun parts."

"Does he store guns taken from Afghanistan?"

Kim nodded yes. "TK has several AK-47s, fully automatic ARs, grenades, smoke grenades, knives, ballistic vests, and other small arms taken from the enemy and some from the army he claimed got lost or taken by the Afghans."

"Kim, we heard TK had a court appearance on the day of the tornado. Did he return to the compound that day or seek shelter in Nashville?"

"He stayed at a shelter in the city. He didn't get back to the compound until this afternoon. He was pissed that the tornado caused the security gate and fencing to lean over, and nobody was working to fix it upright."

"So, you were present when he arrived? Did you help to get the fence upright?"

"Yeah, I was there helping with the fence. TK wasn't in a good mood. After the guys and I fixed the fence, he wanted us to get the gun and fentanyl inventory loaded onto our trucks and ready to move out by sunrise. Because of the tornado, TK said the cops would mainly focus on looters and securing the streets for clearing, not patrolling the roads."

Sam turned to Gabbi with an enlightening expression. "Good to know," said Sam. Knowing that, Sam and Gabbi realized they had to move fast to obtain and execute a search warrant before TK removed the evidence from the commune.

"Kim, I understand Trent had the front gate fitted with a security code. Can the gate be opened remotely?" Sam thought the gate probably could but didn't know for sure. "If it could open remotely, who other than TK had a remote?"

KK bowed his head in thought for seconds before answering. "I know Doc and TK have one, and there's one at the house down the road where some guys stay. I don't know if anyone else has one."

"How do you know those at the house have one?" asked Gabbi.

"That's where I stay. I don't live at the compound."

Gabbi followed up on KK's answer. "Where do you guys keep the remote in the house?"

"TK set up a table at the front picture window. We keep the remote next to the monitor, laptop, and coffee maker. There's also note pads and pens on the table."

KK's mention of a monitor got Gabbi and Sam's attention. Gabbi asked the obvious question. "Why the monitor?"

"There are security cameras on telephone poles. One at the front of the house and another about twenty-five yards from the beginning of the road. We can see any vehicle or person entering the road on the split-screen monitor."

Gabbi and Sam stared at each other, acknowledging how important it was to get that information.

"Gabbi, could you stay with Kim while I confer with Aliyah and Raffi? I'll let them hear Kim's recorded testimony. They may have additional questions for Kim."

"Yeah, Sam. But let's speed it up. We need to get moving on this soon."

After ATF agents Aliyah Mayfield and Rafael Torres listened to KK's recorded testimony, Aliyah agreed to move quickly and secure a search warrant. They didn't need anything else from KK.

"You guys are on the money. We need to hit the compound before they leave with all the evidence. I'll reach out to Jayla Bransford, the US attorney. Based on what Amy Norwood and Kiyoshi gave us, we have the PC to get a search warrant. I'll also contact the special agent in charge to call out our tactical team to report here tonight. We don't have a lot of time. We need to act fast," said Aliyah.

CHAPTER
34

A uniformed police officer stood guard outside the interview room where Billy Lomax sat impatiently, waiting for the police to bring Angie and Ena to him. Max was concerned that Kim might get impatient or spooked by the long wait and leave him stranded without a ride back.

Finally, Sam and Gabbi entered the room and sat across from Lomax. Sam took the lead, displayed his badge, and offered Max water or a Coke.

"I'm not thirsty. I've been waiting almost an hour and still haven't seen my sister and daughter. Where are they? Are they alright?"

"Yes. They're fine. We just need to have you answer a few questions first."

"What questions? I'm only here to get my sister and daughter back home. My sister was supposed to go to the shelter where I work. It's not my fault she didn't go there and was brought here."

"It's not about what shelter your sister did or didn't go to. It's about you and Ena."

Max suddenly felt uneasy, like a ton of bricks had just fallen on his chest. His heart rate accelerated. He could hardly speak. Max coughed, cleared his throat, and shifted nervously in his chair, wondering if he was about to get arrested. His voice was hoarse when he finally responded

"If I answer your questions, Can I leave here with my sister and daughter?"

"That depends on your answers to our questions."

Max realized he was in a no-win situation and tried playing along. "Well, let's get this over with because I have to get back to work."

"What's Ena's last name?"

That question came out of nowhere and was unexpected as Max wondered how to answer it. "I'm not sure why you need to know her last name. What difference does it make?"

"It's a simple, straightforward question. I'll put it another way. Is Ena's last name Lomax? And, if it's not, why not? Certainly, you know your daughter's last name."

Max remained silent. *They're trying to trick me,* he thought. "You already know her name, and you must also know a lot of parents who don't marry have different last names."

"I understand. But how do we know you are Ena's father just because you say so? Without confirmation, we can't release her to someone who only claims to be her father."

Frustrated, Max took a deep breath before deciding not to answer any further questions.

"I don't like the way this is going. Unless you're going to arrest me, I'm leaving. I have to get back to work and have a friend waiting outside to give me a ride there."

Sam grabbed his iPad and brought up the Boston police pole videos showing Ena's abduction sequences. He paused the video where the camera zoomed in on Kim Kiyoshi and Max sitting in Kim's SUV after taking Ena from her school in Boston. "That's you in the passenger seat in Kim's vehicle with Ena in the back after you and Kim kidnapped her from her school."

"That's bullshit. That's not me, maybe someone who looks like me. It's not even that clear a picture."

"We arrested Angie, Max. She gave us a statement. Ena only knows you as Angie's brother, and she was terrified when you and Kim abducted her. That's Kim's SUV, and he's not outside waiting for you. He's in another room detailing everything that will land you in prison for a very long time. We want to know why you think Ena is your daughter."

Max eased back in his chair, realizing they knew everything. But, he figured he could talk his way out of any kidnapping. He then stood upright in his chair, leaned forward with his elbows on the table, and cleared his throat again. "Kim introduced me to Mayumi when our army squad was on R&R in London. Mayumi needed money to pay for medical schooling. So, Kim persuaded her that she could earn enough money for school by having sex with all the guys in our squad. So, I had sex with her twice and later learned she was pregnant. That's how I know Ena was my kid."

"But you said she had sex with not only you but all your army buddies, of which I believe there were about seven other guys. So it makes sense that Ena could have gotten pregnant by any of your buddies."

Max lowered his head, unsure how to respond. Eventually, he came up with what he thought was a convincing answer. He then lifted his head, took a deep breath, nervously cleared his throat again, and replied. "One of those times with her, I didn't wear protection. All the other guys said they always did."

"So you believe whatever the others told you. Does Ena's mother know or think you are Ena's father."

Max leaned back in his chair, thinking over his options. He thought they were playing games with him and wouldn't believe anything he said, so he stood up and announced, "I don't want to answer any more questions. I want a lawyer."

Gabbi stood up and responded. "You're under arrest for kidnapping and endangering a child. You should know we take DNA samples from all those arrested. That will tell us if you are her father. We already have a sample from Ena."

Sam walked behind Max, whispering in his ear. "Kidnapping and transporting a child across state lines is a federal offense. You'll likely face multiple and state federal charges. Unfortunately, Kim, who only tried to help you, will also face kidnapping charges."

"Kim didn't know anything. I didn't have a car and asked if he could help me get Ena from school and drive us to Tennessee, where I was starting a new job. He knew nothing other than my daughter was coming with me to Tennessee."

Sam felt Max's admission should help Kim in court. A uniformed officer escorted Max to the lockup while Gabbi and Sam joined agents Aliyah Mayfield and Torres in Captain Walter's office. The captain had since returned from the church shelter. With everyone in the room, Agent Mayfield briefed them.

"The U.S. Attorney reviewed Amy Norwood and Kim Kiyoshi's statements. She faxed a copy of an affidavit based on their testimony to a federal judge and telephonically spoke to the judge requesting an expedited early morning warrant. I'm awaiting her call back on the judge's approval. Our Nashville ATF SAC called out the Special Response Team and confirmed that all Nashville agents would attend a briefing tonight at nine o'clock here at the PD. Captain Walters has notified the department's tactical team, detectives, and uniformed officers to participate in the briefing. When most everyone arrives here during the next couple of hours, we will prepare the operational plan and assignments to hit the compound and the ranch house that monitors the road tomorrow morning at five-thirty. Any questions?"

Sam thought of something they needed to address for the operational plan. "Regarding Kim's statement about the tunnel from the shed, we should find out if there's a path that leads to a road for him to escape and have that area secured with a team of agents. Aliyah, I believe you had mentioned you had an aerial view of the compound."

"Good point. I have that aerial view photo with me in the case file."

Aliyah placed the aerial photo on Captain Walters' desk as Gabbi and her dad studied it. Gabbi pointed to the old farmhouse on the adjacent property to the commune. "That's the old Holliston farm that was for sale for months. I don't know if it ever sold, but the road in front is North Fenton Road, a short distance west of Warriors Way. There's a clearing here, maybe a pathway, between the trees," Gabbi pointed to it, "that leads to the farmhouse and the road."

"That must be how Killingworth would escape if he has a chance to," said Aliyah, "Let's plan on having agents posted on that street. Thanks, Sam and Gabbi, for bringing that up."

Sam looked at the time and mentioned he had to excuse himself. "I understand the phones are working, so I need about an hour to call my boss and the U.S. Attorney's office in Boston. I also want to call Ena's mom to let her know Ena is safe and going home soon. With your permission, I'd like to invite the two FBI agents working on Ena's investigation in Boston to join us tomorrow. I hope there's no objection."

Everyone looked at each other, then nodded, having no objection. Agent Mayfield said it would take time for the tactical leaders and other team members to get there. "We'll use the conference room on the other end of the building. So take whatever time you need, Sam. Once you get to the conference room, we'll fill you in on the plan.

"Sam, I'm coming with you. Make sure to call Ena's mom on Facetime so we can see her mom's reaction."

"Absolutely. Let's go do it now."

When Ena saw Gabbi and Sam walk into the room, her brown eyes widened, and a radiant pink glow filled her cheeks. She quickly ran to Sam with a hopeful look on her face. "Are we going home to my mom now, Sam?"

"I'm sorry, sweetheart, but the airports are still closed. However, the phones are working again, so we can call your mom. I need to talk to her for only a minute, and then you can speak to her for a long time. I'll use your cell phone."

Excitement was written all over Ena as she went up on her tip-toes and waved her arms, saying, "Okay!"

Sam searched for Mayumi's number and selected the number to call her. It rang seven times before going to voice mail. Disappointed, Sam ended the call without leaving a message. But, seconds later, Ena's phone rang. He saw it was from Mayumi calling him back, but not on Facetime.

"Ena, is that you?"

"No, May, it's Sam Caviello. How are you?"

For a moment, May couldn't speak. She worried that Sam had called with bad news. Her eyes watered even before Sam answered the call. "Please, Sam, don't tell me anything bad."

With that response, Sam realized he had to put Ena on the call immediately. "I have someone here that wants to talk to you, but first, could you call me back on FaceTime?"

"What?" questioned Mayumi. Her anxiety spiked even higher, thinking the worse. "Uh, okay. I'll call you back."

Mayumi assumed Sam was maybe referring to a counseling professional who wanted to tell her the bad news. Her hand quivered as she found the Facetime icon on her phone and called Ena's number back.

CHAPTER
35

As Ena's phone rang, Sam handed it to Ena and told her it was her mom calling. Ena answered the phone and saw her mom on the screen. "Mama!" she screamed with excitement.

Mayumi couldn't control her emotions. Tears flooded her eyes and cascaded down her cheeks like an open faucet. She cupped her hand over her mouth as she sobbed with joy. She was so nervous that she could hardly put words together. "Ena … Ena, my baby. It's, it's you. Are you okay, Ena?" as she continued to weep.

"Yes, mama, I'm okay. Sam and Gabbi found me. Sam is taking me home."

Gabbi became emotional alongside Sam and held onto his arm as a tear rolled down her cheek. Noticing the tear dripping down her cheek, Sam grabbed his hanky and softly wiped it away as they smiled at each other. Gabbi then placed her head on Sam's shoulder. They listened to the happy exchange between a mother and her child for five minutes before Gabbi kissed Sam on his cheek and said she would head back to where the others were planning the raid.

"Stay as long as you like, Sam. I'll fill you in on what you missed later."

Sam let the conversation between Ena and her mom continue for another ten minutes before asking Ena to let him talk to her mom.

"May, I'm so happy for you and Ena. I want you to know we're in Nashville, Tennessee, and it was Billy Lomax, Angie's brother, who took Ena with the help of an army friend, Kim Kiyoshi. We arrested Angie, Billy, and his friend. Unfortunately, we experienced a damaging tornado in Nashville, so the airports are currently closed. So, we can't fly to Boston until the earliest the day after tomorrow. After the airports open, I'll call you back, okay?"

"Okay, Sam. I was worried when you called, but,"— Mayumi became overcome with emotion and started sobbing,—"you made me so happy. You found her, Sam. How do I thank you enough?"

"Seeing your happy faces is all the thanks I need, May. It's an honor to have helped. I'll talk to you later. Ena will be home soon."

Using his cell, Sam left the room and called Donna Ranero, the AUSA in Boston. First, he briefed her on finding Ena, arresting Billy Lomax, his sister Angie and Kiyoshi. He then mentioned the tornado that prevented him from calling earlier. Next, Sam reported the airport was closed and hoped to fly back to Boston the day after tomorrow. Finally, Sam advised her that he and a Nashville detective established enough probable cause for a search warrant on a group making and selling ghost guns, machine gun conversion kits, and fentanyl. "We are waiting for a federal judge's approval for the warrant. We expect it shortly, and we'll execute the warrant early in the morning."

"I'll call the Boston FBI office and give them the good news. Based on your findings on the pole cameras, you should know that they allowed Liang Wu out on bail until they finalize their investigation."

"I'm glad to hear that. But, I also know the FBI won't be pleased that I got involved with their investigation. So right after I end our call, I'd prefer to call agent Kiara Rivers to brief her and invite her to fly down here and participate in the raid, but more importantly, to take custody of those we arrested."

"Good plan, Sam."

"Do me a favor. Don't call the FBI agent in charge. Let Rivers call her boss first."

Ranero agreed.

Next, Sam called FBI Agent Rivers. Her phone rang until it went to voice mail. He left a short message and then ended the call. He was disappointed she didn't answer. While searching for the next number to call, his phone rang. It was agent Rivers.

"I'm glad you called back, Kiara."

"It's Agent Rivers to you, Caviello. Where are you?"

"Hmm, you sound annoyed. Maybe I shouldn't have called."

Knowing she was rude when she answered, she softened her tone. "Let's chalk it up to me not having a great day so far. So why did you call me?"

"I'm calling hoping to make your day better. Please don't interrupt me until I finish what I have to say." He briefed her on finding Ena Oshiro and arresting those involved with her abduction.

"Well, that's good news, anyway," said Kiara.

Sam also informed her that he and a detective developed PC for a search warrant for a commune where ghost guns, bump stocks, gun parts to convert assault weapons, and fentanyl, laced with a poisonous substance, were manufactured. "I don't have time to explain all the details, but ATF and the Nashville tactical teams are hitting the place early tomorrow morning. I'd like you and your partner to fly out tonight and join us on the raid if you can. You can take custody of Billy Lomax, his sister, and Kiyoshi. I'd rather you take custody of the suspects, hoping it leads to a friendly working alliance between us."

Sam's offer pleasantly surprised Rivers, but she didn't say anything, waiting to see if Sam had more to say.

Sam continued. "You may have heard that a tornado caused enormous damage here. The Nashville airport is closed. However, there's an airport not far from Nashville in Huntsville, Kentucky. So maybe you could arrange to fly into Huntsville and join us when we hit the compound. Your boss should be pleased with you participating in a major bust. If you could arrange to fly here using your agency's jet, we can all fly back to Boston together. We could arrange to have a couple of Marshals help secure the prisoners during the flight."

"That might work, Sam, but I'm not sure I could get the plane on such short notice."

Sam sensed Rivers' tone changed when she called him by his first name. "What about Ena Oshiro?"

"She's safe and not harmed. Hopefully, Ena and I could catch a ride with you on the FBI plane back to Boston if you could arrange it. That should also impress your bosses, knowing the FBI participated in bringing Ena back to her mom and the perps who abducted her."

"I'll do my best to get there. Thanks for calling and inviting me."

"Let's get this done together, Kiara. There's an early morning briefing at three-thirty at the Nashville PD. If you miss the briefing, we could fill you in when you get here. Hopefully, you'll get here in time to participate in the raiding party. You have my number, so let's keep in touch." Sam ended the call.

Next, Sam called his boss in Boston and then Major Jack Burke of the Mass State Police, briefing them on all the events since arriving in Tennessee. In addition, he asked Burke to tell Detective Andrea Serrano about the situation in Tennessee and request that Trooper Kojima gets included on the FBI's trip to Nashville. When the calls ended, Sam felt good but tired. He then returned the calls to him by Alli Gaynor, the reporter. Her phone rang only twice before she answered.

"Sam. I've called you a couple of times. Everything alright?"

"Yes, everything is fine. Sorry I didn't call back, but I've been busy as hell. I don't have much time to tell you about a major story you should cover, but it means you have to travel to Nashville now." Sam then briefed Alli on Ena's abduction and rescue and the impending raid at a commune.

After ending the call, Sam rushed to the conference room, stopping for seconds to tell Ena he'd be back with her shortly. He entered the conference room just as the group finalized a draft of an operational plan. Gabbi quickly moved to his side and whispered, "Let's get out of here before my father looks for me."

Gabbi grabbed Sam by the arm, practically pushing him out the door. "I'll fill you in on the plan when we get to my place."

"Your place? Sam asked.

"Yes, my place. There's no sense staying at another hotel when I only live fifteen minutes from here. We could take Ena with us, get a take-out on the way to my condo, and get some sleep before coming back here."

"Okay, but why are you concerned about your father?"

"He's my father, and I'm taking you to my place. That should answer your question?"

CHAPTER
36

After picking up dinner, Gabbi, Sam, and Ena arrived at Gabbi's condo, a two-bedroom unit attached to another condo via the garages. They entered through the garage into the small but nicely arranged kitchen with light brown maple cabinets and relatively new stainless steel appliances. To the left of the kitchen was a large open room merging the dining room with a living room. There was a bedroom and bath on the left side of the living room. A hall containing a closet was on the right side. The hall turned left leading to a closet with a washing machine and dryer and then the master bedroom and bath. Sam was impressed with the living-dining room layout containing designer-looking furniture and large triple windows facing the backyard. Light tan paint covered the walls.

Sam, Gabbi, and Ena shared the contents of the three containers of Asian food, including brown fried rice, mixed veggies, and a combo of chicken and tender steak. Gabbi also ordered a strawberry cream Japanese cake roll and Mochi ice cream for dessert, available for takeout. Sam thought back before his divorce, remembering when his wife, son, and he sat at the dinner table enjoying Asian take-out on a Sunday night, followed by a hot-fudge sundae for dessert. Seeing Gabbi and Ena enjoying the meal and talking together, Sam realized what was missing in his life. He yearned for a return to family life again, if only he could set aside time away from the job to enjoy a similar setting again. *Someday*, he thought to himself.

Gabbi, Ena, and Sam were starving and finished their meal and dessert in record time. When they finished, Sam helped clean up the dining table and put the dishes and utensils into the dishwasher. While Sam cleaned, Gabbi brought Ena into the guest bathroom and set up the tub for Ena to take a bubble bath. Once the bath was ready for Ena, Gabbi put Ena's clothes in the washing machine and returned to set up a small t-shirt for Ena to wear to bed.

With Ena in the bathroom, Sam used the time to call Mayumi via Facetime. He wanted answers about Max's claim to be Ena's dad.

"Hi, Sam. Is everything alright?"

"Everything is fine, May. Gabbi is helping Ena clean up in the bathroom. I'll have Ena take the phone when she finishes."

"When are you coming to Boston? I miss her. Her grandma is here too. We can't wait for her to be home."

"The airport is still closed, but word is it will reopen tomorrow. We have to go before a judge tomorrow regarding the arrest of Angie, Max, and Kim. After that, we'll try to arrange a flight back to Boston. Hopefully, we'll be back in Boston late tomorrow or the next morning."

"That long, Sam?"

"Unfortunately, yes. Listen, May, I need to ask you something. It's personal, but it is an issue I need you to clarify."

"What is it you need to know?"

"I've interviewed Kim Kiyoshi and Billy Lomax. Both of them were in the same army squadron some years ago. They took what the military calls an R&R, a rest and relaxation trip, to London. While there, Kiyoshi said he met you at a coffee shop and then spent the night with you. Do you remember that time? You told him you were attending medical school in London."

"Why do we talk about that? It had nothing to do with Ena's kidnapping."

"Regretfully, it does, May. We never talked much about Ena's father. You only told me he was dead. Can you tell me about him, like who he was and where you met him? Does Ena know who her father was, and has she ever met or talked to him?"

"I only told Ena he died in the war."

Sam wasn't comfortable questioning Mayumi about what he had learned from Kiyoshi, but he needed corroboration that it did happen. "I'm sorry to ask personal questions, but I have to know if Kim was telling me the truth."

Feeling uneasy, Mayumi remembered that Kim promised to keep what happened in London private and would never speak of it to anyone. "What did Kim tell you other than we spent a night together?"

"He said you needed money to pay for school and that he paid you for having sex with him even though you refused any money. Kim suggested that having sex with his friends for money would help pay for your schooling. I ask these questions because Angie's brother, Billy, claims he's Ena's father. Billy was one of the guys in Kim's army unit who paid you for sex. He also claimed he was the only guy who didn't use protection when he had sex with you."

Mayumi became very upset, remembering her indiscretions. Finishing school and becoming a doctor was her dream, and she would have done almost anything to fulfill her dream. Then, with embarrassment and a little tongue-tied with a squeaky voice, she acknowledged what Kim had told Sam. "I did not have sex without condom with any of those men, but I did with Kim only."

Her admission took Sam by surprise. "So, you slept with Kim without protection? Only with Kim?"

"I liked him. We had no condom but still slept together only because I liked him. It wasn't for money. I did not know he would give me money after. It was a lot of money, and when he said I could get more like that, I, uh," she began sobbing, "was so desperate. I needed to pay for my schooling."

Sam gave Mayumi time to compose herself before continuing with his questions. "I understand, May. I get it. I'm not judging you. I'll show you photos to see if you recognize the two men." He first showed her the photo of Kim Kiyoshi.

May nodded yes and said it was Kim.

Sam then showed her the photo of Billy Lomax.

Mayumi looked shocked and shook her head no. "He's dead. They told me he got killed."

Sam didn't understand. "What? Who told you this man was dead?"

"Kim. He told me later Luke was dead."

"Luke? You recognize this man as Luke?"

"Yes. I didn't like him. He was too rough and wanted me to do things I would not do with him. He only gave me twenty dollars when he left mad."

"He said he met with you two times."

Mayumi remained silent before nodding yes. "First time, he was okay and paid me like Kim. Next time, he wanted more and became mean to me. I told him no more."

It was Sam's turn to take a deep breath after Mayumi mentioned Billy Lomax told her his name was Luke Petersen.

"May, the photo is not that of Luke. It's a photo of Billy Lomax. Lomax claimed he didn't wear protection with you."

Mayumi put her hand up to her mouth, giving a muted scream. She couldn't talk for a moment until calming down. "He's lying. I saw him put condom on."

"I believe you, May, and I'm sorry I had to ask these questions. Lomax may very well be lying. I don't like him either," Sam paused to allow May to compose herself before changing the subject. "Listen, Ena is just getting out from bathing and getting ready for bed. I'll have her call you so you two can talk for a while. We have to get up early in the morning, so she should only talk for maybe a half-hour."

"Sam, please don't tell Ena about this. Please."

"Of course, May. Try to put our conversation behind you. Relax and enjoy talking with Ena. I will let you know when we will travel to Boston. Have a good night."

Sam entered the bedroom, where Gabbi sat on the bed talking with Ena. "Ena, I have your phone. Call your mom on Facetime. You can talk to her until it's time to sleep." Sam handed Ena the phone.

As Sam closed the door to the bedroom, he could hear the emotional talk between Ena and her mom. He smiled and saw Gabbi standing nearby, also smiling. However, it wasn't exactly her usual smile. Instead, it was more sensual, and she walked close to him with a sexy swagger.

Oh, no. What is she planning to do now? Sam wondered.

Gabbi strolled close to Sam's face. "I have a question that needs answering, but I'll save it until after we go over the operational plan and the numbers of men we expect to confront at the compound."

"Yeah, let's get that done," Sam said as his anxiety level tapered, "and then I'll answer your, uh, inquisition."

"Oh, I like that answer. I may expand my inquisition, as you call it, and it will require answers no matter how uncomfortable it may make you. Got it?"

Gabbi led Sam to the dining table, where she had set out a diagram of the compound, a list of those who could get confrontational, and her notes taken during the briefing that Sam missed. First, she went over where the evidence was stored and the photos of the suspects. Next, Gabbi plotted the anticipated position and assignments of the teams participating in the raid. Finally, she pointed out where they situated Sam and her as the convoy advanced to the compound.

"They originally put you with Aliyah and Raffi and me with three of my colleagues, but I insisted that we should be together since we're the case officers. Right, Sam?"

"Absolutely. I'm glad you made that clear to them."

Gabbi finished the briefing by answering the 'what if' contingency plans to deal with the trucks loaded with the guns and drugs scheduled to leave the commune. "The tactical teams will recap the final plan during our early morning briefing."

Unexpectedly, Sam's phone rang as Gabbi completed her briefing. He answered the call from FBI agent Kiara Rivers.

"Hi, Sam. I'm at Logan Airport with Gavin and Trooper Kojima, waiting to board our flight to Huntsville, Kentucky. With luck, we should be in Nashville in time for the three-thirty briefing. Realizing we'll need time to deal with extraditing Lomax, his sister, and Kiyoshi, I arranged to have the FBI plan in Nashville by three in the afternoon. Donna Ranero contacted Tennessee's U.S. Attorney Jayla Bransford, who agreed to have a judge available to hold an extradition hearing for the three suspects to Boston. For additional security, I've arranged to have three U.S. Marshals from Boston fly to Huntsville and accompany us on the flight back to Boston, along with you and Ena Oshiro."

"Outstanding, Kiara. That takes a big load off of my shoulders. Thanks. Have a safe journey. I'll see you in the morning at the PD."

Sam briefed Gabbi on what Agent Rivers reported.

"You're leaving tomorrow? Gabbi said with a frown. "I hoped you'd stay a while to help with all the court preparations after the arrests tomorrow."

"I wish I could help you with that, but I'll be involved with court preparations in Boston for some time. But, hey, you could fly to Boston with us and spend a few days giving your testimony in the kidnapping investigation. I'll show you the city of Boston. Then, we can take in a show, have dinner, and whatever.

"I would love that, especially the 'whatever' part," Gabbi slyly emphasized. "Unfortunately, I can't leave all the work to my colleagues since this is my case." Although disappointed with Sam leaving, Gabbi thought only of the time she had left with him. "I already showered, Sam. Why don't you shower while I put away my notes and pack what I need for tomorrow."

Sam left for the bathroom in a hurry hoping she had forgotten about her planned inquisition. He remembered to grab a pair of his workout pants to wear that night. After the shower, Sam put on the trousers and entered the bedroom. He was surprised to see Gabbi waiting there, wearing only a short silk night robe. Seeing her, Sam anxiously asked if she had a pillow and blanket for the couch as he tried passing her on his way to the living room. Instead of letting him pass, Gabbi grabbed his hand, led him to the wall, and gently shoved him against it.

"Is it time for the inquisition?" asked Sam.

"It is, Sam. First, how did you know where Angie and Ena lived? All the houses looked the same, but you magically picked the right one."

"I saw a woman in the window that looked like—"

Gabbi cupped Sam's lips with her hand, stopping him from finishing his sentence. "No, no, no, Sam. I looked where you were looking, and the curtains on that house were closed."

"Why are you bringing this up now?"

"Everything was happening too fast. First, finding Ena in the house, then rushing to the church, where you saved my life— twice, I might add. I was in a tizzy for hours until you and I now have this alone time. So, answer me how you knew what house they were in, and then we'll address the part of you saving my life."

Sam didn't know how to answer. He tried to explain it to others in the past, but they either didn't believe him or thought he was nuts. Sam doesn't understand the weird sensations he receives that steer him to find things or persons. He carried Ena's pendant that he kept on him, but unlike a bloodhound that didn't guide him to the house, the sensations did.

"I honestly can't answer how I knew. I can only describe it as an instinct, a hunch, or a feeling I get. That's the best I could do, Gabbi. I'm sorry if you don't understand or accept it, but it's the truth."

Gabby didn't understand, but she sensed when someone was speaking honestly. She didn't want to pursue it further because she had a plan for the evening and little time to initiate it. "I believe you." She then kissed him. It wasn't a peck on his cheek or lips but a lingering passionate kiss.

Sam, surprised by the intense kiss, was awakened by her. When their lips parted, his only words were, "What's was that for?"

"You saved my life twice today at the church. First, when I would have been crushed to death by that motorcycle hitting the top of the church stairway. Then inside the church, you stopped that asshole, Pitbull, from cutting my throat open. I was scared he was going to kill me.

"Hey, Gabbi, we're partners. We have each other's back. Besides, you saved my ass twice, so we're even. First, you yelled out at the church that the punk was about to stab me. You saved my life."

Gabbi remembered that she did save Sam from getting stabbed. "Well, I guess so, but that was once, not twice."

"My mission coming to Tennessee was to find Ena and return her to her mom. It was your idea to go to the compound with the idea to show Ena's photo to the residents. And your threat to call in more cops got us into the compound, where Amy Norwood agreed to show us where Angie had Ena. So, it was you that got me to find Ena. That was my mission. If I had failed, it would have been a lasting emotional letdown. You saved me emotionally, Gabbi. It's the same importance as saving someone physically."

Gabbi liked how Sam put it. So she decided to show him how emotionally and physically she cared for him. She kissed him again. This time her tongue searched and found his. Her endless kiss and touches stimulated Sam to the point he opened her satin night robe and slipped it off her shoulders. Her beauty and irresistible body mesmerized him. She then removed his attire, gripped his hand, and guided him to the bed. Sam became hypnotized by her passion, which led to intense lovemaking. They never looked at the time, as they remained as one, kissing, giggling, and whispering sweet words to each other. Eventually, they paused their intimacy as Sam raised his head, looking for the time, but Gabbi pulled him down to her lips, wanting to prolong their fun until fatigue led them to sleep in each other's arms.

CHAPTER
37

The alarm clock buzzing resonated throughout the bedroom. The annoying sound finally revived Sam from a deep, hypnotic sleep. His eyes squinted as he scanned the room in a fatigued state, pondering where he was until he saw Gabbi, still unconsciously asleep. That brought him out of his stupor. He sat up, rubbed his eyes, and then reached to shut the alarm. He lightly shook Gabbi to awaken her. She whimpered and protested until Sam mentioned they were late for the briefing, even though they weren't yet. Gabbi peered at Sam and smiled before whispering, "It was amazing, Sam. I felt so connected to you and didn't want it to end."

"Well, right now, I'm heading for the shower. We need to get moving. Otherwise, we'll be late for the briefing."

Sam slid out of bed and moved toward the bathroom. Gabbi stared at Sam's naked tanned muscle-toned body as he entered the bathroom. She thought he was hot, just under six feet tall, maybe a hundred and sixty pounds. She adored his blue eyes, wavy dirty blonde hair, and even his slightly crooked nose from a fight as a teenager. When she heard the water running, she sprang out of bed and stepped into the shower with Sam

"Yow!" she screamed, "That's cold."

"We need to wake up. Turn around. I'll wash your back."

Gabbi curled her hands and arms into her chest as she trembled from the cold water that drenched her. Once Sam finished soaping down her backside, he handed her the facecloth to complete the rest of her body. Sam sped through his shower, stepped out, and grabbed a towel. Seconds later, Gabbi stepped out. Sam already had another towel, wrapped it around her back, and softly wiped the cold droplets from her backside. Not wanting to get frisky, he handed her the towel to finish up.

"Hey, you didn't finish me, and I wanted to use the towel on you too."

"Sorry. I know where that would lead. Finish up and get Ena out of bed. She could sleep in the car on the way to the PD.

Moments later, Gabbi pressed Ena to get out of bed, but Ena complained she was tired, forcing Gabbi to tell Ena it was time to go back to her mom. That remark got Ena to drag herself out of bed and into the bathroom, where Gabby helped her to wash, brush her teeth and get dressed. Later, Sam strapped her in the back seat of Gabbi's car and covered her with a blanket.

Is there a McDonald's or a place like it on the way to the station?" asked Sam.

"Nothing will be open until around five. Besides, someone will have coffee and pastries at the office."

Little traffic was on the road at just past three in the morning, so it was a quick drive into the city. Gabbi pulled into the police parking lot at three-twenty-five. Sam carried Ena into police headquarters and had her grab a donut and a bottle of water before placing her in a room safeguarded by a female officer.

*   *   *

Trent Killingworth supervised the morning's work to gather the products made, packaged, and loaded into trucks and ready to distribute in Tennessee and neighboring states. While overseeing the operation, he continued to call his customers for their drop-off locations. He scheduled last-minute changes and prepared a distribution location list for each driver when they finished loading the product to make their rounds. Work leaders constantly checked totals of finished products and updated TK with new numbers. TK redid the cash totals the drivers needed to collect after making the deliveries. By the end of the day, he figured the total cash in hand would add plenty to the cashbox he kept that would someday allow him to live a comfortable life in retirement. TK would sneak in a perpetual grin when a worker informed him of additional products finished and ready for distribution. When his list was complete, he scrutinized and counted the men working and realized he was short a man or two. TK shouted for Doc.

"Yeah, TK. Whataya need?"

"Where's Kiyoshi and Max? I don't see them. Weren't they supposed to be back by now?"

"Yeah, but I haven't heard from either of them. Neither answered their phone."

"What do you think that's all about? Do you think something happened to them, or did they just decided not to work tonight?"

"Beats me. They should have called to report in by now. KK had to give Max a ride to get his sister and daughter from a shelter. Maybe, something happened to them."

"Did KK say what shelter they had to go to?"

"He didn't mention where."

"Shit. I don't like loose ends. Keep calling until you get them."

*   *   *

The tactical team members and all the officers participating in the raid gathered in the conference room at the Nashville police department. Additional participants were Boston FBI Agent Rivers, Sloan, Mass State Trooper Soshi Kojima, Nashville DEA agents, and the TBI.

Also, part of the operation was the Nashville U.S. Attorney Jayla Bransford, the Special Agent in Charge of the Nashville ATF Office, and Captain James Walters. They made up the command staff for the operation and would position their van near but outside the commune. Agent Jamal Jackson, the tactical leader, recapped the final operational plan for the raid.

The updated plan called for a small group of three ATF and three Nashville tactical team members to first hit the small ranch house that monitors the road leading to the commune. The six-man team's mission was to secure all suspects inside the house, shut down the camera monitoring system on the road leading to the compound, and obtain the remote to open the entrance gate. Once the suspects inside were handcuffed and secured, uniformed officers would enter the house to remove and transport the suspects to the police detention center. Two ATF agents and one Nashville detective would stay behind to search the house for evidence.

The plan called for the caravan of ATF and police vehicles to line up along Old Willow Road, a short distance from Warriors Way, the street that led to the compound. Once the uniformed officers removed the suspects from the ranch house, the convoy would move onto Warriors Way. They would temporarily stop at the house to obtain the remote for the security gate and have the six tactical team members that secured the home join the rest of their team. The tactical leader would then radio the command staff for the signal to commence the raid.

After Agent Jackson reiterated the assignments and how to position their vehicle in the caravan lineup, the briefing ended. Everyone then headed to their trucks and moved to their assigned line position. Once in the appropriate order, the team leader signaled everyone to move out. The long line of official vehicles moved slowly, maintaining a tight line toward Old Willow Road. The armed men and women wearing protective vests, helmets, and eyewear remained quiet while driving to the target location. They all felt apprehension, knowing confrontation and violence were possible when executing search or arrest warrants against a group of trained warriors.

CHAPTER
38

The convoy stretched just short of sixty yards along Old Willow Road. The rear vehicles included two ambulances, a police bus to transport prisoners, and three black and white police vehicles. The last marked cruiser had its lights on, including the blue emergency light bar on its roof, lit but not flashing. All the other cars in line had their lights off except the first armored truck carrying the ATF tactical team. It only had its parking lights on.

The six tactical members consisted of three ATF agents and three Nashville SWAT officers quietly advanced in line from the rear of the ranch house. Close behind were three uniformed police officers. The tactical team covered the ranch windows as they moved to the side of the house and stopped. All six hunched down below the windows as the leader listened for any sound inside the house. Hearing only the sound from a television, the leader motioned with his hand to move forward. The uniformed officers stayed behind until the tactical team leader signaled them to enter the house. When the team got to the front door, the leader moved to the right of the door. Then using a three count with his fingers, he signaled the agent with the steel ram to force the front door open as he yelled out, "Police with a warrant!"

The six tactical officers quickly entered the house when the door swung open, calling out police while their assault weapons aimed at the two men relaxing on the living room couch watching television. The officers ordered the two men to lay on the floor as officers handcuffed them while the others cleared the remaining rooms for any other suspects. Once the officers secured the entire house, the team leader examined the security camera monitors on the table by the front window, shut them off, and grabbed the compound's gate remote. The uniformed officers then entered the house to remove the two suspects for transport to the police station lockup. Once the officers led the suspects out of the house, the tactical leader called for the caravan to enter Warriors Way.

* * *

Helen Holliston, who rented the neighboring farm to Trent Killingworth after her father passed away, drove home early that morning along North Fenton Road after visiting a sick friend. As she passed her old homestead, she noticed two cars parked on the road outside the farm. She slowly passed them, rubbernecking, trying to see why they were there. Then, not far from the two cars, she saw two officers sitting in their patrol car. Concerned, she drove to the end of the road and turned left onto Old Willow Road.

Less than a half-mile along the road, she came upon a whole line of vehicles, including ambulances and police vehicles. She wondered if there was an accident up ahead. A police officer exited his cruiser and held up his hand for her to stop when she got close. As the officer approached her, Helen pushed the button to lower her window.

"Sorry, ma'am, you'll need to take a detour by taking a right turn here. Go to the second stop sign and make a left. Then, drive about a mile and a half that will take you back onto Old Willow Road."

"Is there a bad accident up ahead?"

The officer hesitated in answering at first. "Just police business, ma'am. Follow the detour I gave you, and you'll be past the area in just a few minutes."

As Helen Holliston turned right, she was perplexed by the number of police vehicles and ambulances, many with their lights turned off. When she got to the second stop sign, she wondered if it any anything to do with the commune at the end of War Way Road or whatever they called it now. She sat at the stop sign, asking herself if she should worry about renting her property to that 'fella,' Trent Kilworth, or however you said his name. Then, before taking the left turn, she grabbed her phone from her purse and called that guy.

TK looked at his screen's phone, thinking it might be a customer but recognized the number of the older woman he rented the adjacent farm from after her dad died. Doc tried to get his attention, but Trent held up his finger for him to wait a minute. He wondered why the woman would call him so early in the morning. He thought about not answering her call but was curious about such an early morning call.

"Ms. Holliston, how are yah?"

"Well, I'm not sure. I just saw a line of police cars and ambulances on Old Willow Road just before your street, whatever it's called now. Is everything okay up there where you're living?"

That information immediately concerned TK, but he convinced Holliston that things were fine and for her not to worry. However, as soon as he ended the call, Doc rushed to tell him no one answered at the ranch house. That, plus what Holliston just told him, spelled trouble.

"Forget about loading the rest of the inventory. Secure the basement, and let's move, out. I think we're about ready to get run over by the cops. Come on, everybody, finish loading up and let's roll!"

"TK, how will we get past the law driving toward them?" asked Doc.

"Everybody follow me through a backway!" shouted TK. "We're in for a fight, so arm yourself with everything you have to fight back. Then, when we hit North Fenton Road, head out to your assigned stops and unload the product as fast as you can. When you're done, stay out of sight of the cops. Don't come back here. We'll connect later."

TK reached behind his truck's seat for his AR-15 and grabbed extra magazines. Next, he unlocked a metal box hidden under the front seat and pulled out two grenades, a distraction device, and three smoke bombs. He then slid onto his driver's seat, with Doc climbing into the passenger's side carrying his AR-15. Doc was surprised to see the grenades TK brought into the truck.

"What's with the grenades, TK? Killing cops could end up getting you the electric chair, for chrissake. So let's run instead of having a shootout with the cops."

"If the cops get us with our product, we'll spend the rest of our lives in prison. I don't know about you, but I'm not going to jail. If we could cash out after we sell what we have today, we could live a good life in Mexico or South America."

Doc's only thought was that TK wasn't thinking straight. *This isn't Afghanistan. We can't kill the cops,* Doc thought.

Doc lowed his window and waved to the trucks to follow behind them. TK headed toward the shed. Sparks followed in his van with two SUVs behind him. All the men had their weapons next to them. Approaching the rear fence, Trent reached for his remote clipped to his visor and pressed the device's control. He momentarily took his foot off the gas, waiting for the gate to open fully. Then, TK waved to the drivers behind him to follow him. TK started driving towards the open gate as the three trucks followed onto an overgrown dirt path that led to the old Holliston Farm that TK had told no one he had rented.

"TK, when did we put in a rear gate?" asked Doc.

"It's been here since the fence went up, but I didn't say anything about it. We have too many people here with big mouths. I didn't want the word to get out because of what's happening now. The cops don't know about it, so as they charge through the front gate, we disappear through the back."

CHAPTER
39

After receiving the all-clear signal from the ranch house, the convoy turned onto Warrior's Way and stopped at the ranch house. The convoy leader, Agent Jackson, received the gate remote while the six tactical team members who raided the ranch house joined the rest of the team before the convoy continued to the commune. At that point, the entire raid team was intact. Agent Jackson then radioed the command staff they were ready to hit the commune. The ATF agent in charge gave the go-ahead as the convoy rolled ahead toward the compound's entrance gate.

A short distance from the gate, Jackson saw taillights from a line of vehicles on the west side of the compound. From twenty-five yards from the entrance, Jackson pushed the remote button, and the gate slowly opened wide as the lead ATF vehicle drove through it.

TK's truck, the first in the line of the four trucks, drove through the rear exit as the police convoy entered the front entrance.

"Crap, those trucks are heading out a rear gate. They must have known we were coming!" radioed ATF Agent Jackson from the lead truck. "We're going after them."

Hearing the communication from the lead armored truck, Sam radioed the ATF agents and police officers stationed on North Fenton Road outside the Holliston Farm. "Agent Caviello to team three, the suspects escaped heading in your direction. Ensure readiness and good cover. These guys are army special forces and well-armed."

"10-4, Caviello. We're ready for them."

"Sam, we only posted three cars on Fenton Road. Maybe we should go there to help them rather than searching for evidence, most of which the suspects are taking with them," said Gabbi.

"The ATF tactical leader radioed, seeing three or four trucks leaving. That means anywhere from four to maybe eight suspects leaving the commune. We have two tactical teams in pursuit. That's twenty-plus specially trained swat members and six officers waiting on Fenton Road. The tactical team could handle the suspects," said Sam. "Let's park over in front of the barn. There're suspects to arrest and evidence to seize here, especially the equipment used to make the gun parts and drugs. This was our assignment, so let's finish it first. Then, if the tactical teams need additional help, they'll call on us."

Two SUVs parked along Gabbi's sedan as she stopped in front of the barn. Gabbi, Sam, four ATF agents, and two Nashville detectives stormed into the barn with guns drawn.

"Police, don't move and place your hands up high," several officers shouted to the three remaining suspects, two men, and a woman.

All three suspects stood still, raising their hands. The agents handcuffed all three and sat them down on nearby chairs. In the distance, they heard an avalanche of gunfire. Radio chatter immediately followed.

"We're taking heavy fire from the suspects. They formed a line with their trucks in front of the farmhouse, using them for cover," said Agent Jackson. "Wait—oh shit— grenade! Hit the ground!"

TK threw two grenades, one toward the tactical team vehicles and the other at the two cars on Fenton Road. The loud sound of exploding grenades deafened the ears of the men kissing the ground behind their trucks while shrapnel spewed against the tactical truck. While on the ground, the tactical team heard two more blasts, one after the other. They remained with their heads down, hoping to avoid scattered shrapnel. They continued to hug the earth, wondering if the suspects had additional grenades to heave at them.

Moments later, Agent Jackson heard vehicle movement. Puzzled, he slowly peeked around the fender of his vehicle. The only thing visible was a vast cloud of greyish smoke.

Jackson quickly pressed his radio mic. "The suspects threw smoke grenades to throw us off. We heard vehicle movement, looked to see what was going on, and couldn't see ten feet in front of us. My guess is the suspects are on Fenton Road heading north. We're going after them. Put out a BOLO on their vehicles. Jackson had his men back in the trucks and ordered them to drive north to search for the two pick-ups, an SUV, and one van.

Sam knew Gabbi was familiar with the area, especially since she's been on North Fenton Road often and knew the different directions the suspects could spread out from there. He looked over the situation in the barn and assumed the other officers could handle it without them. Sam got the attention of an ATF agent.

"If you guys feel comfortable securing the suspects and searching the barn, Detective Walters and I will leave to help search for the suspects who escaped."

The four other officers agreed and told them to go.

"I think this is the right thing to do, Sam. We need to find Killingworth with the goods. He's our main target." said Gabbi."

"You were right, partner. Let's go get him."

Gabbi reported to the command staff that she and Sam were joining the search for Killingworth and his associates. A command staff member confirmed her message as she turned onto North Fenton Road.

"Our hunt for these guys will be like finding a needle in a haystack. We should focus on the crime districts where the drug dealers operate," suggested Sam, "or where Killingworth and his crew hang out in the city. They'll need to meet somewhere after they get rid of the product. They certainly aren't going back to the compound." Sam always thought ahead. "Gabbi, can I assume your department has an intelligence unit?"

"Yeah, but the command staff should have all the intel background on these guys. I think the ATF agent in charge would have everything they have on the group too."

"Would you call the command center and get what you could on any known girlfriends, family, or close friends the men have outside the commune, and where any of them, especially TK, hang out, like a bar or clubs, or whatever? Also, get the description of all vehicles they use, especially the license plate numbers. I'll call Agent Mayfield and get ATF's intel on this group."

As Gabbi drove by the Holliston Farm, she and Sam saw traces of smoke lingering from the road to the farmhouse. Sam's phone dinged with a text message as they passed the farmhouse. The text was from a burner cell phone number that Sam recognized. It was a message from Alli Gaynor. Her text asked if he was available for a call. He answered with one word—later.

Gabbi took the second right leading into West and North Nashville and began crisscrossing through the Bordeaux area streets. She didn't drive sixty yards before she got a call back from her dad, who reported the license plate numbers of the five known vehicles belonging to the commune residents, including Killingworth's black Dodge Ram pick-up truck. Sam jotted the plate numbers on his notepad as Gabbi repeated them.

"At least now, we know what trucks to look for during our search," said Sam.

From that point on, Gabbi and Sam carefully surveilled every driveway, parking lot, and alleyway on the streets they passed. It became frustrating that they didn't spot any suspect vehicles on the multiple streets they passed. Gabbi then swung onto Crescent Street as her sedan crawled by one apartment building after another. Finally, when they passed by a small salon and liquor store building, Sam spotted three men unloading boxes from the tail end of a vehicle protruding from the rear corner of the building.

"Gabbi, don't stop. Keep going and turn around at the next intersection ahead. Then drive back toward the salon slowly with your lights off. I'll tell you when to pull over to the curb." Sam waited until he could view the back of the salon. "Pull over here."

Sam grabbed the pair of binoculars on the seat, aimed it at the license plate, and read the plate number to Gabbi.

"That's on the list, Sam. I'll call it in for backup."

"Ask if one of the tactical teams is close by to respond. There are at least three of them by the truck and maybe more inside the building. We don't want to go in for an arrest shorthanded."

Gabbi made the call, gave her location across from the salon, and waited for a response. The Nashville tactical team leader responded within seconds that a team was only about five minutes out.

"Have your emergency lights on when entering Crescent Street, and I'll put on my flashers, so you'll know where I am. I have agent Caviello with me," said Gabbi.

"10-4, detective. Stay put in your car until we have control of the situation."

CHAPTER
40

The ATF tactical team van came speeding down Crescent Street behind Gabbi's sedan and turned into the salon driveway behind the suspect vehicle. The team quickly exited the van, yelling "Police" several times as they surrounded the SUV. It took several minutes before the tactical team leader reported they had secured the suspects and property. The leader then called for an ATF evidence collection team to respond at the scene.

Gabbi and Sam joined the team inside the back of the salon to assess the seizure. It included two boxes containing twelve ghost guns each, one box containing six bumper stocks, one small box containing a dozen conversion kits, six packages containing 100 packets of fentanyl pills, and one long box containing two Russian-made AK-47 machine guns.

"We also found an AR-15 and two ghost guns with plenty of ammo in the SUV," said one ATF tactical team member.

Sam stepped outside and called ATF Agent Aliyah Mayfield to get ATF agents to the scene to seize the firearms. Next, he called Alli Gaynor, summarized the situation, and suggested she go to the commune and then the PD. "I'm not going to have time to talk now, but I'll try calling you later. The FBI is bringing in one of their planes to transport the abductors of Ena Oshiro back to Boston. Ena and I will be on that plane. Try getting to Boston after getting what we need here so you'll be at Logan airport to capture the scene when we bring Ena back to her mom." Sam ended the call as Gabbi came out of the salon.

"Did you hear from any other team?" she asked.

"No. I called agent Mayfield regarding the seizure here."

Sam then saw Gabbi taking a call. When Gabbi's call ended, she filled in Sam. "A Nashville patrolman spotted another suspect truck and asked for a tactical team to respond. The command center is asking the team here to respond and for us to stay until the evidence unit arrives?"

Gabbi and Sam agreed to stay and returned to the salon, where four suspects were handcuffed and laid face down on the floor. They only had to wait ten minutes before two ATF agents, one Nashville detective, and two patrol officers arrived to take over the scene. When Gabbi and Sam returned to their car, a Nashville police van, or paddy wagon as they are sometimes called, arrived to transport the prisoners to the police lockup.

"Well, it looks like two down and two to go," said Sam.

"Do you want to keep looking or head back to the station?"

"Find out who they found at the other location. If it wasn't TK, let's keep searching. He's the guy we want to find."

Gabbi called the command post and learned it wasn't Killingworth, but they found an ample supply of fentanyl in the Shepherd Hills area. Consequently, Gabbi and Sam continued to comb the Bordeaux area without success.

Sam wasn't ready to give up so early in the search. "Gabbi, you have the names of two hangouts that TK reportedly frequents. So let's take a ride by those two."

Gabbi first drove east to a small bar near the end of a narrow dead-end street in the Talbot's Corner area of the city. Sam didn't see Killingworth's black pick-up truck parked on the road near the bar.

"Looks like a tight squeeze by the trucks parked on the narrow driveway to the rear," said Sam, "but we should take a look in case his truck is in the back."

Gabbi had a tough time wedging her mid-sized sedan between the larger trucks and the bar's sidewall before turning into the back of the building.

Unfortunately, Killingworth's truck was not among the six pickups parked in the crowded backlot, nor any vehicle they had listed from the commune. As a result, Gabbi had difficulty turning around because of the limited space between the trucks parked on both sides of the small backlot. Because of the tight room, Gabbi had to maneuver back and forth until she managed to cram her way down the narrow driveway and onto the road. She then continued to drive through the Talbot's Corner area, searching the section for Killingworth's black pick-up without finding it.

"Okay, Gabbi. Let's check out Killingworth's other known hangout by the Cumberland River northeast of here. While combing the streets around the Heron Walk section, it became misty as water droplets hit the windshield. Gabbi used the intermittent windshield wiper while searching for the black pick-up truck but struck out again. She then headed to their last venue along the Cumberland River.

Gabbi had patrolled River Road numerous times as a uniformed officer. The road was extra wide to allow for perpendicular parking. There was one large city parking lot near the end of the row of eating establishments, not far from the first of six eateries overlooking the river. Most of the smaller cafes lining the road opposite the river bank didn't have separate parking lots. However, the widened street allowed ample parking for customers in front of their favorite establishments. Regretfully, the police had reported that suspected drug dealers operated within three of the cafes.

As the remaining dark clouds rolled east, the moon lit up the star-filled sky. The first three cafés and saloons Gabbi drove by were situated on a slight slope requiring patrons to walk up a flight of stairs to the entrance. As Gabbi drove passed the fourth tavern, the hill flattened and became more level when reaching the two more up-scale restaurants closer to the city parking lot.

Gabbi and Sam focused on the Cumberland Waterfront Tavern, the third venue they passed on the slope, where Killingworth was known to frequent. As they slowly drove past the tavern, they were disappointed in not seeing Killingworth's pick-up on the street. Killingworth was ATF's primary target, and not arresting him diminished the success of the morning raid.

Although Sam counted plenty of cars and trucks parked along the broad road in front of places to eat and drink, he recognized only one had a limited parking lot on the side of their building. Gabbi continued to drive by the different eateries.

The first three cafes they passed were close to each other, while the next three were spaced more apart because of large decks on the side of the eateries for outdoor dining overlooking the river. Sam asked Gabbi to make a U-turn, drive past the restaurants, and make another U-turn for a slow drive-by for a closer look at the first four places.

"Drive even slower. I want to study if there's a way to park in the rear of any of the cafes. I'm looking for a way TK could hide behind his favorite hangout." Sam had his eyes glued on the grassy hillside between each cafe they passed.

"Stop—okay. Go slow." Sam's focus turned on one particular area as Gabbi slowly rolled ahead. He then asked Gabbi to back up a few yards. When she did, Sam had her stop while he pointed to the slope running along the side of the second tavern.

"The tracks don't lead to the rear of TK's favorite hangout next door, but he could have used any possible lot in the back of this bar and walked next door to the Cumberland Waterfront Tavern," said Sam.

Gabbi glanced out the open passenger window to see what Sam saw there. "What are you looking at, Sam? I don't see anything."

"Focus on the slope about five feet to the left of the building. There's no driveway, but I see tire tracks in the overgrown grass leading to the top, which tells me vehicles had driven up the hill and probably parked in the rear of the building. It may be nothing or where the owner parks, but let's check it out to be sure."

Gabbi found an empty parking space. Sam exited the car, while Gabbi, unsure if looking behind the café was worthwhile, hesitated while still sitting in her car.

"Gabbi, you could stay here if you want. I can take a quick look and come back here."

"No, no, Sam. I'm coming. I'm your partner. We have to stick together."

Gabbi joined Sam as they hiked up the slight uphill grade to the corner of the café. The on-and-off mist began again, probably because they were close to the river. Sam peaked around the corner at the top of the slope and saw three or four vehicles parked there. So he moved around the corner and walked toward the parked trucks with Gabbi tracking behind him. Sam stopped at the first SUV and checked out the makes of the other three parked up against the back of the building. The first and second trucks parked with the front of the vehicle facing the building, as was the last car. However, the third was a black truck that backed in, hidden between the pick-ups on either side. Sam didn't see a front license plate on the black truck, so he and Gabbi gradually moved closer to it, where Sam saw it was a Dodge Ram model. He felt the temperature of the truck's hood.

"It's still warm. I'm going to check the back plate. Here's the list of plate numbers. I'll read out the number while you check the list."

Before moving to the rear, Sam first glanced into the cab but couldn't see much because of the dark tinting of the window. He then moved to the pick-up's cargo bed when he began to feel the shakes coming on. His body shuddered while a slight twinge traveled down his spine.

Gabbi saw Sam shaking and abruptly jolt backward as if something stung him in his back. "Sam, what's going on? Are you alright?"

The episode lasted only seconds. "Yeah, I'm alright. I just suddenly felt a cold chill."

Gabbi had seen Sam tremble once before outside the house where they found Ena. She didn't feel any chill in the air and thought maybe it wasn't a chill that caused Sam to shake.

When the sensation subsided, Sam moved to the cargo bed, saw two boxes, and grabbed both but found them empty. So he went to the tailgate, lit up the plate with his mini-flashlight, and whispered the license number to Gabbi.

"That's it. It's Killingworth's truck," said Gabbi. "I'll call it in."

"No, not yet. We don't know if TK is in this place or his usual hangout next door."

"Well, we can't go into these places."

Sam thought about it, though. He saw the café had a back door and a small window to its left. There was no visible light seen from inside the window. Sam had to verify if Killingworth was inside either of the two bars without putting Gabbi in danger. Once he decided he was going in, he got up close to Gabbi, cupped her cheeks in his hands, and kissed her nose.

Her face lit up, asking, "What was that for, Sam?"

Sam wanted to soften her up before telling her he was going into the bar alone. "I'd prefer you stay outside to call for backup if things get haywire when I go inside. I won't stay long. If he's in there, I'll come back out and have you call the tactical team."

"You shouldn't go inside there. I'm familiar with this bar. It's a hangout for gang members, prostitutes, and drug users. They don't like strangers coming in without knowing you. I'm pretty sure I heard detectives say the word on the street is that the owner of this place, Tyrese Drackler, is a real badass. Because of his last name, the gang members started calling him Dracula. He liked the nickname so much he had his canine teeth sculpted to a sharp point."

"Whoo! Are you saying a blood-thirsty vampire is lurking inside there? Trust me. I'm not going to socialize with anyone inside, especially a vampire. There's no light on in the back area. The door probably leads to a storage room. I'll sneak into the back room and peek into the bar area to see if TK is inside. It's in and out as fast as I can before I get bitten by the vampire."

"Oh, now you're a comic, making fun of me." Her somber expression lasted seconds before a smile crossed her lips. Then, surprisingly, Gabbi wrapped her arms around Sam and kissed his lips softly before stepping back. "Make it fast, Sam. I want to see you out that door within five minutes."

"I promise I'll be out in no time. I'm putting my phone on silent mode. Even so, whatever you do, don't call me. Even in silent mode, someone might hear it vibrating."

Gabbi agreed and patted his butt as Sam moved toward the tavern's back door. That pat on the ass reminded Sam of his little league coach doing the same to motivate him to get a hit and drive in the winning run.

He considered Gabbi's pat was similar for him to confirm TK's presence, like getting a hit and returning safely with the winning proof. Sam got a kick out of Gabbi's free-spirit. His feelings for her grew by the day. She was sweet-natured and fun to have as a partner. Her personality was something he once had, and he wanted to be like that again. At the door, Sam stopped and put his ear against the old grey paint-peeling door. He listened for any voices before turning the loose doorknob. Luckily, it opened, so he slowly pulled it toward him, then stopped when he heard a click, and the lights inside the room came on. He looked up and saw a switch of sorts inside the door jam. He clicked it back to the right, which shut the inside lights off. Sam then gradually wedged himself inside, closing the door behind him. Sam heard loud voices and music coming from inside the bar.

As he thought, the backroom was a storage area. It was dark, so Sam didn't move until his eyes adjusted to the darkness. He didn't want to stumble into anything that created noise. Sam pulled out his mini flashlight to light up the room. He didn't recognize any boxes similar to those used by TK. To Sam's right was a steel cabinet secured with a heavy padlock. While scanning the rest of the room, he suddenly heard footsteps, so he stepped behind the cabinet to hide. He thought for sure someone was walking toward the storage room. He heard more footsteps and realized the steps came from above him, not from the bar. He then heard water running down a pipe behind him where he hid. Sam never figured there might be a second-level floor in the building. The floor above squeaked as someone moved around. Next, Sam heard a voice as the storage room door from the bar swung partially open, allowing some light into the room. Fortunately, Sam had his flashlight under his armpit and pressed it off. His anxiety spiked, dreading the thought of getting caught.

"TK!" yelled the tall thin black man known as Dracula. "TK, come to the door, man!"

Sam heard the squeak of the upstairs door open.

"Yeah, Drack, did you get a hold of Missy," said TK.

"No, man, she's not answering her phone."

"What about those two sexy gals? I don't remember their names. I think they were sisters."

"You probably mean Jada and Julene. They're not sisters. They're lovers. I could call to find out if one can come over unless you think you could handle both of them."

"Yeah, either way. One or both is fine."

"Okay, you're the man, TK. I'll get right back to you." Drackler closed the door.

Sam relaxed once the door closed. At least now he confirmed Killingworth, or TK as he's called, was in the café. Before leaving, he switched the flashlight on to study the storage room again. Sam couldn't see all the boxes in the room since the larger ones hid others. Regardless, he decided it was time to go, not wanting to press his luck. Sam had what he came in to find out. He shifted toward the rear door, and his arm accidentally bumped into something, which was a metal pipe. It made a loud noise as it fell and rolled along the floor. Sam wanted out quickly and pushed the back door open without thinking, causing the lights to come on. Thinking he might get caught, Sam stumbled out the door, fell to the ground, rolled to his feet, and ran like hell.

CHAPTER
41

oston FBI task force members, Agents Kiara Rivers, Gavin Sloan, and Massachusetts State Trooper Soshi Kojima returned to Nashville police headquarters after participating in the early morning raid at the commune. After freshening up, Agent Rivers wanted to meet and talk to Ena Oshiro. An officer escorted Rivers to the secure room where Ena drew in a children's coloring book.

"Hi, Ena. My name is Kiara. I'm an FBI agent from Boston, and I'm here to take you back to your mom."

"Where is Sam? He's taking me to my mom."

Kiara thought about how she should best answer. "Sam is helping the police find some bad people. He'll return here soon."

"Can you bring Sam here when he comes back?"

"Yes, of course, I will. How are you doing, Ena?"

"I'm fine. Sam saved me and arrested Max, and that guy, Kim, for taking me. They took my phone and wouldn't let me call my mom. Sam arrested Angie, too. She wouldn't let me call home either. But Sam called my mom and let me talk to her for a long time. He's taking me home today."

"Yes, I arranged for our FBI airplane to come here so you, Sam, and I could fly to Boston together."

"Oh. Thank you. I hope Sam comes back soon. I want to go home."

Kiara realized that Ena was very much attached to Sam, and she couldn't take that away from her. "As soon as Sam gets here, I will send him to you. It was nice meeting you. You tell the officer outside the door to get me if you need anything, okay?"

Ena shook her head yes and began coloring in her book again.

* * *

Sam found cover behind the first parked truck as floodlights lit up the back area of the café.

"Sam, are you okay?" whispered Gabbi.

"Yeah. Stay where you are. I'll come to you."

Hidden from view, Sam peeked back at the door and saw who he thought was Drackler peering out in Sam's direction. Seeing nothing, Drackler closed the door but left the outdoor lights on.

Sam crept low toward Gabbi, maintaining cover until he reached her waiting behind TK's truck.

"TK is in there on the second floor. Let's get back to your car and call for the tactical team to arrest him. I suspect TK sold products to Dracula," said Sam jokingly. "I mean Drackler, but I don't have any evidence. So, we'll have to hope the arrest team sees something incriminating during the arrest to get a search warrant."

Keeping low and hugging the vehicles, Gabbi and Sam scrambled back to Gabbi's sedan. Then, without delay, Sam called agent Mayfield and filled her in on finding TK's truck in the back of a tavern and the conversation he overheard between TK and Drackler.

Mayfield told Sam she'll scramble the tactical team out to his area, estimating their arrival in about twenty minutes. "Keep an eye on the place in case he leaves."

"I'm pretty sure he is in for the night. He ordered two escorts to join him in the room upstairs. I'm guessing it's a bedroom of sorts. The stairs leading up to TK's room are off the back storage room. I'm guessing Drackler, a reputed drug dealer, purchased products from TK."

"Good to know. Hopefully, the women will keep him occupied when the team hits the place."

"One other thing. I recommend that uniformed officers be the first to enter the bar with the tactical team behind them. There are quite a few cars parked in front of the bar, a known gang hangout. With uniformed officers entering first, it will put the occupants on notice immediately that it's the police."

"I'll make your recommendation known to the tactical team leader. Thanks, Sam."

Gabbi re-positioned her sedan with a view of the tavern's front entrance and the rear left corner of the building while Sam took a position behind a bush on the slope to watch the back door.

It took thirty minutes before Gabbi spotted the tactical van and three black and white police cruisers approaching from the right.

Gabbi instantly called Sam. "The troops are here, Sam. The ATF tactical van and three cruisers are out front of the place. Are you staying there or heading back down to me?"

"Get out of your car and make sure they send two guys to cover the back and let them know I'm up here."

Gabbi quickly exited her car and rushed toward the van as the tactical team poured out from the van. Gabbi saw two members head to the side of the tavern building and yelled out, "ATF agent Caviello is at the top of the hill, watching the rear door!"

The two agents shouted, "10-4," as they continued to move up the slope.

Sam moved out from the bush to show himself with his ATF badge embodied vest and his hands up by his head showing no weapons. The two agents recognized him as they moved toward the back door.

"I'll back you guys up until everything is secured inside!"

Once the agents in the back confirmed they were in position, three uniformed officers entered the front entrance of the tavern and shouted, "Police, no one move and show your hands," as the tactical team filed in one after another. The first four team members charged to the back storage room, moving quickly through the door and up the stairs, where they yelled "police" as they forced the second-level door open and entered the room with guns drawn.

CHAPTER
42

Two naked women screamed as the agents called out, "Police, don't anyone move, show your hands," as they circled the foot of the bed. Still on his back and naked, TK was dazed and stunned that the police knew he was hiding at the tavern.

Two agents struggled to pull TK up into a sitting position. When they did, they cuffed his hands behind his back with plastic ties and pulled him out of bed onto the floor face down.

The two agents were surprised by the size of the thirty-eight-year-old TK, who stood six feet, four inches tall, about two hundred and forty pounds of muscle, with thick wrists.

A third agent, a female, ordered the two women to the side of the bed away from TK. The agent ordered the women to dress and then kneel on the floor, where she cuffed them in the back.

Under one of the pillows, an agent found a loaded ghost gun. He secured it with surgical gloves to avoid adding his fingerprints, cleared it of ammunition, and placed it into an evidence bag and into the side leg-pocket of his tactical pants.

TK complained about his treatment. "I'm a decorated army veteran, and you guys are treating me like shit. Could I get some clothes on instead of lying here bare-ass?"

"We'll get to that after we make sure you don't have any other weapons here," responded an ATF agent.

Once the agents completed a search in the area, the female agent and another agent escorted the two women out the rear storage room door and to the street, where a police van waited to transport them to the police department. The remaining two agents helped TK stand up. After removing everything from TK's trousers, an agent stood in the back of him and had him lift each foot into his pant legs one at a time. The pants were then pulled up and buttoned. Next, the agent grabbed TK's shirt from the floor and forced it over his head and down to his waist. Next, the agents ordered him to lay on his back on the bed while one of the agents pushed boots onto TK's feet without his socks. The agents pulled him off the bed and escorted him to the open door. The agents signaled they secured the prisoner and would head out the back with him. After hearing the agents had the suspect in custody, Sam and the two agents covering the back door began moving back to the street.

With TK in custody, one agent walked down the stairs in front of the prisoner. He had his back to the sidewall, keeping an eye on his prisoner. TK followed behind, planning his escape. There was no way he was going to jail. The second agent stepped behind TK. The agent had TK's shirt lifted to maintain a tight grasp on the plastic cuffs. While they descended the stairs, TK waited for his opportunity. Three steps from the bottom, the agent in front turned his back to TK to watch his final steps to the floor. That allowed TK to put his quick-thinking idea into action. He lifted his right foot and, with a powerful kick, drove his boot into the back of the agent in front of him. The blow forced the agent to fall, hitting the floor hard with his head striking the wall. He followed the kick using his head and solid upper body to forcefully thrust back against the agent behind him, causing the agent to fall back against the stairs releasing his grip on the plastic cuffs. TK dropped one step, jumped over the remaining two steps, and gave another pounding jolt with his foot to the back of the agent on the floor. He then raced to the back door, drove his right shoulder into it, tripped as he lost his footing, and fell to the ground with a thud and a groan. Then, like a practiced procedure, he rolled onto his side. With his shirt still lifted, he brought his knees up against his chest. TK stretched his long arms down, forcing his hands below his butt and then over his feet. Next, he rolled forcefully to his other side and up on his feet with his cuffed hands now in front of him. He spotted his truck and ran toward it.

Sam had heard the thud and groan from TK hitting the ground. He turned back and jogged toward the rear door to see what caused the commotion. The two tactical members followed. Sam immediately recognized TK as he moved toward his vehicle.

How the hell did he escape? Sam wondered while aiming his Sig Sauer pistol at TK, shouting, "Police, stop, or I will shoot."

Spotting the two tactical team agents with their automatic weapons behind Sam, TK pivoted between his Dodge Ram pickup and the tan truck parked adjacent to it. Sam quickly paralleled TK's movement on the opposite side of the Ram truck. As they both reached the back end of the vehicles, Sam yelled again to stop. Avoiding Sam, TK side-stepped around the tan truck to the other side and crouched down low, nudging toward the truck's tail end.

Sam slid between the Ram truck and the tavern wall and carefully began side-stepping around the tan vehicle. At the same time, the two tactical agents cautiously stepped toward the tan truck. Still hunkered low, TK waited patiently. Then, when he saw the barrels of the weapons carried by the two agents facing down, he sprung out from behind the truck and aggressively tackled both agents with his two hundred and forty pounds of muscle. He swiftly grabbed one of the AR-15s from one agent and slammed the butt end of the stock against their heads, knocking one unconscious and leaving the other in a daze. TK grabbed the weapon from the other agent and flung it out of reach into the tall grass behind the tavern. Then, still holding one of the weapons, he raced toward the back of the neighboring saloon, the Cumberland Waterfront Tavern.

Sam peeked over the truck's hood and saw TK sprinting toward the nearby bar. He was about to give chase when he saw his two colleagues down on the ground. He stopped to check on them while pressing his radio mic to report the situation.

"This is Caviello. Be advised Killingworth has escaped and now armed with one of the ARs taken from the agents in the back of the bar. He's running towards the neighboring tavern south of here. Our two agents in the rear are down and need medical assistance. I'm going after the suspect and need backup."

Hearing Sam's call for help, Gabbi instantly rushed to back up her partner. As she ran up the slope between the café and the neighboring tavern, Sam shouted for her to cover the front side of the tavern, and he'd deal with the back.

TK heard Sam's footsteps coming in his direction. When he reached the far corner of the tavern, he peeked around it, hoping to see someone walking to their car so he could hijack it and speed away from the area. Unfortunately, TK saw no one but heard the voices of cops chasing from behind. He surveyed the open back field and decided he had no choice but to run toward the high grass fifteen yards in back. He darted up the slight slope to the line where the nearly four-foot-high grass began in the meadow. TK looked back to his right and saw the silhouette of Sam jogging toward him. He moved into the field thinking back to when he was in Afghanistan. Twenty yards into the field, he decided to flop down on the ground and get ready to ambush his enemy as he approached. TK never noticed Gabbi advancing from the road up the slope from his left flank.

Seconds later, Sam cautiously approached the tall grass line and stopped to scan the field in front of him. He searched for TK but didn't spot him anywhere. Knowing TK's military training, Sam sensed TK could be lying in wait to nail him dead. While scanning the field, he immediately began feeling a weird sensation throughout his body that he took not to mean elevating anxiety but a warning sign of a threat nearby. Sam ducked low, pausing to adjust his sight on the tall grass ahead of him for any movement. There was no wind in the air, a clearing sky, and a bright moon giving sufficient light to notice any slight sway in the grass. Any movement would indicate something other than a breeze causing it. Staying low, Sam guardedly took small steps forward. He held his gun, aiming ahead as he took one short step at a time.

Not far from Sam's position, TK lay in wait for the kill. He struggled to break open the plastic cuffs holding his wrists together, with no luck. He found it challenging to position cuffed hands to hold the gun steady without his left hand supporting the forestock while using his right-hand finger on the trigger. As Sam stepped forward in a crouched position, TK saw a slight movement in the tall grass. However, he waited for a clear head or chest shot before pulling the trigger. He assumed the agent hunting him caused the shift in the grass but didn't want to take a shot without seeing a body to hit.

Sam stopped his advance when feeling the threat sensation in his body elevate. Realizing TK had the upper hand, he decided to use a tactic to confirm TK was near. It would only take a second to employ his trick. Sam stood up and shouted, "Police. You're surrounded," and immediately dropped to the ground.

Seeing Sam's head as he stood, TK instinctively pulled the trigger, but not quick enough, missing his target while Sam, on the ground, heard the 5.56 round whizzing through the air just above his head. Glancing up to the sky, Sam let out a breath, whispering, *Thanks again, Michael, or whoever.*

TK could hear the voices of cops scrambling toward him in the distance. He had no time to play games with the agent nearby. Impatient and pissed that the agent duped him, TK decided he had the advantage to rush the agent, who hid with his face down on the ground. He'd shoot him dead and quickly disappear into the high grass field.

Without warning, Sam heard grass rustling and slowly lifted his head to glance at what had caused it. *Shit,* a stunned Sam thought as he lifted his head and saw TK standing above him with an assault rifle pointing at his head.

"Say your prayers, dead man," announced TK.

CHAPTER
43

Inside the café, the uniformed police and agents had all the patrons, primarily gang members, street drug dealers, and pot-heads, searched and identified, resulting in the arrest of five of the dozen at the bar. The police searched behind the bar where Drackler stood with his hands up. They found a loaded short-barreled shotgun and a ghost gun close to where Drackler stood. He was arrested and handcuffed. The two guns gave the agents cause to seek a search warrant for the premises. The ATF tactical team leader called the command center to procure a search warrant and request additional agents and police at the scene.

* * *

With a contentious grin, TK put pressure on the trigger to end Sam's life. The sound of a gun blast then filled the air. Then silence. Most bullets travel faster than the speed of sound. TK stood immobilized by the pain as a bullet penetrated his jaw. Then, a second and again, a third bullet hit him, burning a hole in his chest. He stood frozen in shock with glossy eyes looking straight ahead at a shadowy figure aiming a gun at him. Gunshot residue gasses floated in the air from the gun barrel that fired at him. The weight of his assault weapon became heavy as TK lowered it while he plummeted to the ground like a free-falling elevator crashing to the bottom floor. He landed on the AR-15 with the selection switch on a three-shot burst and his finger still on the trigger. When TK hit the ground, it caused his finger to pull the trigger with the barrel pointed at his chin.

Pop-pop-pop! The rapid fire sounded muffled as the three-round blast tore into TK's head.

Thinking he was shot dead, Sam wondered why he didn't feel the bullet from the gun blast. Even though Sam didn't feel it, he thought he was dead. His eyes were closed when he saw the bright light, not knowing it came from the three-round flare from TK's weapon. An image of his son appeared accompanied by a warm feeling of his love for him. Then, unintentionally, Sam's eyes opened. His peripheral vision awakened him from his thoughts of being dead. He stared at an unrecognizable fragmented bloody face on his left.

Sam raised his upper body to look behind him. The cool air blurred his eyes, making it difficult to recognize the person holding a gun pointed in his direction. He wiped his eyes to clear his vision and caught sight of Gabbi standing behind him, still holding her gun straight ahead. Sam lifted himself off the ground, glanced again at TK lying dead before him, thinking it could have been him, and then moved to Gabbi's side. She had a lifeless look of a zombie with wide lackluster eyes, mouth partially open, pale-looking, and clammy while she trembled. Sam reached for her gun's slide, held it tight to prevent an accidental discharge, and lowered her arm. He softly asked her to let go of her weapon. When she released it, Sam placed it in his rear pocket and then wrapped his arms around her, holding her tight.

They stood there for a moment in silence, with Sam firmly holding her before Gabbi finally spoke. "I just killed a man. I never did that before, ever."

"You did the right thing, Gabbi. He was going to kill me. You saved my life."

"I wouldn't let him do that, Sam," Gabbi paused, then whispered, "I love you." Her bulging eyes swelled with tears.

Sam dabbed her tears and then kissed her cheek. At that moment, Sam heard the trudging sounds from the slope below. Police and agent footsteps moved up the hill, shouting, "Are you guys okay?"

*　　*　　*

When Sam and Gabbi returned to their car, Sam slid into the driver's seat, knowing Gabbi was still unsteady. He looked over at her to check her demeanor and saw her fixated on him.

"What?" he asked.

"I'm sorry I spaced out up on the hill. I saw that bastard sneak up on you with a gun. I didn't even call out 'police.' I just shot him. I don't even remember how many times. I thought I might have missed, so I just kept shooting. I couldn't let him hurt you." A tear fell from her eye as she spoke in a sedated tone. "I went blank after seeing him fall." Her lips quivered but managed to continue. "Thanks for the hug and support, Sam. I never asked if you were okay. Are you?"

"I'd be lying if I didn't admit I was out of it. When I heard the gunshot, I thought TK had shot me. You saved my life, Gabbi. It was a good shoot," said Sam convincingly. "I almost died twice in the past two days, but I'm still here breathing, thanks to you."

Still numb from the incident, Gabbi peered out the back window, assessing the activity surrounding the taverns. "Is the team still searching the cafe?"

"Yeah," responded Sam. "I heard the team was getting a search warrant, called for more help, and the coroner."

"Should we stick around to help?"

"No, Gabbi. We did enough. We found our guy, and he will no longer hurt anyone. We're not needed here, so I'm taking you back to the PD. We both need some downtime."

"When we get back there, let's not stay long. Okay, Sam? Let's head to my place, grab something to eat, and shower. My body feels drenched."

"I'm with you on that, and it will be my pleasure to wash the sweat away."

"Hmm. I like that, Sam. After cleaning up, we could rest for a while in bed before returning to the PD."

"Resting, huh? Is that what you have in mind or something else?"

"You know exactly what I mean," Gabbi said with a sensual smile. "You mentioned earlier the plane was not arriving until four this afternoon. That means it needs to get refueled, and the pilots have to check in and chart their flight. The plane probably won't leave until close to six. So, we should have plenty of time for some deserved time together."

"You got this all figured out. When you said rest in bed, I suspect we're not going to rest but get a workout?"

Gabbi's face shifted from a withdrawn look to a glowing, enthusiastic one with a beaming smile. "Let's call it a rewarding show of appreciation to each other for our great work today."

CHAPTER
44

The first thing Sam did when he returned to police headquarters was to meet with FBI Agent Rivers to confirm the flight to Boston. He searched and found her in the detective's unit.

"Seems like you had a productive morning," said Rivers.

"I'm dead tired but feel relieved that it's over. What's the status on the plane landing here this afternoon?"

"The latest I heard was it will land in Nashville later than expected, between four-twenty and four-thirty."

"That's good. Thanks. It will give my partner and me time to take Ena to a local kid's shop and get her something new to wear home. She's been in the same clothes for a few days now. Has the court arranged for an extradition hearing to have Max and the others transported to Boston?"

"Yes. The hearing is scheduled for one this afternoon."

"Let's hope the judge approves the extradition so we can leave for Boston with them. Anyway, I'll contact you around three to check how things went in court."

Next, Sam searched for the room where the police watched over Ena. It only took a few minutes to find it. Ena jumped off her chair and ran to him when he entered. Sam picked her up in his arms, hugged her, and asked if she was hungry.

"Yeah, but when are we going home?"

"After we eat at Gabbi's place, we'll come back here, then go to the airport."

"Can I call my mom again?"

"You sure can, Ena. First, we're buying you something nice to wear home. Then, Gabbi will take us back to her place, where we'll clean up and have something to eat. After that, we'll call your mom, and you could tell her that you're going home today. Okay?"

"Okay, yeah."

Ena held Sam's hand as they walked out of the room to find Gabbi. He found his partner in the detective's unit in conference with Aliyah Mayfield and others, including an unfamiliar black woman. Aliyah waved them over to the gathering.

"Sam, I'd like you to meet U.S. Attorney Jayla Bransford. I believe you already know Kiara, Gavin Sloan, and Soshi Kojima. Everybody, this is Ena Oshiro from Boston."

First, everyone smiled and waved hi to Ena. Then the U.S. Attorney spoke right up. "I'm pleased to meet you, Sam. I've heard a lot about you. I've had extensive talks with Attorneys Donna Ranero in Boston and Debra Durrell in Hartford. They spoke very highly of you. I'm impressed with the incredible work you did in Boston. Now, here you are in Nashville doing the same for the good people of Tennessee. I wanted to thank you in person. I've scheduled a press conference at three this afternoon and request you be front and center to say a few words to the citizens of Nashville and maybe take a few questions from the press."

Sam stood there thinking about how to put into words why he didn't want to partake in the press conference. "Uh, well, I appreciate what you said, Jayla. However, I prefer that Detective Gabrielle Walters and Agent Aliya Mayfield receive recognition for the investigation leading to the arrest of all those involved at the compound. You should also recognize Detective Walters for arresting the gang members at the church shelter. I have no problem with you mentioning Detective Walters and I worked together to rescue Ena and arrested those responsible for her abduction. Also, I'd appreciate it if you mentioned FBI agents Kiara Rivers, Gavin Sloan, and Massachusetts State Police Trooper Kojima for taking custody of those responsible for Ena's abduction and transporting them to Boston for prosecution."

Attorney Bransford was taken aback by Sam's assertion to spotlight others rather than himself.

"That's very commendable of you, Sam, but you should get the recognition for what you did while in Nashville. Why are you shying away from well-deserved recognition?"

"I came to Nashville for one reason—to find Ena and return her unharmed to her mom. That was my sole mission. Detective Walters knew where to find the information leading to where the abductors held Ena. Her advice and support led us to Ena and those responsible for taking her. I might add, Detective Walters saved my life twice, once at the shelter and again this morning when Killingworth escaped and would have killed me if it wasn't for the detective's quick action."

Sam paused for Attorney Bransford's response but only got her nod. "ATF Agent Mayfield provided the intel and background on the suspects and their illegal activities at the commune. In addition, she managed the enormous job of planning and executing the search that led to the arrests. But more relevant to your question, these two investigators serve to protect the people here in Nashville and the state of Tennessee. I'm not from here. I'm leaving today, but they remain as part of this community. Once I leave, the Nashville citizens won't remember my name. However, they will and should remember these local officers who serve them and thank them for the top-notch job they did today. They're the ones deserving recognition from the people here in Nashville."

Attorney Bransford and Gabbi's father, Captain James Walters, stood impressed with what Sam said and the thoughtful way he put it into words.

Feeling more like herself, Gabbi took hold of Sam's arm and whispered, "Let's get out of here. We have a lot to do in the little time left before getting back here later. I know a place close by in the city that sells children's clothes. It's only five minutes from here."

"Sounds good. Let's go," Sam, holding Ena's hand, followed Gabbi to her car. On their way, Sam leaned closer to Gabbi and whispered. "Ena has to like what we find for her before leaving the store, including getting her underwear. That'll be your job."

"That should be easy."

It took longer than Gabbi anticipated to get to the children's store, maneuvering around city trucks that were cleaning up debris on the city streets.

At the store, Ena picked out a dress, blue jeans with tears at the knees that she said her mom would never buy for her, and a stylish top to go with it. Ena was undecided about which one of the three underwear garments Gabbi selected. Sam decided for her—he bought all three and added a sleep shirt for Ena.

Before driving from the store to her apartment, Gabbi phoned in a take-out order and picked it up on the drive to her place. Once at her apartment, Ena's first request was to call her mom, but Gabbi insisted she bathes first and then have lunch before calling home. While Gabbi helped Ena get ready for her bath, Sam quickly took a shower knowing Gabbi might insist on joining him. Later, when they sat at the dining table to have lunch, Gabbi noticed Sam's hair was wet, and he had changed into his workout attire. She was disappointed since he promised to wash away the clammy sweat from her body.

They enjoyed a Japanese chicken and rice soup made with dashi, a flavorful soup broth, and sweet onions. Instead of ice cream, Gabbi ordered a strawberry cream Japanese cake roll for dessert. The dessert was light and airy and filled with whipped cream. Sam and Gabbi enjoyed fresh coffee while Ena sipped down a milkshake.

"Can I call my mom now?" excitedly asked Ena.

"Yes, you can," answered Sam, "but don't talk for a long time. You should take a nap before we go back to the police station and wait for the plane to arrive. Then, you could talk to your mom again when we arrive at the airport."

Sam was with Ena when he used Ena's phone to call Mayumi on Facetime. Mayumi answered the phone in two rings and saw Sam.

"Hi, Sam. Where is Ena," asked Mayumi. "Is everything alright?"

"Yes, May. I'll give the phone to Ena in a minute. Ena and I are flying to Boston tonight. Our flight is scheduled to leave here around five-thirty and land at Logan Airport around seven-forty, give or take a few minutes. I'll give the phone to Ena so you two can talk. Ena needs to take a short nap before we head to the Nashville airport, so talk for only an hour, and then let her take a nap."

Sam handed the phone to Ena, and as he closed the bedroom door, he could hear two jubilant voices talking Japanese at high speed like two young happy kids. Sam didn't see Gabbi in the dining room, so he headed to her bedroom. Gabbi had just stepped out of the shower when he walked in. Seeing him enter the bedroom, she quickly dropped the towel and walked into the bedroom. Sam stood in a daze, staring at her, admiring her beauty.

Gabbi wondered why he just stood there. "What are you thinking, Sam?"

He didn't answer immediately but gawked at her a little longer. "I'm thinking how beautiful you are and how lucky I am to be with you."

"Are you ready?" she said.

CHAPTER
45

Sam and Gabbi were fixated on each other while their bodies were closely linked, taking a short break from the so-called rest they enjoyed while Sam whispered sweet nothings in Gabbi's ear, often causing her to giggle.

"I can't believe you gave me so much credit to the U.S. Attorney, Sam. I'm so humbled and grateful, of course, but we are a team, and the recognition should be for both of us, even more for you. I don't deserve all the honor. You alone"—Sam interrupted her with a kiss. When their lips parted, Sam put his finger on her lips to stop her from continuing.

"Don't do that, please. Don't ever sell yourself short. You deserve so much recognition for what you did over the past few days. You're amazing, Gabbi. Plus, I meant what I said. I don't need all the atta-boys. I only want to be left to do my job without all the fuss. I'm in Nashville because I promised myself I'd find Ena and bring her back to her mom."

"Why aren't all men like you?" Gabbi said with conviction.

"I'm sure there are plenty of good men out there, Gabbi."

"You can't convince me of that because I haven't found any like you. What drives you, Sam? Part of you, especially when with Ena, you're more like a parent to a kid. You're nice, generous, and a real gentleman, but you're like a wolf hunting your prey on the job."

Sam snickered. "I am nice to nice people, that is. But for those who are not nice, like TK, they bring out the other side of me. I'm a public servant and take it to heart to serve the good people and protect them the best way I know. I'm good at what I do but don't need the plaques or certificates of appreciation. My reward is the success of helping victims, especially kids. My motto is, get out of the way and let me do my job."

"Well, I can attest you're doing a heroic job. You just have to loosen up and not be so serious. I can help with that, as you know."

"I know, and you have done a good job at it. If you know what I'm referring to. I can get used to being less tense and more tranquil. Now it's my turn. Tell me about your mom and your dad. Do you have brothers and sisters? What kind of kid were you? What are your favorite things in life, and what do you enjoy doing outside work?"

"You're good at changing the subject, Sam." Gabbi had more questions she wanted to ask Sam, but it could wait. "Hmm. First, what I enjoy doing the most is what we do together," Gabbi chuckled, causing Sam to join in laughing, which got out of hand when he started tickling her. "Okay, okay, let me finish. I mean everything we did together, not just the fun times," she then cracked up laughing again. Gabbi was a fun-loving woman but more so when with Sam. She enjoyed working as 'equals' and felt safe around him. Sam saved her life more than once. She trusted him like no other. Sam was different from the men she knew or dated. The private moments they had were magical, romantic, and cozy. The intimacy they shared was passionate but fun and playful. She felt a strong emotional attachment to a guy for the first time.

Eventually, Gabbi stopped her giggling and got control. "Okay, more seriously," she laughed again. "Hmm, okay—I grew up in a ghetto neighborhood until my dad finished community college in criminal justice and got hired by the PD. I had a lot of girlfriends in school, but I wasn't interested in boys until I was fifteen. My mom insisted I attend a private middle and high school. Most of the students there were white and didn't pay attention to me until, you know, I began developing some and caught the eye of a soccer player who was an honor student. My dad was overprotective and discouraged me from dating. But my mom, whom I was close to, always supported and encouraged me to do what was right for me, not for others. My mom is beautiful, with blondish hair, and what caught my dad's eyes were my mom's amazing blue eyes. They dated in high school. He was tall, good-looking, and a star football player. Like most people in school, my mom thought he had a chance to play professionally and take her out of poverty. Unfortunately, dad was injury-prone and didn't get offered a scholarship to college, so after graduation, he worked two jobs to pay for school earning his two-year degree."

Sam looked at the alarm clock and said he should check on Ena.

"No, Sam, not yet," she said, not wanting her time with him to end. "I'll check on her in a while. But, first, I want to finish what I was telling you. To make a long story short, my dad was never home, going to school, or working, and it never stopped after getting the job with the police department. My mom needed attention. I love her, but she began seeing another guy on the side, and my dad eventually found out."

"Does your mom still live in the Nashville area?"

"No. She remarried a guy with a great job in South Carolina. We often talk on Facetime and text, but I haven't visited her for almost two years."

"Everything good between you and your dad?"

"Yes and no. As the unit's captain, hmm, now about to become a deputy chief, he encouraged me to become a police officer, taught me the job, and guided me to get promoted to detective. However, he continues advising me on finding the right man and starting a family. He is dead set on me not dating anyone in the department. I did it anyway, and he gloated when it turned out he was right because the guy turned out to be a real jerk. Enough about me, it's your turn to tell me more about you, especially how you knew what house Max rented and held Ena. So you know, I've heard from unnamed sources that you have a unique gift for finding people."

Eventually, everybody gets around asking what I can't explain, reflected Sam. "It's a mystery to me. By choosing that house, you could call it a hunch, or better yet, a feeling I had that it was the right house. That's my honest answer, Gabbi. It all happened when I was a kid sick in intensive care at a local hospital. My older brother told me the hospital staff called my mother to return to the hospital. When my mom and brother arrived, the doctor said I had passed. My brother later constantly joked that when my mother went into my room and kissed my forehead, I awakened from the dead."

"What?" said a puzzled Gabbi. "You're kidding. It's a joke, right?"

"See. That's what I mean. You and everybody else would say I was joking. Before you say another word, I was in a coma and didn't remember a thing. Was this the reason I subsequently received these unexplained feelings? I have no idea. I can't explain it and can't even believe it myself. For some unknown reason, I get these weird feelings. I can only describe it as instinctive feelings that warn me of a threat, and the feelings steer me to whatever I'm searching for. That's all I can say about it because I don't have a better answer for you. Anyway, we should start getting ready to get back for the press conference. You're going to be the star hero and deservingly so."

Gabbi sensed Sam didn't want to talk about his 'instinctive feelings' anymore. It was an issue for another time. "Let's have more workout fun before we go. Just a few minutes. I promise."

Sam took in a deep breath and looked at the clock again.

"Sam, I'm crazy about you. I'll miss you big-time when you leave for Boston. Can you give me a few more minutes of love, please?"

Sam didn't hesitate. He kissed her tenderly. Their feverish intimacy lasted longer than a few minutes—it sizzled, filled with sweet but suggestive words and much laughter—it was a fun time they would never forget.

CHAPTER
46

Ena smiled when looking in the mirror as Gabbi combed her hair back into a ponytail fastened with a colorful matching barrette. Ena liked her new outfit—designer jeans and a swanky multi-colorful top that she hoped her mom would like. Ena chose this outfit instead of the pretty dress Gabbi wanted her to wear to Boston.

"I can't wait to see my mom—and my grandma. Oh, my teacher and friends at school, too."

"I'd love to be there when you and your mom see each other at the airport," said Gabbi. "I'm sorry I can't be there because I have to work. But, I promise I'll visit you soon. So let's show Sam how you look before getting back to the police station and catching a ride to the airport."

"Okay," said Ena as she glanced one last time in the mirror.

When Sam saw them coming out of the bathroom, Sam was impressed by telling Ena how he liked her new jeans and how pretty she looked. His eyes then caught Gabbi, seeing her in tight black pants and a low-cut V-neck top. "Wow, you are pretty too." He moved up close to her so Ena wouldn't hear his whisper. "You're so hot."

Gabbi hugged him and whispered, "So are you, Sam."

Although Sam was anxious to return Ena to her mom, he felt uneasy about leaving Gabbi. "I wish you could fly to Boston with us and witness the reunion. As I promised, I'll show you the city, dine you at great Italian restaurants, take you to the theater, and, you know, much more."

"Uh, huh, I'm glad you included the 'more.' That's what I want most," said Gabbi in a sassy tone.

"Oh, that goes without saying."

With that said, Gabbi's eyes welled with tears as she turned away to hide her emotions, saying, "Let's get moving. We can't be late."

Sam had made concise phone calls, first to his boss, then to AUSA Ranero, his son, and finally to Major Burke, notifying them of the flight schedule. Additionally, he recommended that Burke send a cruiser to transport Ena's mom and grandmother to the airport since they might need security from the anticipated crowd greeting Ena's return.

They got back to police headquarters in plenty of time for the press conference. FBI Agent Rivers confirmed the plane was on its way with a scheduled landing in Nashville at four-thirty-five. U.S. Attorney Jayla Bransford went over the plan and positioning on the steps outside the police department for the press conference, where the street was closed to make room for the reporters and on-lookers.

At three in the afternoon, the press conference began with the Chief of Police making initial remarks about the successful investigation and announcing Captain James Walters' promotion as the next Deputy Chief of the Department. Walters was brief, thanking the Chief and citizens for their support and congratulating the investigators for such a heroic job.

The U.S Attorney was brief in announcing the arrest of numerous suspects for manufacturing and dealing in tainted fentanyl and illegal guns. She thanked the fine officers who participated in the raid and arrests, particularly those most responsible.

"I must recognize two officers in particular for their incredible investigative work. In just one day, these two rescued an eight-year-old girl kidnapped in Boston and transported and held here in Nashville. They arrested three suspects responsible for the abduction. A couple of hours later, they arrested two gang members for assault. That same day, they developed probable cause for a search of the commune that led to the arrest of twelve co-conspirators for the illegal manufacturing and trafficking of illicit fentanyl and guns. She then introduced Agent Sam Caviello and Detective Gabbi Walters of the Nashville PD. As agreed, Bransford kept her promise to keep the press conference short by asking Detective Gabbi Walters to say a few words. Gabbi nervously read a brief statement she had prepared without Sam's knowledge.

"I want to thank all the officers and federal agents who helped make the investigation a success, and thank God we all went home safe and unharmed. I want to thank the department, especially Deputy Chief James Walters, my father, for his mentoring and trust in my ability to serve and protect the citizens of Nashville. But, most of all, I have to thank and recognize the man who was most instrumental in the success of rescuing the young kidnapped child. If it weren't for his determination to find her, we would not have arrested the kidnappers and the two gang members. We also would not have succeeded in obtaining the warrants for the commune. The citizens of Nashville, the city of Boston, and ATF owe enormous gratitude to an extraordinary special investigator, ATF Agent Sam Caviello."

Although appreciated, it was Gabbi who Sam wanted the spotlight on, not him. But he nodded to Gabbi in thanks for her comments.

Alli Gaynor, the national news correspondent who stood among the reporters, was not surprised that Sam was again the investigative hero. She also noticed that he always managed to partner with a beautiful woman detective.

Attorney Bransford ended the conference by also recognizing ATF Agent Aliyah Mayfield and FBI Agent Kiara Rivers for their exceptional investigative support, planning, and arrests of the suspects named.

As the conference ended, the reporters rushed to Attorney Bransford for additional information. Alli, however, reached out to Sam and Gabbi.

"Agent Caviello, Detective Walters, can I have a moment for you to say a few words for the national news?"

Sam was pleasantly surprised to see Alli and asked that the three of them step inside, away from the crowd. "Gabbi, this is Allison Gaynor, the local Hartford reporter who wrote supportive articles about me when the contemptuous father of a guy I was investigating for the kidnapping and murder set me up in an assault scheme resulting in my arrest. I owe her a lot for being the only reporter who provided support to me in the local papers."

"Oh, wow, Sam, you never told me about being arrested," expressed Gabbi.

"It must have slipped my mind."

Sam and Gabbi gave Alli ten minutes to interview them. Alli wanted to meet Ena and ask her to say a few words before the camera, but Sam wouldn't allow it. "Not until her mom has her back in Boston and gives her okay to it. I assume you'll be in Boston after you leave here. Maybe, once Ena is home, her mom will allow you to talk to her."

"I'll come to Boston as soon as I can. Thank you both. Talk to you later."

As Alli left them, FBI Agent Kiara Rivers reached out to Sam. "It's time to head to the airport. It's nearly five o'clock. You and Ena could ride with us."

"Detective Walters will drive Ena and me to the airport. We have some investigative matters to discuss on the way. So we'll follow you there."

"For your info, we ordered food and soft drinks for the ride to Boston. The plane is limited to a coffee maker and bottled water. Also, our plane is specially set up for cell phone use while in the air. I thought that might be helpful if you needed to make a call."

It was a twenty minutes ride to the airport. Gabbi followed the large-size black Chevy Tahoe used by many federal agencies through a separate gate on the side of an airport terminal out to where the FBI plane was parked and fueled. Sam, Gabbi, and Ena talked and laughed the whole way. It was evident to Sam and Gabbi that Ena expressed animated excitement about going home to her mom.

The Captain exited the plane when seeing the Tahoe arrive. Gabbi parked at an angle to the Tahoe to stay hidden from view, knowing she'd get emotional when she hugged Ena and Sam goodbye. She had tears rolling down both cheeks as she hugged Sam, not wanting to let go. He wiped away her tears and passionately kissed her, not caring if the FBI agents saw them.

"I'll miss you, Sam. Something terrible. Will you come to visit me?"

"Yes, I will. Make sure the prosecutor needs my testimony on these cases. You also have to promise to visit me in Boston. I plan to have the state police recognize you for helping find Ena. I'll insist they pay for your trip and hotel stay. That will ensure you'll visit Ena and me too. Right, Ena?"

"Yeah, come visit me, Gabbi."

Gabbi hugged Ena again, "You are a brave little girl. I'm glad we met and are lasting friends. I'll miss you and so happy you're going home to your mom."

"I'll miss you too, Gabbi. Thank you for helping me go home. Come visit me, please."

Gabbi hugged Sam again. "I hope you know how I feel about you. Remember our time and work together, especially our private time. Don't forget me, Sam."

"Oh, I can never forget you. Promise me you'll be careful out on the streets and stay safe."

"I promise. You two have a safe flight, and I'll see you again soon. Bye."

Ena held Sam's hand as the captain welcomed them. The captain bent over in front of Ena. "Hi, Ena. I'm Captain Alex Willard. I'll be flying the plane to Boston. You are our special guest passenger, and I wanted to say hi and welcome you aboard. Once we get up in the sky, if you'd like to visit up front where we fly the plane, you are welcome to see how we do it."

Ena looked up to Sam to get his approval.

"That would be fun. Thank the captain, and tell him okay."

"Will you come with me?" asked Ena.

"Yes. I'll be right there with you."

Sam guided Ena for the first four steps up to the plane's door and lifted her to the top landing as they stepped into the small jet. Sam pointed to the cockpit where the captain flew the plane. He then directed her to the two empty seats on the left side of the aisle. Agent Rivers, sitting with Agent Sloan in the back of them, moved to sit in the single seat across from Sam and Ena.

"We have to wait a while. The marshals are not here yet. They texted me that they were a few minutes out. Will Ena be alright seeing the suspects come inside the plane?"

Sam explained to Ena that because they arrested Max, Angie, and Kim, they had to take them to Boston, where a judge would send them to jail for taking her from Boston. "So they will be on the plane with us. They'll be here in a few minutes. Three federal police will guard them and keep them away from us. They will sit in the back of the plane and won't bother us. Will you be alright with them being on the plane?"

Ena only looked at Sam, perhaps waiting for him to say it was okay.

"Kiara and I will be right here with you. Nothing bad will happen. When they enter the plane, you could look out the window and not look at them if you want to. Okay?"

Ena nodded that it was alright then.

Nearly ten minutes later, the marshals escorted the three prisoners. The Marshals had Max and Kim shackled at the wrists and ankles and Angie cuffed at the wrists in front. When Max and the other two entered the passenger section, Max saw Ena sitting next to Sam. He stopped where they sat and began mouthing off.

"Why did you arrest my sister? She was not involved. She only watched over my daughter while I worked. She didn't even know I took her."

A marshal told Max to move to the back and shoved him forward.

Ena stared out the window as the marshals shuffled the three prisoners to the plane's rear.

Sam turned to Kiara and asked if there were any results on the DNA samples from Max and Kim.

"The lab personnel told me they wouldn't have the results until tomorrow."

At that point, the passengers heard the whining sound of the turbine jet engines starting up. The captain turned on his speaker to make an announcement.

"The tower advised we would be next in line. So we should be on our way in a few minutes. Ensure your seat belts are fastened, relax and enjoy the flight. Our estimated flying time to Boston is two hours and fifteen minutes.

EPILOGUE

The flight had a smooth takeoff and settled to a cruising speed of over four hundred miles per hour, as reported by the pilot. Sam and Ena chatted continuously during the flight. In only a few days, the two of them established a close connection, similar to that of a father and his daughter. During the talk, Sam asked Ena how she liked her teacher and what her favorite subjects were in school. Ena loved to talk about her teacher and told him the names of the three students she liked the most. She also described what and why science and math were her favorite subjects. Next, Sam tested her skill in adding and multiplying double numbers in her head. Sam was impressed with how quickly she answered. It took him longer to confirm her correct answers.

When Kiara arrived with sandwiches, Ena selected tuna, and Sam turkey. They shared the French fries. Afterward, Ena asked Sam question after question. First, she wanted to know about his job, was it was scary, and if he liked arresting bad people. Sam answered some questions but avoided explaining details of his investigative techniques and eventually changed the subject.

"Ena, would you like to visit the pilots flying the plane?"

Excited about going into the cockpit, Ena gave him an emphatic yes.

Sam asked Kiara if the pilot was ready to have Ena and he visit him in the cockpit. Kiara returned shortly. "The Captain said he's looking forward to your visit. So, I'll escort you both to him."

When Ena was at the cockpit's open door, Captain Willard invited Ena to sit in the jump seat behind the co-pilot's seat. Sam remained standing by the door.

Captain Willard first explained how the airplane takes off and flies in the open sky. "We have jet engines that move the plane very fast, causing the air outside to move over the wings. As the plane moves faster, the air on the wing's top section is less than on the bottom. So as the plane moves faster, the difference in the air pressing on the wings forces the plane to lift up into the sky."

The captain explained more about how the Gulfstream G550 plane lifts during takeoff. He then described the cockpit panel and devices and the purpose of each one. Next, he pointed to different instruments, including the speed indicator telling Ena how fast they were going and the gauge showing how high they were from the ground. Finally, he explained how he would land the aircraft.

"When we get close to Boston, we slow the plane down, pushing down on this wheel called the yoke." The captain pointed to the wheel in front of him, saying it reduced the air going over the wings allowing the plane to start going down toward the airport. "We maintain the proper speed as we travel lower, and when we approach the airport, we lower the wheels and land on the runway. Easy, right, Ena?"

Ena shrugged her shoulders, not knowing if it was easy.

"Do you have any questions, Ena?"

Ena shook her head no.

"Well, Ena, do you want to stay here or go back where we sat?" asked Sam.

Ena pointed toward the back.

"Okay. Thank the Captain, and let's go back to our seats."

Ena thanked the captain, and when he asked for a high five, she slapped his hand with spirit. Once back in her seat, Ena had a request.

"My teacher has students' parents come to the school to talk about their job. Would you come to my school to talk about what you do in your job? I think the class will like hearing about your job better than the others."

"Of course, I will, as long as your teacher and mom say it's okay."

"Do you like my mom, Sam?"

Sam didn't expect that question. Puzzled, he wondered if Ena asked if he liked her as a friend or something more.

"I like your mom because she loves and takes good care of you. That's the way I like her."

The captain interrupted the chatter saying they started their descent toward Boston and should touch ground in about twenty minutes. Continue to have your seat belt buckled until landing."

The captain's announcement also took Ena's focus away from the topic of liking her mom. Instead, Ena stared out the window, watching the aircraft as it slowly got closer to the ground below. She then tapped Sam on the shoulder. "It's taking a long time, Sam."

"We're almost there. Just a few more minutes," Sam said, noticing Ena's anxiousness.

Sam heard a phone ring and saw Kiara answering the call. She spoke for a couple of minutes before the call ended. Then, Kiara leaned toward Sam and whispered that a large crowd was waiting at the airport's reception area to greet them.

"Thanks. I assumed there might be a big gathering to greet Ena. If I don't get a chance to talk to you again tonight, thank you for all you have done, especially arranging the flight back. I appreciate it and hope we stay in touch now and then."

"Well, thank you, Sam, for calling and asking me to partake in all that happened in Nashville, especially for having me recognized with Gabbi and you during the press conference."

Sam extended his hand, and they both shook hands with a firm grip and a smile.

They heard the landing gear going down as the captain announced they would land momentarily.

Ena looked at Sam with a beaming smile. "Is my mom here?"

Sam nodded yes. "Your mom and grandma are here waiting for you. Many other people will also be there, including news reporters. They are here to take pictures of you and your mom. Don't look at them or care about them. When you see your mom, just run to her."

Ena was visibly excited as she bounced between looking out the window and back at Sam. Finally, the plane touched down as the plane's wheels and brakes screeched, hitting the pavement. When the plane's wheels hit the pavement, Ena grabbed tightly on Sam's arm. Sam put his arm around her and whispered, "It's okay. The plane just touched the ground. We're back in Boston."

Sounds from the aircraft landing increased as the whirling noise from the wing's spoilers helped slow the plane down. As the aircraft turned toward the terminal, Ena gazed out the window and saw the airport in the distance, then turned to Sam with an anticipating look. "I can't wait, Sam."

Sam noticed Ena was trembling. He rubbed her back and told her everything was fine. "Don't be nervous, Ena. You're back home now. I'll be with you until you see your mom."

When the plane finally stopped, Sam helped Ena unbuckle her seat belt. They sat until the exit door opened, and Kiara took the lead to disembark. Sam held Ena's hand and followed behind. Sam allowed Ena to step down the stairs on her own while holding on to her. The driver of a black SUV waited near the bottom of the stairs. Kiara asked that FBI Agent Sloan and Trooper Kioshi sit in the third-row seat and Sam and Ena sit in the middle row. Kiara climbed into the passenger seat. A U.S. Marshal's van parked several yards behind. The SUV driver headed to the terminal and stopped several yards from the lower level terminal door so the crowd greeting Ena's arrival could see her exit the SUV from the glass window on the upper floor.

Kiara opened the door for Sam and Ena and asked Ena to look up to the large window on the upper terminal level to see her mom and grandma waving. Sam lifted Ena from the car to the pavement and pointed to her mom. Ena waved while jumping up and down with excitement, showing a wide smile. When she saw someone open the lower terminal door, she began to run toward it. Sam yelled for her to wait for him as he ran to catch up to her.

The woman holding the door asked Sam and Ena to wait until the other officers got inside and then would escort them all to the waiting group upstairs. The woman directed them into an elevator. When they reached the floor, the elevator doors opened. Ena practically pulled Sam out of the elevator when she heard the cheers and shouts of her name. Ena turned to see her mom and grandma waving at her. With tears in her eyes, she released her hand from Sam's and screamed, "Mom," then darted toward her mom's open arms. Mayumi and her mother cried out as they embraced Ena tightly, not wanting to let her go. Flashes from the reporter's camera lit up the scene.

Sam stood motionless, absorbing the beautiful backdrop of a young child returning to embrace her mother. A scene he would never forget. While several reporters shouted questions that no one answered, Sam's son, Drew, left the crowd of reporters and strolled up to stand with his dad.

"This is quite a scene," whispered Drew. "Hey, is that a tear, I see? What are you thinking right now, Dad?"

Sam didn't have to think about how to answer and spoke from his heart. "This is a fairytale scene. It's the most gratifying moment of my career." Sam wanted to freeze this moment to capture it in his memory forever. "This is what our job is all about, Drew—helping victims who can't fend for themselves, especially when the victim is a young child."

Finally, Ena's mother released her grip on Ena and put her down. She then fixed her watery eyes on Sam. She put her hand over her heart and bowed slightly in respect to him. Then, she whispered something in Ena's ear, causing Ena to run back to Sam. Seeing Ena racing toward him, Sam knelt and opened his arms as Ena charged into him and wrapped her arms around his neck.

"My mom says thank you for bringing me back to her."

"It was my pleasure, sweetheart. I am happy you're back with your mom and grandma. I hope we see each other again."

"Will you come to my school like I asked you to?"

"Yes, I will. I promise." Sam walked her back to her mom. There, Mayumi and the grandmother hugged Sam, thanking him repeatedly.

"Please come to dinner soon to celebrate with us. Okay, Sam?" asked Mayumi.

"I will, thank you, May. Ena told me you are a great cook. Would it be okay to invite the police detective who helped me find Ena to join us? Her name is Gabbi Walters."

Ena heard Sam mention Gabbi. "Yes, mom, have Gabbi come too."

"Hai, yes, please bring Gabbi too," said Mayumi.

Reporters continued barking out questions for Sam to answer. He had been up since two in the morning and tired. He held up his hands, trying to stop all the questions. "I'm not answering questions. Tonight, my only statement is that there had never been anything in my career that was more rewarding than finding Ena and bringing her home to her mom and grandma. It was an inspirational sight for me to witness the joy and love this family has for each other. I will cherish this moment forever." Sam's voice quivered a bit as he finished his words. "It is and will always be the highlight of my career." Internally, Sam's body tingled, feeling exhilaration and gratitude while accompanied by humility and serenity. He thought how lucky he was to have brought such happiness to Ena and her mom. It affected his whole self-worth that he was able to accomplish such a precious moment. With his son beside him, he hoped Drew would someday achieve such a gratifying moment like this.

As the state police escorted Mayumi, Ena, and the grandmother away, the reporters trailed along, soliciting questions and comments. Once the final reporters left, Major Jack Burke, and the federal DA, Donna Ranero, commended him on bringing Ena back safely and the success in closing down the illegal gun and fentanyl ring in Nashville.

"Sam, take some time to relax and think of all you have accomplished in such a short time. Rest up. When you're up to it, come see me. We have a lot to discuss. And, just so you know, Detective Serrano desperately wanted to be here, but she's not feeling well," said Major Burke.

Sam's boss patted Sam on the shoulder and asked Sam to prepare the required investigative reports and get them to him as soon as possible.

Figures, Sam thought.

Ranero took her praise further by hugging him and whispering, "You're a genuine hero, Sam. I'm not sure those here and those who will read about it in the news tomorrow will appreciate the immeasurable investigative achievement you made over the past several weeks here in Boston and

Nashville. My boss and I will have a press conference tomorrow, and we want you there to say a few words."

"Please, Donna. I'm just a public servant doing my job. Bringing Ena back safely to her mom and seeing their display of emotional joy and love was my reward. Nothing will top that."

"Sam!" yelled out FBI Agent Rivers, walking back toward Sam. "I just got a call from Nashville. The DNA results show that neither Max nor Kiyoshi are a match with Ena. Neither one is Ena's father."

"Interesting," he shouted back. "I'm glad they're not Ena's father for so many reasons, and whoever is her father will be Mayumi and someday Ena's business. Thanks for the info, Kiara."

Drew placed his arm on his dad's shoulder. "Well, Dad. What a day. You want to get going to my place?"

"Yes. I'm wiped out. Let's get outta here and back to your place to relax. I'm sure you have many questions, and I want to spend time with my son."

The two of them walked together. A man in a dark suit waited near the terminal exit.

"I hope this is not another reporter," whispered Sam.

"Agent Cavello, I'm Secret Service Agent Don Hadley. I have instructions to take you to the Boston Waterfront Bay Hotel for an urgent meeting with Senator Evelyn Alvarado-Thornton."

"For what reason?"

"That will be explained to you by the senator when we get there."

"Well, tell the senator I've been up since two this morning, and the only place I'm going to is my bed for a long-deserved sleep. Here's my card. Have the senator call me in the morning, but not before nine."

"But this is urgent. If you don't already know, the senator is the favorite to win her party's nomination to be the next President of the United States."

"I'm very happy for her, but the election is months away, and I need to sleep now. She should call me in the morning. I'll be much more attentive to listen to her by then."

Sam and Drew walked away as the Secret Service agent yelled, "It should take only a few minutes to meet with her, Agent Cavello."

"Senators never take a few minutes to ask for something they want—and Agent 'Badley', my name is Caviello, not Cavello. Sam continued walking, waving goodbye to the agent as he and his son exited the terminal.

ACKNOWLEDGEMENTS

My gratitude remains to ATF, the agency where I worked for nearly thirty years. The agency provided a lasting community of friends and colleagues I served with including the Special Agents, Industry Operations Investigators, and the administrative and technical professionals. The men and women of ATF dedicate their lives to serving and protecting the great citizens of the United States.

Special thanks to Dominic Wakeford, U.K. Editor, for his tremendous insight and constructive overview of my story. He provided exceptional feedback pointing out the story's strength and highlighting where the prose needed bolstering. In addition, he identified and suggested areas of the story that needed descriptive amplification. I place Dom in the top tier in the realm of book editors. Thanks, Dom.

My wife, Donna, spent hours proofreading my books accurately and provided suggestions that made sentences and paragraphs more readable and meaningful. Her tiresome editing is much appreciated, with love as always.

Again, I'm indebted to my friend and former colleague, author Wayne Miller, for his continued input, advice, recommendations, and encouragement. Thanks, Wayne.

I'm grateful to my coach, Geoff Affleck, and his associates, for mentoring and guiding me through the challenging process of launching and promoting my books through the complex steps of self-publishing and optimizing sales. I couldn't have done it without his expertise.

To my friends, former classmates, relatives, and ATF colleagues, I appreciate your praise, encouragement, and support for my stories.

To my son, Paul, and of course, my wife, Donna, thank you for the everyday encouragement to write and give everlasting support in my work.

ABOUT THE AUTHOR

Stan Comforti is a thirty-year law enforcement veteran. He was a federal air marshal before becoming a Special Agent with the Bureau of Alcohol, Tobacco, Firearms, and Explosives (ATF). As a field agent, he worked numerous investigations against drug dealers, outlaw motorcycle and street gang members, and felons who possessed, stole, traded, or trafficked firearms, including illegal sawed-off shotguns and fully automatic weapons. Many of his field assignments involved working undercover. Subsequently, as a supervisor in Massachusetts and Connecticut, he directed many high-profile investigations, including a murder-for-hire case where a father paid an undercover agent to kill his daughter by placing an explosive device under the car she drove. ATF arrested the father before any harm came to his daughter. Another investigation involved the unlawful sale and possession of firearms, including a machine gun that involved police officials, one of whom was also engaged in a major police exam-scam operation. Also, for seven years, Mr. Comforti was a leader of Boston ATF's Special Response Team. He led many early morning arrest and search warrant raids against drug dealers and gang members who illegally possessed and used firearms in their illegal operations.

THE SAM CAVIELLO FEDERAL AGENT CRIME MYSTERY SERIES

Book 1: *A Cry for Help*

Book 2: *Chasing Terror*

Book 3: *Finding Ena*

Available at Amazon and other book sellers.

If you enjoyed this novel please leave an Amazon review.

Connect with the author at stancomforti.author@gmail.com, or visit StanComforti.com. You also scan the QR code to reach his website.